The Body in the Birches

ALSO BY KATHERINE HALL PAGE

Small Plates

The Body in the Piazza

The Body in the Boudoir

The Body in the Gazebo

The Body in the Sleigh

The Body in the Gallery

The Body in the Ivy

The Body in the Snowdrift

The Body in the Attic

The Body in the Lighthouse

The Body in the Bonfire

The Body in the Moonlight

The Body in the Big Apple

The Body in the Bookcase

The Body in the Fjord

The Body in the Bog

The Body in the Basement

The Body in the Cast

The Body in the Vestibule

The Body in the Bouillon

The Body in the Kelp

The Body in the Belfry

The Body in the Birches

A Faith Fairchild Mystery

Katherine Hall Page

HARPER LUXE

An Imprint of HarperCollins*Publishers*

THE BODY IN THE BIRCHES. Copyright © 2015 by Katherine Hall Page. All rights reserved. Printed in the United States of America. No part of this book may be used or reproduced in any manner whatsoever without written permission except in the case of brief quotations embodied in critical articles and reviews. For information address HarperCollins Publishers, 195 Broadway, New York, NY 10007.

HarperCollins books may be purchased for educational, business, or sales promotional use. For information please e-mail the Special Markets Department at SPsales@harpercollins.com.

FIRST HARPERLUXE EDITION

HarperLuxe™ is a trademark of HarperCollins Publishers

Library of Congress Cataloging-in-Publication Data is available upon request.

ISBN: 978-0-06-239311-1

15 ID/RRD 10 9 8 7 6 5 4 3 2 1

To Danielle Bartlett Emrich
Friend and HC Publicist, in Honor
of Our 11+ Years Together
and
To the people of Deer Isle and Stonington, Maine
Those whose roots have been embedded in the
granite for hundreds
of years and those who arrived later, including
the ones From Away

After a good dinner one can forgive anybody,
even one's own relations.

—OSCAR WILDE

Acknowledgments

Many thanks to the following not only for their various expertise, but also for their friendship: Dana Cameron (author and character-name high bidder at the Malice Domestic charity auction); Dr. Robert DeMartino; Michael Epstein; my agent, Faith Hamlin; my editor, Katherine Nintzel; Thomas E. Ricks; Dr. Thomas Risser; and Captain Jamie Robertson, Robertson Sea Tours & Adventures, Millbridge, Maine.

Chapter 1

Sophie Maxwell had not remembered it taking quite so long to reach the island. Darkness had fallen hours earlier, and now it was a dark only lonely roads in Maine produced.

The journey had started many hours ago. After an uncharacteristically panicked phone call from her mother, who was somewhere on a yacht in the Aegean with her third—no, wait, fourth—husband, Sophie had taken a train to Connecticut from Manhattan and a cab from the station to the house to pick up a car for the drive. She hadn't been home for over a year, but she knew the keys would be in the same drawer as always. Mother changed mates but never her beloved 1892 Victorian that sat high up on a peninsula jutting out into Long Island Sound. The shingle and stone house had been a wedding gift from her parents thirty years ago when Babs had married her college beau Sandy Maxwell. Less than two years later she'd found a receipt for a diamond-studded Piaget watch with instructions for engraving in the pocket of one of her husband's suits that she was taking to the cleaners. The initials weren't Babs's. They were his secretary's. She was dumping him for adultery, she told her friends, but even more for a complete lack of originality—"tacky is as tacky does."

There was no question about keeping the house. Over the course of his successors, Babs had added on and continued to restore the place until it became her own best jewel, one worth a cool ten million now.

There was also no question about keeping their daughter, Sophie—Babs demanded and got full custody. Despite her penchant for serial nuptials, no one could ever say Babs was not a good mother. Early on she'd decided Sophie was going to be her one and only child, directing her efforts toward her daughter's appearance, manners, and even intellect—"You need to be smart, but you don't need to flaunt it"—in much the same way she scoured the Connecticut countryside and auctions for the right salvaged chestnut to match the original flooring, the right dining room table and other furniture for the twin parlors with their ten-foot ceilings, and the right mantels for the six original fireplaces.

Thoughts of her mother had crowded Sophie's mind as soon as she'd unlocked the front door (bright red with a lion's head brass door knocker). It was impossible not to think of Babs when every inch of the house reflected her perfect taste and something more— something antiques dealers referred to as "an eye." You couldn't learn it. You had to be born with it. So far Babs's only lapse in visceral judgment had been Sanford Maxwell, but she'd told Sophie that was why she never drank gin. "TMI," Sophie, sixteen at the time, had told her. It did still bring a smile to her face, though, especially as her mother had always made sure that Sophie understood she was well worth the slip. Babs wasn't demonstrative—she was a New Englander after all— but she loved her daughter. And she loved her house. It had six bedrooms, six full baths, two halfs, assorted other rooms including a conservatory, and of course a state-of-the-art kitchen that Babs had remodeled every four years.

Sophie loved the house, too, but her room in the turret at the front of the home was her favorite, and she headed straight for it. Although it was not as large as the other bedrooms, she preferred her own private tower room, resisting her mother's attempts to get her to move as she got older. Babs had had a curved window seat installed under the windows that looked straight out to the water. Built-in bookcases that curved as well still held Sophie's books charting her progress from girlhood through adolescence—*Anne of Green Gables* to *The Bell Jar.* Sophie greeted the volumes like the old friends they were as she dug out a large suitcase and a duffle from the closet. She didn't know how long she'd be staying in Maine, but she knew that even in July she'd have to bring some warm clothing.

Mother's current housekeeper had unpacked what Sophie had dropped off before she'd left for England and after she'd returned to New York in late spring. She'd been bunking with a friend from law school until she could find a job and there had barely been room for her interview outfits in the apartment, a studio on the East Side. Closet space had been sacrificed for a doorman and a tony address. Almost everything she owned was here in Connecticut.

"Why shouldn't I spend the night?" Sophie'd muttered to herself as she added a rain jacket to the pile. She had gotten in the habit of softly talking aloud to herself as a child and it had stuck, unlike the nail biting that Babs soon put a stop to by painting her daughter's fingernails with something so foul Sophie gagged just looking at them. Babs took her for a manicure and had the salon paint tiny daisies on Sophie's nails. Worked perfectly. The daisies were so pretty Sophie couldn't bear to destroy even one.

"I could get up early and be there by midafternoon tomorrow," she said a little louder, addressing the warm burgundy-colored walls. She knew she was trying to convince herself and knew she wouldn't, but it was such a temptation. The room had always served as a refuge, and she had never needed it more than now.

She looked up from her packing. The window seat was beckoning. Donna Tartt's *The Goldfinch* was in her bag. She could run to the Firehouse Deli in Greenwich, get one of their delicious, humongous Reubens to go, and given that the house had a well-stocked wine cellar courtesy of spouse number three, she could curl up and read, drowning her sorrows while clogging her arteries.

But her mother had been adamant that Sophie get to Sanpere Island as soon as possible. Sooner. It was a ten-hour drive with no stops, and she'd be lucky to get to The Birches by one in the morning. She sighed and continued tossing clothes into the luggage.

When she'd seen her mother's name on the cell display, she'd almost let the call go to voice mail. It was the realization that Babs was many, many miles away that had made Sophie pick up. Had Mother been in the same time zone, Sophie was pretty sure the call would have been one of the all-too-frequent ones she'd been getting since her return from London. "How's the job hunt? Where have you applied?" and so on. And so on. It had to be something more important if Babs was interrupting her trip. Her mother had cut straight to the chase.

"Sophie, you have to get up to Sanpere right away. You'll have to go to the house first. There's a ten thirty out of Grand Central. Don't take any of the other cars. Be sure to take the Lexus. You'll need to pack a few things. I don't know how long you'll be staying. I can't get there for at least three weeks. You probably don't have any cash. I've wired some to your account, so stop at an ATM. God knows you won't find one on Sanpere. You'll get there late, but they know you're coming."

Sophie had finally been able to get a word in. Two, in fact.

"What's happened?"

Her mother's annoyance reached all the way across the globe. "It's been over a year since Aunt Priscilla died, but Uncle Paul is just now getting around to telling us her last wishes. Not just wishes, but instructions— instructions about The Birches. As in who gets it."

"Why do I have to be there? She surely didn't leave it to me."

"Of course not," Babs had snapped. "If she was going to specify anyone, it should have been me."

"So who is it going to?"

The Birches had been built by Sophie's great-grandparents, Josiah and Eleanor Proctor, as a summer "cottage" in the late 1800s. It was an ark of a place on Little Sanpere Island, connected to its larger neighbor, Sanpere, by a now well-paved causeway and to the mainland by an elegant suspension bridge, a WPA project that some on Sanpere continued to regret. "Got everything I need right here," Old Joe Sanford said. He had never been over the bridge in all his ninety-four years and didn't intend to make the trip ever, even in a pine box. The Sanfords got planted almost in Joe's backyard and he'd saved room in the family plot for himself and his wife.

The Proctors had been "rusticators," joining other wealthy Bostonians and New Yorkers in pursuit of the simple life. Bracing swims at dawn in Maine's frigid waters, sailing in the same, hikes on Mount Desert Island or climbing Mount Katahdin farther afield. The simple life didn't extend to cooking one's own meals or washing one's own clothes. An army of servants accompanied their employers on the two-day steamer journey from Boston, longer from New York.

The Birches was situated at the end of a point overlooking Eggemoggin Reach. Its rocky beach was home to a lighthouse, and over the years the owners of similar houses on adjacent lots—The Pines, Eagle's Nest, Ferncroft (those owners claimed Scottish ancestry)—had constructed several docks. Now a flotilla of pleasure craft bobbed at moorings that were passed down as carefully as the family silver.

Sophie's great-aunt Priscilla had been the youngest of her generation and her death marked the end of an era in some ways, but not in others. Just as Priscilla and her siblings had grown up at The Birches, spending their days on the water or in it, collecting and identifying flora and fauna, doing jigsaw puzzles or reading the slightly musty books that had accumulated from generation to generation, so had Sophie and her cousins. The family prided itself on lack of change. Inevitably the twentieth and the twenty-first centuries had crept in through the screen doors that always banged shut and the windows, swollen from the damp, that didn't. There had always been indoor plumbing—there was a limit to roughing it but electricity replaced gas and a furnace was added. A telephone was the first real thin edge of the wedge, with a TV following, and Sophie had heard that her uncle Simon had installed Wi-Fi so he could telecommute.

Babs was the oldest in the next generation and Sophie knew she loved The Birches, and not only because of her love for a whole lot of pine beadboard. It was a love for the entire island as well. Babs Proctor Maxwell Rothenstein Williams Harrington had spent every summer on Sanpere until she went off to Wellesley, returning for only part of the summer until Sophie was born, and then she began to stay until Labor Day again. Sophie had never given much thought to what would happen to The Birches in the future. She vaguely knew that Aunt Priscilla took care of things. She was the one to whom you went when you found things like a leaky pipe or hornets' nest under the eaves. The Birches was just there and always would be.

"You are wasting precious time!" Babs had snapped in answer to Sophie's question, rapidly adding, "She didn't leave it to anyone but instructed Uncle Paul to get family members interested in the place to come for July. At the end of the month, he'll announce who will get it."

Aunt Priscilla and Uncle Paul were childless. "Why can't it just go to the three of you?" Sophie suggested.

As soon as the words were out of Sophie's mouth, she knew why. Babs and her brother, Simon, a year younger, had never gotten along. The idea of their sharing even a peanut butter and jelly sandwich was impossible. In turn they both loathed their cousin Sylvia, who had never moved on from her infatuation with all things tie-dyed and infuriated Babs with constant exhortations to "Stay loose." Sylvia's father had been the middle Proctor son, Babs and Simon's the oldest. Priscilla had been the only girl.

Her mother didn't even bother to answer Sophie. "Just get up there and stake a claim. I want you there before the Fourth. It's always a big deal at The Birches. I can't cut the cruise short. It's not the money, but—"

This time Sophie *had* been able to squeeze in a few words.

"Admit it, Mother. You want to stay. You've fallen for real this time. Ed is more than a nice guy. He's a keeper. "

Babs had, of course, managed to have the final word. "Not that you'd recognize one. Now, get going. Uncle Paul always liked you. So did Aunt Priscilla."

The words had stung. Not the last part of the sentence, but the first. Stung like an entire hornets' nest.

Sophie had stopped at the Firehouse Deli for a sandwich to go, and she ate it at the first rest area in Maine near Kittery, getting out so she would be sure to keep the Russian dressing from dripping on the SUV's leather seats. As she'd driven, she'd cataloged the number of relations who might be turning up at The Birches, or were already there.

Paul McAllister was Aunt Priscilla's second husband. Her first, George Sloane, had died before Sophie had been born. With no children of her own, Priscilla's nieces and nephews, and eventually their offspring, were much doted upon substitutes. Sophie was the oldest in her generation by a few months, but it had always been her cousins, Simon's twins Forbes and Felicity, who decided what they and the kids from the other houses on the Point were going to do each day. Although both lived in Manhattan, Sophie hadn't seen them in a year or more. Neither was married yet, but Felicity was engaged, which currently seemed to be her full-time job. Like Sophie, Forbes was a lawyer. Only he was steadily making his way up the rungs to partner, while she had jumped off the ladder.

"Jumped." She whispered the word aloud. One summer when she was ten, Forbes had decided the boathouse roof would make a swell diving board at high tide. He'd put a ladder up and declared that Sophie should go first, since she was the oldest. It was lucky she hadn't killed herself on the submerged rocks, only breaking her ankle. It wasn't until many years later that she realized just what Forbes had been doing: seeing if it was safe before he tried it. Aunt Priscilla had made Sophie a nook in one of the rooms off the kitchen, where she'd slept until her ankle was healed. Sophie had spent her days reading Priscilla's old books—*A Girl of the Limberlost, Daddy-Long-Legs*—and learning to knit. It turned out to be one of the happiest summers ever.

Surely Forbes wouldn't be able to get away from his job for more than a few days around the Fourth, which was a relief, and Sophie doubted that Felicity would be there. She'd long ago made it clear her idea of a beach was one in the Hamptons or the Caribbean. Maybe the South of France, but then there was all that smelly cheese and suspicious animal organs, plus garlic.

Which left Simon and his wife, Aunt Deirdre, plus Simon and Babs's cousin Sylvia, who might or might not be with someone at the moment. It was hard to keep track of free-spirited Sylvia's status. She had three children who were Sophie's second cousins or cousins once removed? She had never mastered these genealogical distinctions. Sylvia's oldest, Autumn (better than "Fall," but Sophie still felt sorry for her, saddled with the name, no way to shorten it even), was only a few years younger than Sophie, but seemed much younger. Partly because Sylvia believed in "letting children be children," a philosophy that translated to something others might call benign neglect. The last time Sophie had seen Autumn, she'd been wearing a Raggedy Ann outfit, with the striped tights and all, but very little else. The pinafore and dress were so sheer that had she a little pink heart tattooed, it would not have been hard to spot. Autumn's brother Rory was twenty, several years younger, and Daisy was the baby at twelve. Despite the fact they all had different fathers, they looked identical—strawberry blond with china blue eyes. Sophie wondered if they'd be there "auditioning" along with their mother. Sylvia lived out on the West Coast in Marin, but she was a fixture each summer at Sanpere and had acquired a local reputation as the woman who was always first in line at any yard sale no matter how early it started.

Sandwich finished, Sophie made a quick stop at the restroom, did some yoga stretches, and got back in the car. Although she'd crossed the border into Maine— THE WAY LIFE SHOULD BE the billboard announced— she tried to keep herself from thinking she was almost there. The island was still a very long way away.

"I don't like it."

Ursula Lyman Rowe; her daughter, Pix Miller; and Faith Fairchild, their friend and neighbor both on Sanpere Island and, in the inclement months, in Aleford, Massachusetts, were all sitting in Bar Harbor rockers on the front porch of The Pines, a summer retreat that had been in Ursula's family for generations. It was a grande dame of a cottage, the term a misnomer for what easily slept ten with cots on the sleeping porch for others.

From their perch overlooking the waters of Penobscot Bay, the women had not been watching the sailboats and an occasional windjammer as they tacked down the Reach, but another sort of human activity. There had been a steady stream of arrivals at The Birches, located down the hill and on the other side of a birch grove, hence the name. It was visible to the naked eye of its lofty neighbor, but for good measure, Ursula had her binoculars out.

"Don't like what?" Faith and her family had a summer cottage that really *was* a summer cottage across the causeway on Sanpere itself. Little Sanpere and Sanpere had a year-round population of 2,400 that doubled in the summer—quite a few of the locals considered this yearly onslaught worse than that of the blackflies.

The Fairchilds—the Reverend Thomas Fairchild, Faith, fifteen-year-old Ben, and twelve-year-old Amy—were adding a much-needed extension onto the original small house they had already remodeled once and had taken Ursula up on her offer to stay at The Pines, at least until all the walls were intact.

"Sorry, dear," Ursula said. "We were talking about something before you came and it was still on my mind. Always annoying to walk into the middle of a conversation you don't know anything about. I'll start from the beginning. Pix won't care."

"I'll get a pitcher of iced tea," Pix said, getting up. "Spying on the neighbors is thirsty work."

"I hid some of the brownies I made yesterday from the kids. They're in an old Bremner Wafers tin in the pantry." As a caterer, Faith's thoughts were never far from food. "Now, tell me everything, Ursula. When I got here, your binoculars were trained toward The Birches. Is that what this is about?"

"It is. Although Priscilla died over a year ago, Paul has waited until now to carry out her wishes regarding the property."

This sounded intriguing, Faith thought to herself. Last wishes. Inheritance. It had all the makings of a page-turner. Aloud she said, "I was sorry to hear of her death. How is Paul doing?"

"Pretty much the way any man who is widowed does. Still inundated with food of every kind and invitations of every nature from dinner to marriage."

Faith laughed. "It's the same way on the rare occasion I go out of town. Suddenly all Tom's handmaidens of the Lord line up to bring dinner and provide I dare not think what kind of other distractions. When he's away, it's me, the kids, and a chick flick DVD once they're asleep."

"Paul is no fool. It would take more than tuna noodle and a Merry Widow to trap him. He adored Priscilla and she him. It was a second marriage for her—she'd been widowed young—but a first for him, and they never had any children. Plenty of nieces and nephews, younger cousins, too. I have the feeling we'll be seeing each and every one of them before long."

Pix emerged from the house with a tray, which she set down on a sturdy wicker table. All the furniture at The Pines was sturdy, having stood the test of time. Plus the wicker had been repainted so often the paint itself would have supported a skyscraper let alone a tray with iced tea and brownies, even brownies laden with walnuts and dried cherries.

"What did I miss?" she asked.

On Sanpere, Pix and her family lived a few coves over from the Fairchilds. In Aleford the Millers were next-door neighbors as well as parishioners at First Parish. Pix and her lawyer husband, Sam, were older than the Fairchilds, with their children, Mark, Samantha, and Dan, well positioned over the years to be Fairchild babysitters. Pix was also Faith's guide through the labyrinth known as parenthood, as well as life in the small suburb west of Boston. Faith's own childhood had been spent in the Big Apple. The more bucolic orchards of New England, her husband's native land, continued to baffle her periodically.

When Mark, the Millers' first child, was born, they decided to buy their own place on Sanpere rather than live at The Pines with its steady stream of guests. Ursula and her husband had always filled the place with friends and relatives, especially ones that sailed. Pix's late father, Arnold, considered an entire day on dry land a day wasted.

Pix handed her mother a glass of tea. Faith noted with approval that she'd gone to the garden behind the house for fresh mint.

"Thank you, dear. Perfect timing. I'd just gotten to Priscilla's last wishes. All spelled out and notarized by the way, not that Paul would have disregarded them, but she apparently didn't want him to have to deal with any objections. The long and the short of it is that Paul was to summon all those relatives interested in inheriting The Birches to visit during or for the entire month of July, after which time he is to select the legatee. And to repeat myself: 'I don't like it.'"

"I can see why you might not like to see him put in the position of ultimate decider—is that the word I'm looking for? It somehow rings the wrong bell. Well, judge, authority, and so forth. But other than that, why?" Faith said.

Pix put her glass down. She shook her head and sighed audibly.

"Oh, Faith, I thought after your years here—and in Aleford—you'd know what this sort of thing can lead to. At best, people stop talking to each other. At worst—"

Her mother interrupted and said grimly, "It can be murder."

Miles away from both The Pines and The Birches and many hours later, Sophie felt as if she had been driving for days. She'd stopped in Bucksport for gas, knowing from experience that it was the last available. The convenience store with the pumps was the last anything until places opened very early in the morning—4 A.M. on the island for the fishermen.

She bought a Coke and some granola bars. Even if the coffee sitting on the hot plate hadn't looked like something that might be found under the hood of a car, she didn't want any. She'd had so much today, it would be a while before a cup of joe would appeal to her. There was no point in pulling over for a nap. The caffeine would prevent sleep, and it was also impossible to see whether she'd be pulling onto a shoulder or into a ditch.

The radio signal had turned most broadcasts to static and she'd gotten tired of trying to find a station that wasn't a call-in or not her kind of country music. She hadn't thought to check whether her mother had CDs in the car, and now she didn't want to stop and look.

After all, she had her thoughts for company. Too many. They crowded unbidden and unwelcome into her mind as she drove through the darkness. It had all started last September . . .

Meeting Ian Kendall had been a fluke. The law firm where she worked was huge, occupying many floors in the Citigroup Center on Lexington Avenue. Intellectual property, Sophie's specialty, was geographically far away from mergers and acquisitions, Ian's.

The chance encounter was a Meg Ryan movie moment. Pretty girl dashes for the elevator, the doors close in her face, and a handsome stranger appears at her side, commiserating, "I hate when this happens." He had a warm smile, thick well-cut ash-blond hair, Paul Newman blue eyes—and a British accent. Roll credits.

By the time the next elevator arrived, they had agreed to meet after work for a drink. He didn't know the city well. Would she be willing to act as his guide? Happy to oblige, she'd responded.

Back in her office, as she'd opened her e-mail, one part of her mind was registering the fact that besides being attractive, he was significantly taller than Sophie. Everything she looked for in a man on the surface. Especially the height. In middle school she had shot up alarmingly, like Alice after sipping from the DRINK ME bottle in Wonderland. Sophie wasn't just the tallest girl in her class, but the tallest student period. When Babs wasn't around she slouched. In high school the boys and some of the girls caught up; at the same time Sophie's braces came off; she stood up straight and stopped feeling like the ugly duckling.

Since then she'd never lacked for male attention, but there had never been anyone who'd swept her off her feet. Maybe it was all of Priscilla's happily-ever-after books at The Birches or a penchant for movies like *The Holiday,* but Sophie was a hopeless romantic under her Armani power wardrobe. She wanted a man who would knock her socks off, not just remove them—although that was nice at times. After all, a girl well shy of thirty couldn't live like a nun.

And Ian had done both. He was in New York representing a UK company in a complicated merger with a U.S. one represented by Sophie's firm. The drink— Sophie had taken him to the St. Regis King Cole Bar for Manhattans—had turned into dinner. That night, and every night thereafter, except for the ones both had to work, which was more often than not. It was good to be with someone on the same insane schedule. Sophie's promotion a year earlier had included her own office, albeit not a corner one. The first thing she had done was move in a couch she could sleep on. It was rare for her to leave work before midnight and often easier just to sleep there. One desk drawer held some toiletry essentials, and she kept a change of clothes in a coat closet that held an unsurprising number of her colleagues' spare outfits as well.

Despite their hectic agenda, she did manage to squeeze in tours of her NYC favorites for Ian—including a trip on the Staten Island ferry and one to the top of the Empire State Building, this last at his insistence when she confessed to never having been there. In turn he promised to take her to the Tower of London, which he hadn't gotten around to in like fashion.

Ian, like Sophie, ate everything, and they hit Michelin stars one night and hole-in-the-wall places another. He didn't send flowers but instead sent thoughtful gifts like a pair of earrings she'd admired in the museum shop after they'd seen an exhibit at the Metropolitan and funny little windup toys for her desk. And once a gorgeous rainbow silk infinity scarf he'd seen at Barneys that he told her was "her." They loved the same music, the same books, the same artwork. And eventually they loved each other. Sophie had read *The Rules* and a bunch of other advice books for singletons, but more to the point she'd lent a sympathetic ear and a shoulder to cry on too many times after a friend had blurted out "I love you" only to hear he wasn't, in the classic phrase, "all that into her," before departing at the speed of light. But Ian said it first. Said it and repeated it while holding Sophie in his arms. He gave her a ring that had been in his family—a Victorian flower ring, one perfect pearl surrounded by turquoise and garnet "petals." Babs had declared it "very sweet" and suggested Sophie walk Ian, whom Babs had met and liked, past Tiffany's windows if not for what she considered a suitable replacement for "at least, darling, something to sparkle around your neck or wrist."

The only hitch was time. Ian would be returning to London just before Christmas. Their days—and especially their nights—took on a new intensity as November became December.

"I can't bear to leave you, my love," Ian had said over and over. "Why doesn't your firm have a London office? Surely you can arrange one," he'd added with that smile. That totally captivating smile.

Of course she couldn't, but what she did do was ask her boss for a leave of absence.

"I wish I could, Sophie, but we've just put a new policy into effect. I know you'd come back, but too many people haven't. Of course if there's a"—he coughed—"physical reason . . ."

Sophie had blushed furiously. "No, no maternity leave required."

Finally, despite his admonitions—"I can't tell you in all honesty that you could walk back into your job even in a few days. You know what it's like . . . ," as well as a strongly worded appreciation for her work and plea not to go—Sophie resigned.

That night she booked a table at The River Café on Water Street in Brooklyn and prayed for a table by the window overlooking New York harbor and the Manhattan skyline. It had all worked out, even the stroll there in unseasonably mild weather across the Brooklyn Bridge, the one very romantic and quintessential city experience she hadn't fit in so far. Over champagne and oysters she told Ian what she had done.

"You're mad, utterly mad," he had said, immediately getting up and enveloping her in his arms before kissing her to the applause of the adjoining tables.

Babs was not as enthusiastic, especially as Sophie couldn't sublet her rent-controlled West Side apartment and had to give it up.

"Burning one's bridges is never a good thing," she'd said crossly. "Pay the rent and leave it empty. I wish you had talked to me about this. You could have taken vacation time until after New Year's and then decided."

Instead Sophie packed for what she knew would be a typically British rainy winter, purchasing a new Burberry in anticipation and following her besotted heart, moving into Ian's spacious Kensington flat off the High Street in time to celebrate the holidays.

London at Christmas! The decorations throughout the city and especially on Regent Street made New York's appear in need of higher wattages. The tree in Trafalgar Square, a gift from Norway, dwarfed poor Rockefeller Center's. Sophie and Ian drank mulled wine, ate mince pies, skated in the flooded courtyard of Somerset House and at a smaller rink by the venerable Science Museum on Exhibition Road. At the nearby Victoria & Albert they asked a perfect stranger to take their photo in front of Helen and Colin David's Christmas installation, "The Red Velvet Tree of Love." It seemed as if everywhere she turned, there was another good omen.

Sophie had always liked London, happy when work or a vacation took her to the city, but now she was on her way to truly being a Londoner, with a "myWaitrose" card for the upscale grocery and one for Boots, the chemists—she'd had no trouble switching from "drugstore" to the British word. Just as she also switched from Clarins to Molton Brown, coffee to tea, all for her new home. All for love . . .

Ian's family lived in Kent. Sophie had spent a weekend with them. The house was everything she'd imagined: the British equivalent of shabby chic except it was authentic. The furniture had been in the family forever and the Colefax and Fowler was vintage. A trio of King Charles spaniels had greeted her uproariously. Their owners less so, but as the weekend wore on, Sophie thought she had made a good impression, especially when Ian's mother had pressed a jar of locally made gooseberry jam into Sophie's hand when saying good-bye.

Sophie had assumed they would be spending Christmas in Kent, but the "mater and pater" Ian had told her would be going to his sister's in Yorkshire and he wouldn't inflict that on her "for the world." Sophie had thought Christmas in Yorkshire had an enticing Ye Olde English ring to it, but then thoughts of the Brontës intervened, and on Christmas morning she was glad to be in Ian's warm flat next to the tabletop tree she'd decorated, opening gifts ranging from Agent Provocateur lingerie—"I rather think these are for you, Ian darling"—to a gold bracelet from Links of London—"If it's good enough for the Duchess of Cambridge . . ." he'd said.

New Year's Eve had been wonderful beyond imagining . . .

After the stop for gas, she'd soon left any semblance of main roads. The shape of a dark cluster of trees loomed up in front of her as she took a curve too fast.

She slowed down and tried to keep her thoughts on what was in front of her. What she could see of it, that is. Not only was it dark but also foggy, and it didn't seem to make a difference whether she used high or low beams. Or the fog lights. Sophie began to switch among them, yet even that activity couldn't keep her from revisiting what had been the happiest night of her life. December 31.

"We're going to meet some of my mates at Babylon to watch the fireworks," he'd told her. It was amusing the way these Savile Row–clad men referred to one another as if they were getting together for a pint and darts, she'd thought more than once. She'd liked Ian's friends and they had accepted her as one of them, even offering advice about how she could get a job with a firm based both in the United States and the UK. Though Sophie did notice that all the women who had jobs seemed to be doing something vague for a magazine or dropping by "to mind the till" in a Mayfair boutique. A few of Ian's friends were married, and those women weren't working at all, busy doing up the flat and giving little dinner parties to help their mates, as in husbands, get ahead.

The Roof Gardens at Babylon were located a few blocks from Ian's flat on the top of what had been a department store in the 1930s. Sir Richard Branson purchased it in the 1980s, transforming it into a restaurant and private club. The rooftop, a hundred feet above the High Street, sported seventy full-size trees and three resident flamingos, an oasis in the middle of London. Sophie tended to forget how temperate the climate was when confronted by palm trees and palmettos amid the oaks.

It had rained most of that last day of the old year—had rained almost continuously since Sophie had arrived in the city, not that she minded. When it appeared to be letting up, they had taken the Underground to Holborn and Lincoln's Inn Fields, deserted with not a lawyer in sight. The sun came out, a long low late-afternoon light that made the grass emerald and the Tudor brick buildings look like a stage set. They strolled up to St. Paul's and then down along the Embankment before the crowds made it impassable. For a brief moment, Sophie had wished they weren't going to a party but could stay and be part of the throng watching the fireworks quayside. Just the two of them. But back at the flat, she changed her mind when she saw the look on Ian's face after she emerged from the bedroom dressed in the posh frock she'd splashed out on at Harvey Nichols.

It was like nothing he'd ever seen her in. Nothing she'd ever owned, in fact. For one thing it wasn't black or gray, but hot pink. Very hot. It was an Alice and Olivia lacy cocktail dress (she'd been amused that the department store had a whole department for "le cocktail"). The fabric hugged her body like a glove, and the dress had a low but not plunging neck in front. The wow factor came when she turned around—a keyhole back open to the waist. Ian had pulled her close, running his hand appreciatively over her bare skin, then lower.

"No bra I can tell," he said. "No knickers . . . ?"

"No knickers," she whispered in his ear.

"Maybe we should stay in," he said.

Sophie had been tempted, but the dress was having an interesting effect on her, too. It had started when she'd put it on and stepped out of the dressing room to look in the three-way mirror. The saleswoman had gasped. A customer had said, "Luv, whatever it costs, get it."

Her dark hair—thick and shiny—was longer than it had been since she was in her teens and it almost brushed her shoulders, the ends curled under. The dress was short. Her legs seemed to go on forever; especially with the strappy high-heeled Jimmy Choos she'd bought in the shoe department after she realized the all-purpose black pumps she'd brought with her would kill the effect. She'd tried the whole outfit on back at the flat and instantly felt sexy, desirable—like a whole new Sophie. New year. New girl.

No, they didn't stay in but went off to Babylon where she'd lost count of how much champagne she'd had and afterward only recalled the feel of Ian's lips on hers at midnight as the fireworks went on and on and on.

A week later she found a part-time job in an antiques store while she continued to apply to firms with offices in both countries. Ian took her to Paris twice through the Chunnel, easier than getting from Manhattan to Brooklyn—and shorter than that trip during rush hour. Babs called less frequently and Sophie was both relieved and disappointed. It had been annoying to have her mother constantly ask when she could send out Save the Dates, then when she stopped asking, Sophie felt her mother was giving up on her. Ian started to work even longer hours than usual, which she understood all too well from her lawyer days. His parents had gone to Spain to escape the weather and he promised when they returned he'd talk with them about a date. He'd shown Sophie his list, all in late June or early July. She'd called her mother to announce that they were getting closer, but Babs had been underwhelmed. "Just let me know, dear . . ."

Spring came in a rush. One day London was cheerless and wet, the next sunny and blooming. On such an afternoon, Sophie arrived at the flat, her arms filled with fragrant lilacs from the flower stall outside St. Mary Abbots at the start of Kensington Church Street. Letting herself in, she heard voices coming from the bedroom, which meant that Ian had come home early as promised and had the television on. He was a self-confessed news junkie.

Except the only news was the redhead in bed with him.

He'd smiled that smile. "Sorry you had to find out like this, darling."

Only he wasn't sorry. Not one little bit, she realized.

She'd bolted down the stairs, smacking into Gillian, who lived in the ground-floor flat and had just let herself in the front door. Gillian had taken one look at Sophie's tear-streaked face and promptly steered her down a few streets to The Hereford Arms, guiding her to a booth in the back corner of the pub before going to get drinks.

"Gave you the push, right?" Gillian said when she'd returned with the glasses. Through the haze of her emotions, Sophie remembered they'd had drinks here once before—with Gillian and the man she called "my non-live-in lover."

The venerable pub had been a haunt of Alfred Hitchcock's when he'd lived close by, and the entire back wall was covered in posters from his movies. The more Sophie imbibed, the more she thought about adopting the techniques used in some of them.

"Okay, enough," Gillian had said when Sophie had begun to get maudlin, reciting the names she had picked out for their first baby (Alistair if a boy, Sarah Jane if a girl). She had steered Sophie out into the cold night air and put her to bed on the sofa in Gillian's flat.

As Sophie closed her eyes, trying not to see the image of Ian and the redhead in bed that was burned on the back of her lids, she'd wailed, "But he gave me a ring! His great-grandmother's!"

"Oh, luv," Gillian had said, tucking a duvet around her. "He has a drawer full of them."

She got a plane out of London to New York the next day, but it had taken Sophie a week to call her mother, who—to her credit—had not said "I told you so" until after the first five minutes of conversation. Getting another job was not going to be easy in this economic climate, even with her credentials and experience, but Sophie hadn't realized how bad things were. She had been in full panic mode for some time when Babs called, sending her on this odd mission to Maine. What exactly was it she was supposed to do on Sanpere to guarantee her mother as Uncle Paul's choice?

A happy sight greeted her as she drove up and over one of the hills that she knew meant she was in Penobscot and not far from the bridge to Sanpere. She spotted taillights up ahead. Another human being. And what was more, a path to follow. She accelerated. She didn't want to lose sight of them.

Suddenly they were too close for comfort. She hit the brakes but not soon enough, and felt a faint *thunk*. Seconds later a man bolted out of the car stopped in front of hers. He was shouting. She rolled the window down in time to hear the last part loud and clear.

"What the hell! You hit me!"

He was tall, dressed in dark clothing, and angry.

"What the hell were you doing stopping short in the middle of the road!" she retorted with equal vehemence.

"I don't know where you come from, lady, but in Maine when you see a deer crossing the road smack in front of the hood of your car, damn straight you stop."

Sophie opened the door and got out. "Well, I didn't know there was a deer. I was just trying to stay in sight of your taillights."

Her heart sank when she got a closer look at the car. It was some kind of vintage, read expensive, sports car, sleek and low to the ground, which also explained why she hadn't seen the lights when the road dipped.

The man, who appeared to be around her own age, was grumbling audibly about women drivers, specifically women drivers from away. "I don't see any damage," Sophie interrupted before he could get on to a further subcategory.

He turned abruptly and went back to the car, returning with the largest flashlight she had ever seen, directing it toward his car's rear bumper. The lights were intact and all Sophie saw was a slight indentation. Very slight.

"Of course I will pay for any damage."

She got her purse, and they exchanged information. She was so tired now, she was tempted to pull over and sleep when she got to the Eggemoggin Country Store just ahead.

The man, whose name was Will something—she was too exhausted to remember—was still training the light on his beloved car's bumper.

"Would you mind if we got going? I've driven from Connecticut today and still have a ways to go."

"Connecticut!" The sneer in his voice was perceptible, although Sophie realized he was not from Maine, either. He had a slight Southern accent.

"Yes, you have a problem with that?"

"No, no problem at all. Not with that."

With one last furious glance back, he slammed his car door and shot off into the night. Sophie got in her own driver's seat and leaned over to put the registration back in the glove compartment. The lid wouldn't shut. Something was stuck.

She turned the interior lights on and pulled out a bunch of maps—quaint of Babs—a small tissue box, an Altoids tin, and at the bottom a heavy object loosely wrapped in suede. Some of the fabric had caught. She worked it free and suddenly Sophie wasn't sleepy at all.

Babs had been particularly insistent that Sophie take the Lexus rather than one of the other smaller cars at the house. She'd told her daughter twice she wanted it to be on the island. Wanted it because of what Sophie now held in her hand?

A gun.

Her mother had a gun?

Chapter 2

Sanpere celebrated holidays in a big way. At Christmas Santa arrived at Granville not in a sleigh with reindeer, but in a lobster boat decked out with lights accompanied by a flotilla of similarly adorned crafts. Most of the island was waiting on the town pier and escorted the jolly old elf to the Community Center for cocoa, hot cider, and other potables more potent in the parking lot. When a local team returned from a competition on the other side of the bridge—athletic sports as well as the nationally ranked chess team—islanders lined Route 17, the main road that circled Sanpere, waving banners to welcome the kids home, win or lose.

But all these observances paled in comparison to the festivities at the Fourth of July. After years of equitably alternating the parade and the fireworks display, the island had settled on Sanpere Village for the morning parade—this year's theme was "Our Beautiful Island"—and the much larger harbor at Granville for the evening's pyrotechnics. The rivalry between the two towns gave way to practicality.

"It seems strange not to have one of the kids decorating a bike or marching in the parade," Faith said to her husband. They were at the cottage, waiting for their original builder, Seth Marshall, to come back from Barton's Lumber. Two of his crew were adding the steady rhythm of hammering to the cries of the gulls circling overhead. With the Fourth only several days away, Faith was feeling nostalgic. "We won't even be able to have the picnic here."

"Come on," Tom said. "You've always wanted to see what the clambake at the Point is like. All those old Yankee families. We wouldn't be invited if we weren't staying at The Pines with Ursula."

"Don't get your hopes up for anything special to eat. They will have lobster, too, but unless some of the islanders who work for them make the potato salad and pies, it will be the equivalent of the millimeter of anchovy paste or chicken salad on white bread crusts off they serve at funeral collations."

"Wait a minute! Aren't you making something?"

Faith laughed at the sound of slight panic in her husband's voice. He was what her aunt Chat called "a big hungry boy," and he had stayed annoyingly slim over the years no matter how many carbs he tucked into his tall, rangy body. Ben was the same, and it was a job keeping the larder and fridge stocked.

"Don't worry. I'm bringing two kinds of bread pudding—chocolate and a new recipe I want to try that calls for buttermilk. Since Ursula's garden has a bumper crop of strawberries—way more than we need for jam—I want to use them instead of raisins."

Tom, and for that matter Faith, had never met a bread pudding they didn't like. "Phew," he said and gave her quick hug. "I guess I won't go hungry."

"I'm bringing barbecued chicken, too."

"So there *is* a God."

"Obviously, because here comes Seth. And you thought a run to Barton's meant a lengthy stop at the new coffee place."

While Starbucks meant driving many hours to Portland, and even a Dunkin' Donuts was forty minutes away, islanders had never lacked for good coffee. Up until now the Harbor Café and Susie Q's had met the need. Two young local women, however, had started roasting beans themselves in what had been the old high school, a white frame building, in Sanpere

Village. The smell was intoxicating, and they were, too—both more than pretty and endowed with a hefty dose of Maine humor. The shop had become a favorite hangout for everyone from the fishermen to the many artists living on Sanpere.

Seth was carrying containers of coffee that Faith recognized were from the new place.

"Sorry, I would have brought some for you, too, if I'd of known you would be here," he apologized. "You want to look at the tile, right?"

As they followed the builder into the garage where he'd put the boxes, Faith realized that her nostalgia for her children threading red, white, and blue crepe paper streamers through the spokes of their bikes was tied to the cottage's new addition. Years ago when they'd bought the original twenty-four-foot-by-twenty-four-foot dwelling, they had gutted it, creating an open kitchen/living area with floor-to-ceiling windows overlooking the cove. The twenty-foot-by-twenty-foot wing with a tiny bath and tinier bedrooms had been moved closer to the road and put on a concrete slab. It was supposed to be used as a garage, but Faith had long given up any hope of getting a car in. Besides Tom's workbench, it was filled with a ride-on lawn mower a neighbor was getting rid of; life vests, paddles, and other marine paraphernalia; finds from the dump and flotsam and jetsam from the shore; and always a mound of assorted items Tom thought too good to toss. Occasionally Faith sneaked out something like a bucket with a large hole, just as she culled sweaters he wore in college unraveling at the elbows—and cuffs and collar—from his wardrobe. The Fairchilds were the embodiment of the New England tendency to hold on to "string too short to be saved."

In place of the twenty-foot-by-twenty-foot, they had attached a two-story addition with a dining area, bath, and bedrooms for each kid plus a guest room on the first floor. Above was another bath, master bedroom, and small study for Tom. It had all worked fine when the kids were small—literally. Now with Ben close to six feet and Amy, a teenager in September, as she reminded them almost daily—a thought Faith preferred not to contemplate—the family needed more space.

There was also the fact that Tom had to go over to the Millers' or other friends' to watch Red Sox and Celtics games, an activity that convinced him they needed a TV. A big TV. And so over the winter, they'd talked with Chris Scovel, their architect friend who'd done the first plan, and he'd designed a generous family room with a roof angle echoing the other addition and suggested tile with radiant heat as flooring instead of the hardwood in the rest of the house. Tom and Faith had selected the tile at a Home Depot in Massachusetts and specified the Sanpere delivery. Seth had called this morning to say it had arrived, and they'd driven over to make sure the order was correct.

It was the right tile and they walked back to the house. The wall between the new addition and the rest was still open, but the whole thing had been framed in. Faith was encouraged.

"When do you think we'll be able to move back in?" she asked. "I know you're working as fast as you can. It's just that I hate to inconvenience Ursula."

Seth had done work for both Ursula and the Millers. He picked what he called "reasonable" jobs. Capable of building just about anything, he had turned down offers to put up million-dollar-plus McMansions. "Don't belong here." And he didn't mean the houses.

Hard to tell how old Seth was, Faith thought, like so many island men. He was starting to go gray, but his unlined face was tanned from working outdoors a great deal and his body was fit. He could be anywhere from thirty-five to fifty-five. No wife. Told Tom that he'd tried it once and had decided to do the "poor woman" a favor and let her divorce him. He played in a local band. Not the Melodic Mariners, which kept things hopping at dances at the Legion Hall, but The

Urchins, who entertained at Camden hot spots and, closer to Sanpere, Bar Harbor. Sanpere's female population had long ago given up any hope of being the next Mrs. Marshall, or just Seth's steady girlfriend. He liked people, but liked to keep to himself equally, he'd told them.

Seth grinned. "I'm sure she's more than happy to have you," he said. "The Rowes have always had a full house over there to The Pines." He paused a moment. "And I guess it's going to be the same and more at The Birches." His grin became broader. One of the things Faith liked about Seth was his broad knowledge of island gossip, despite his solitary status, and readiness to share good dish with her—once he got to know her, that is. They had bonded over the now historic skunk episode during the first remodeling. In the words of Elwell Sanborn as he ran to his truck after shooting out of the crawl space below the new section like a cannonball—"By Thundah! It's a mumma skunk and babies!" Faith had been in the yard at the time and Seth had turned to her. "Elwell's religious. That's pretty strong language for him. Doesn't much like any animals except for deer in his crosshairs." It had been an ordeal, not funny at the time, luring the little family out. Seth had not kept a thing to himself. Now she was glad for his loquaciousness and grabbed the chance to find out his take on what was going on next door to The Pines.

"So you've heard that Paul McAllister is going to have a lot of company this month?" she said.

"Ayuh." Seth was no more a geezer than Tom, but he liked to affect an old geezer Maine vocabulary. "Gorry, wouldn't want to be in his shoes. Glad I don't have anything to leave except my tools. Already told my nephew he can have the trailer if he wants it, sell it if he doesn't. But those people at The Birches—don't expect it's going to be pretty and besides . . ."

At that interesting moment Ben came racing up on his bike. "Mom, Dad! I got a job! Hi, Seth." He was flushed and the words continued to spill out as he climbed up into the new construction. "I'm going to be washing dishes at the Lodge. And Tyler is working there, too. You don't have to worry about driving me because there's a girl, who's working in the kitchen, Mandy Hitchcock, and she can drive us. And I've got my under-sixteen working papers all filled out. You just need to sign."

"Slow down, son," Tom said. "I thought you were going to be working at the day camp."

Ben gave his father the look of irritation that automatically descends on a teenage face, pimpled or not, at the stroke of midnight on his or her thirteenth birthday.

"I *told* you and Mom that they weren't sure they could pay me and that I was going to try to find something that did."

Tom looked at Faith, who responded, "And I remember saying that jobs were scarce on the island even for kids older than you, so you'd better take the day camp offer for the experience it would give you."

Seth judiciously walked away to talk to his crew.

"I *went* to the camp and last summer I pretty much was a CIT, so I have all the experience I need. The Lodge is a real job. If you're thinking how it's going to look on a college application I'm sure the fact that I want to earn some money will be impressive and I can do something to save the world the rest of the year."

When did her sweet boy turn into this snarky stranger? Faith wondered. "The Lodge" was The Laughing Gull Lodge and one of the most beautiful spots on the island. In the 1940s a retired marine biology professor from Bowdoin had purchased the land and put up a rustic main building with a number of equally rustic cabins. With his wife in the kitchen helped by local women, guests were provided with three squares—very square, but filling meals—a day. The professor provided nature walks and talks. The faithful returned year after year for an affordable and enriching vacation. In the late 1960s, ill health forced the couple to sell, but not before ensuring a hefty chunk of their acreage would never be developed by giving it to a land trust. Since then the Lodge had changed hands, and incarnations, many times, but never its name. New owners were giving it a try this summer, and Faith wasn't sure what it was being marketed as now.

She could see Tom was annoyed. More and more, father and son were locking horns. She knew from the books—and Pix—that this was normal and even healthy, but it didn't make being with them any more delightful. Before her husband could say anything, Faith jumped in. "Of course we're not thinking about what is going to look good on your college applications." It was a white lie. "We just want a bit more information. Your hours, for instance. They're serving dinner now, right? So it could be late."

Apparently deciding to rope his mother in as good cop, Ben said, "There are four kitchen crew who can be dishwashers. We're going to rotate shifts so no one ends up staying late often. And because of my age, I'm limited to the hours I can work anyway. Besides dinner is like at six and I should be done way before nine. I really want to do this. Tyler's parents have no problem with it." He smiled. This was clearly his trump card. Tyler was one of Nan and Freeman Hamilton's grandsons. The Hamiltons, eight generations and maybe more on the island, were the Fairchilds' closest neighbors on Sanpere. The four had been through a lot together two years ago when another grandson had been mistakenly arrested for murder. It was the kind of experience that fortunately few people have, Faith thought, but when you did, it either made you shy away from one another once the crisis was over, or created an unbreakable lifetime bond. It was the latter with Nan and Freeman, plus their entire family, which constituted a sizable proportion of the local population.

Ben's strategy worked. "I'll talk to Freeman," Tom said. "See what he knows about the new owners, but it looks like you have yourself a job. And we'll figure out the transportation thing ourselves. I don't like you having to depend on someone else, especially someone we don't know."

With a "now what" look, Ben said, "Ask Mr. Hamilton about Mandy, too. She's like a straight-A student and very responsible." He scowled. "If we lived in Maine, *I* could drive myself."

Faith decided to ignore the last part and Ben took off to tell Tyler his parents had said yes, so Tyler could tell his parents the Fairchilds were all for it, and that Tyler better call his grandfather fast—neither boy thinking this particular craftiness was anything other than a commonsense strategy for the care and handling of parents.

Seth came back over and, looking at Ben's energetic retreat, said, "Think I can just about remember having that much energy. Especially on a day like today. Hear they're frying eggs on the sidewalk in Granville."

It had been hotter than anyone could remember since the middle of June and only an occasional rain at night kept the gardens alive. Faith had even waded into the Reach from the rocky shore by The Pines before the numbness in her legs convinced her that attempting a swim would be sheer madness.

"What do you know about the new people at the Lodge?" Faith asked.

"I don't travel in those kind of circles, deah, but I think you can safely trust your boy to the kitchen there. Don't know how long the operation will last, though. Rich couple bought it, the Otises, and they're the owners on record, but they've turned the day-to-day operations over to their son Derek. They have a big pile over in Blue Hill and doubt they'll be around much. The son is a kid, just shy of thirty, been bouncing around from place to place and wants to try inn keeping. Hasn't been in a rush to open. Still finishing getting it staffed, but brought in some big-deal chef from Hawaii. And last spring they upgraded the cabins and put in a fancy rec hall—place for video games, big-screen TV, air hockey, the whole shebang—to keep the kids out of their parents' hair."

So much for nature walks, Faith thought. "What about this girl Mandy? Should we let Ben drive with her?"

"Mandy's a good kid and smart. Been on the top of the honor roll every year since her family moved to the island. Her mother's a Sanford, married a guy from potato country she met when she went off island for a taste of freedom."

"In potato country?" Tom asked, momentarily diverted from his son's issues.

Seth laughed. "No, the two of them were working at a Wendy's in Orono. Think Leilah—that's Mandy's mother—had some idea she might get to be a student at U Maine that way or maybe meet one. Instead she ended up with Dwayne."

Detecting an undisguised note of disgust in Seth's voice, Faith said, "Why don't you like him?"

"Lazy pissant. Lives off Leilah—she works at Denny's in Ellsworth now, helluva commute—and claims disability from some bullshit accident he supposedly had when he was working at the mill in Bucksport.

"But don't worry. Ben will never see him. Sleeps until noon, then takes a nap. Now, if the tile is a go, I'll get back to work so my employers don't think they're bein' took to the cleaners."

Driving back to Ursula's, Faith tried to put what she was feeling into words. "I know it's a cliché, but it all goes by so fast. Our kids aren't kids anymore. Well, of course they're kids, but . . ."

Tom reached over for his wife's hand and gave it a squeeze. "But they're trying their wings. At least Ben is. I don't think you have to worry about our Amy jumping out of the nest—at least not this summer."

Faith nodded. Amy, unlike Ben, had never wanted to go to sleepaway camp; didn't even like a night away until her friends had started having slumber parties, though she was always happy to stay with Tom's parents, Marian and Dick, down in Norwell in the house where Tom had grown up, one of four kids. Dick Fairchild was retired and loath to travel anywhere except into Boston for a Sox game and an unvarying meal at the only place he'd eat—the Union Oyster House (Wellfleet oysters on the half shell, cup of clam chowder, baked scrod, baked potato, and Boston cream pie). Marian, in contrast, had decided to fly the coop. Not permanently, she'd declared, but she intended to see more of the world than the South Shore of Boston, Cape Cod, Fenway Park, and the Haymarket. Dick had fussed at first, but she was so attentive when she came back from Machu Picchu or other trips, that he had grown to accept her wanderlust.

The Fairchilds were as different from Faith's own family as two families could be. In dog terms, the Fairchilds were bouncy golden retrievers, the Sibleys well-trained borzois. Faith's father, Lawrence, was a man of the cloth, as her grandfather had been. She and her sister, Hope—one year younger—had grown up in that fishbowl known as a parish, although it was quite a nice one on New York's Upper East Side. Both girls had sworn to avoid those waters, no matter the lure of little fairy-tale castles and exotic aquatic plants. They well knew the constant peering in and the rather limited view out. Hope had stayed true to their oath—sailing through an MBA and ever more prestigious jobs carrying the kind of leather cases "When your own initials are enough"—marrying Quentin, whose only collars were buttoned down. Faith had fallen—fallen head over heels—for Tom who was in New York to perform the ceremony for his college roommate's wedding, which Faith was catering. The good reverend had changed his collar before the reception, so Faith hadn't had a clue. When he told her what he did for a living many hours later, it was too late. It had been a *coup de foudre* for them both. She'd tried to hold out in the weeks that followed but had eventually listened to what her heart had been telling her all along. Tom had insisted that times were changing and she would not have to be involved in his "gig," but could move her catering firm, maintaining an independent career. She'd humored him, poor darling, and prepared herself for what lay ahead, hoping she could at least avoid the Sunday school Christmas pageant for a year or more with its dissonant parental chorus of "Why is my kid a shepherd again!"

Unlike her sister, whose first words after "Daddy" and "Mommy" were "Dow Jones," Faith took a more circuitous path to her vocation, also happily her avocation. While it took her family time to understand why their older daughter wanted to labor over a hot stove, once Faith set up her own firm, called Have Faith, after years of study and apprenticeship, it was a different matter. Have Faith—she received the occasional inquiry of a religious nature and, especially in the beginning, some more lascivious—became one of the most sought after caterers in Manhattan. Having the attractive Faith Sibley as a guest at gatherings had been desirable; having her supply delectable food soon became a cachet in the same circles. She knew that once married and living in Aleford, Massachusetts—a place more foreign than most places around the globe for her—she would start up the business again. Someone had to wean those poor people away from boiled dinners and overcooked vegetables. And Have Faith had been just as much a success in Massachusetts as it had been in New York. Last summer, during July and August, she'd left the business in the hands of her assistant and now co-owner, Niki Theodopoulos, who was more than capable of managing things, to be in Maine with her family full-time.

"I just have a funny feeling that this will be the summer I remember as the last one when the kids were even partly kids," Faith continued. She was feeling wistful.

"I was working when I was fifteen," Tom said. "And since Ben will be getting a paycheck, he'd better open a savings account up here at the bank in Granville. Maybe we should start charging him rent."

"Tom!"

"Kidding, sweetheart. Kidding. Not about the bank, though. Do you think Amy is going to be happy at the day camp if Ben is off doing something as glamorous as earning money dishwashing?"

Faith considered it. "She likes babysitting at home, and maybe we can spread the word here for some jobs. How about camp only three days a week, unless she wants to go more? I don't think Ben's job will be an issue." The kids had passed through the "She's always messing up my stuff" phase some time ago, although as Faith spoke she also felt a slight misgiving at what adolescence might bring—all those hormones, all that unpredictability.

They were pulling into the long private road that led to Ursula's and the other houses. The trees on either side were casting long shadows, but the thermometer on the dash read that it was ninety-two degrees outside. And there were people who didn't believe in global warming? They also probably still thought the world was flat and the sun revolved around the earth and you could get AIDS from toilet seats and . . .

Sophie slept in. When she'd arrived in the wee hours of the morning, Uncle Paul had been waiting up in the kitchen, drinking tea and reading. She knew that he had always stayed up late reading like this—Aunt Priscilla had often chided him for missing the best part of the day, since he rarely rose before nine, but he'd told her *she* was missing the best part, and they let it go. Perhaps the schedule suited them. Time together, time apart.

He'd apologized that since it was almost a full house, Sophie had the choice of the little room off the kitchen or the bunkhouse, built in the 1950s for the Proctor offspring and friends, which was unoccupied at the moment. She'd happily picked the kitchen room and was starting to tell him about her memories of recuperating there when he'd told her that her eyes were closing and there would be plenty of time in the morning— actually later in the morning.

There must have been sounds of breakfast preparations, but Sophie hadn't heard them. For a number of summers, Bev Boynton, who had worked many years for the McAllisters as the housekeeper in their Weston, Massachusetts, home, had been coming with them to Maine as well, moving between the two places when they did. She was in the kitchen now hulling strawberries for shortcake.

Sophie popped a particularly juicy-looking berry into her mouth and Bev lightly slapped her hand. "There's a bowl of them for you to have plain or on cereal. Leave these alone. I've already had half the family here snitching them."

"You're the best," Sophie said, giving her a quick hug. Bev wasn't much for overt affection, so Sophie wasn't surprised when the woman didn't return it but pushed her slightly away toward the bowl of fruit. Food was Bev's way of communicating.

"So who's here?" Sophie asked as she poured a little cream over the ripe strawberries.

"Your uncle Simon and aunt Deirdre. And your

cousins should be arriving soon. Forbes called from Belfast to say they'd stop and have lunch somewhere on the way."

"Felicity and Forbes!" Sophie was astonished—and dismayed. She'd assumed work and other matters would keep them in Manhattan. Besides, she'd viewed the whole selection process as one involving her mother's generation; Sophie was a placeholder until Babs could get there. There was another member in that age group. "I'm assuming Sylvia is here, or coming."

Bev nodded. "Got here two days ago. Picked Mrs. McAllister's room."

Aunt Priscilla had moved into what had been her parents' room—the largest, looking straight out to the lighthouse—in her last years. Uncle Paul stayed in the one that had been theirs. Trust Sylvia to grab the prime spot, Sophie thought. Looking up at Bev's expression she knew the housekeeper was thinking the same thing. Suddenly she desperately wanted her mother to have The Birches. Babs would let everyone else use it, Sophie was sure. But if it went to anyone else, Sophie would be saying good-bye to the spot forever when Uncle Paul died. The whole thing began to feel unbearably distasteful and she didn't even want to finish her breakfast. She went to get some Saran Wrap to cover the bowl.

"Not hungry?" Bev said.

"You're just very generous. More than I can eat now. I'll finish them later, but thank you. It's so hot! Why don't I make some sun tea and we can have it iced?"

"Already did that, but you could do a big pitcher of lemonade [see recipe, page 241]. You know how much Mr. McAllister likes it."

Was she being coached? Reminded of what her uncle liked? Sophie wondered as she went to get sugar to make the syrup for the authentic, old-fashioned version of the drink.

"And all her kids are coming, too," Bev said. "Sylvia's. The little one, Daisy, came with her. No idea when the other two are turning up. Lord knows where we'll put everyone. Daisy didn't want to sleep in the bunkhouse by herself, so she's in with her mother for now. The bedrooms on the top floor are all set up, but it's hotter than H-E-double-hockey-sticks up there."

Despite being off the kitchen, Sophie's room had been nice and cool. She'd had no trouble sleeping, although she'd been so tired she could have been in the biblical fiery furnace and slept like a log—well, a biblical log that didn't burn. Uncle Paul hadn't mentioned the rooms upstairs that had been servants' quarters back in the day. She allowed herself a slightly smug inward smile, thinking of Forbes and Felicity up there or in the very rudimentary bunkhouse as she put the sugar syrup into the fridge to cool before adding water and fresh lemon juice.

"I'm going to pick some mint before it gets too hot out. We can leave it in the shade on the counter in a glass of water to put in whatever drinks people want," Sophie said.

"Pick me some tarragon if you would. I'm making chicken salad and other cold dishes for dinner. It's too scorching for anything else," Bev said.

Outside the heat *was* a shock. It never got like this in Maine, especially not at The Birches, normally cooled by the winds off the Reach. Yet there were no winds today; any sailboats out would be motoring to their destinations. Sophie headed quickly for the herbs and crouched down to cut some sprigs of mint. It was taking over the garden the way mint does; she'd have to get out here and weed once the heat broke.

A shadow fell across the patch and she looked up, squinting into the sun.

"You!" she said.

It was the obnoxious man from last night. She'd almost forgotten about the whole episode and now here he was, obviously tracking her down so he could hurl more abuse. "What do you want? I gave you all the information you needed to make a claim on the little bitty dent to your precious car's bumper!"

He appeared to be as astonished as she was, looking from her to the house and back again before saying, "Don't tell me you're one of the relatives, the ones who are going to try to outdo each other in the charm department this month." He almost spat the words at her.

"Whoa, mister. You haven't told me what *you* are doing in my uncle's yard, and how do you know about this anyway?" Sophie stood up, aware that her position low to the ground was not giving her much of an advantage in what was clearly an argument. She was happy to note she was almost as tall as he was. Taller if she'd been in heels.

"Your *uncle*"—he managed to make the relationship sound dubious—"is my grandmother's brother. The car you damaged belongs to him."

"Wait a minute. Uncle Paul is your uncle, too? And I've never seen him with a sports car like that."

"That's because he kept it at my family's house outside Savannah and drove it when he was down there. That's Georgia, by the way."

Sophie knew Uncle Paul was originally from the South and still had family there. He and Aunt Priscilla had spent part of every winter in the warmer clime, but she'd never really paid attention where. She *was* a regionalist, she thought with sudden shame. Not that she was about to let this man know that.

"Why is it here now? The car?" She was tempted to add, *and you*.

"Not that it's really your concern, but I'm pretty fond of Paul and offered to bring it up for him and drive him around this summer—I've never been up here—plus do anything else for him he might need. I have a little free time for the next two months, and I thought he could use my help."

Your help protecting him from his wife's family, Sophie thought, before another idea entered her mind. Could Paul leave The Birches to anybody? Or was Aunt Priscilla specific that it be a Proctor descendant?

"I'm sure there are any number of cars available on the island for sale or rent," she said. "I don't get why you had to drive this old one all the way up here."

"Woman! This isn't just any old car! For your information it's a 1973 Triumph Stag, just about the ultimate sports car Britain ever produced. It's Paul's baby. He's owned it for years."

At that moment, Paul McAllister himself came down the back stairs. "Sophie, Will! Glad you two met. I was keeping an eye out for you, Will. What did Forrest think of the car?" He was looking at them both in an approving manner. Sophie's heart sank. Someone must have told her uncle about Ian, and now he was going to play matchmaker.

"Forrest?" she said.

"Forrest Nevells," Paul said. "He's a local guy. A wizard at restoring cars. I knew he'd get a kick out of seeing this beaut."

"He did—and he said if you ever think of getting rid of it, he's first in line."

"You'll see Fod, that's his nickname, in the parade, Sophie. He and his wife, Margie, always drive one of their cars. Last year's had a vanity plate that read 'WA2SEXY.' I'm thinking of getting one for the Triumph. Maybe not exactly the same, but something that befits a car that James Bond drove."

"I doubt Sophie would have seen those movies, Paul. She strikes me as more the *Pride and Prejudice* type."

"And you strike *me* as the Mister Darcy type—in the first chapters," Sophie shot back. "Now, I have to get these herbs inside before they wilt."

"The same goes for me," Paul said. "Coming, Will?"

"Sure, but I want to put the car in the garage. Wouldn't want anything to happen to it."

Sophie stopped where she was. If her face hadn't been red from the heat, the blush of shame at what she'd done would have been obvious. She'd hit Uncle Paul's car. His treasured vehicle. She turned around and followed Will. He saw her and paused where he was. "What now? Maybe you could do something to the roof with those scissors. The canvas is thick, but you seem like a very determined type."

"Is there some way we could get the dent fixed right away?" Sophie tried to keep her voice from trembling.

"So you don't have to tell him who did it?" He folded his arms and stood in front of her. He was wearing a red baseball cap with a bulldog on it, the same one she'd seen in the light from the flashlight last night, but today she could see that the hair sticking out was the color of hay and his eyes were green, deep green. Like the herbs she was clutching. For some reason this annoyed her even more.

"No!" Sophie knew she had shouted and lowered her voice. Her uncle was still making his way back into the house. "I just don't want him to be upset."

"Well, fortunately Fod was able to take care of it, so you can stop worrying." He smiled, a "Dennis Quaid *Big Easy*" crooked smirk. "About that, anyway."

"Now what the H-E-double-hockey-sticks was that supposed to mean?" Sophie said softly to herself once he was well out of earshot.

With the arrival of Felicity and Forbes, the house was bursting at the seams, and Sylvia's two oldest children would be adding to the numbers late tonight or tomorrow. Bev served dinner buffet style and people took plates out to the porch, where it was marginally cooler. Household groups gravitated toward one another, and without a next of kin, Sophie found herself with Uncle Paul and Will, whose last name she'd learned was Tarkington. Booth Tarkington was well represented in The Birches's bookshelves. The summer she'd spent recuperating, Sophie remembered making her way through every title from *Penrod* to *Gentle Julia*. She doubted Will had ever heard the author's name, let alone read him. This Tarkington struck her as a *Car and Driver* devotee, oh, and James Bond, but the movies, not Fleming's books. She'd been dismayed to discover Will was camped out in the boathouse at the end of the largest dock, so avoiding him would be a challenge. Now he was sitting next to his uncle and she was on the porch floor. She moved down a step.

"So, Sophie." Her cousin Forbes's voice was carefully modulated to sound slightly superior, but not arrogant. She imagined he practiced to strike just the right tone, one that said "I'm better than you, but it

would be such bad taste to flaunt it." She steeled her-
self for his next words. She knew what was coming.
"Sorry things didn't work out with you and that Brit,
Ian. How's the job hunt coming?"

Felicity quickly chimed, "You must have been dev-
astated. So, so sorry." It was an almost convincing demonstration of how very very caring and sympathetic her
cousin was, Sophie thought.

"Thank you both, but I'm fine. And the job hunt is
going well." She tried not to grit her teeth. And who
had told Forbes Ian's name?

"Oh?" Forbes said. "Which firms?"

"None you'd be familiar with."

"Try me. My net is a broad one."

"That reminds me," Uncle Paul said. "We're going
to need lobsters for the Fourth. I'd better call Charlie
Sullivan."

Sophie gave him a grateful smile.

"Seems to me those are caught with traps, not nets,"
Will said, getting up. Sophie's smile vanished. Was
Will trying to steer the conversation back? Then he
added, "Anyone want more lemonade? I can bring the
pitcher out."

"Where's Bev?" Aunt Deirdre said. She had been
quiet—rare for her. Sophie figured she was basking in
the pleasure of being with her three favorite people:
her husband, her son, and her daughter. The question

clearly indicated that she thought fetching lemonade fell under the purview of the help.

"I told her to go lie down," Paul said. "Keeping all of us fed in this heat is too much for her."

How could I be so thoughtless, Sophie thought. Bev was easily in her seventies. She was always shooing people out of the kitchen, but from now on Sophie wasn't going to let her. She would start by cleaning up once everyone had finished.

"This heat is getting to everyone," Uncle Simon said. "Can't remember it ever being like this here at The Birches."

"That's because we're destroying the earth," Sylvia said. "Poor Daisy won't have anything but an ash heap."

The twelve-year-old looked so startled that Sophie hastened to reassure her. "I'm sure not. We certainly do our part here, and people are much more aware now all over the world."

"Sophie, I do not believe in telling my children anything but the truth, so please don't tell Daisy what we all know is a lie. The polar ice cap is melting rapidly and as for fossil fuels—"

Paul jumped in. "The only fuel I need now is the strawberry shortcake I happen to know Bev made. The real kind with biscuits, not that spongy stuff you get in restaurants. *And* real whipped cream. I'll bet you can eat two, Daisy."

Sylvia opened her mouth and seemed about to say something, but changed her mind. His distraction worked. "If she does, she'll be sick. Come on, Daisy, and we'll bring a plate back for you, Paul."

Sophie watched them go into the house. She had to hand it to Sylvia. She never veered off course. She'd come of age during the Summer of Love and had never left. Along the way she'd toyed with just about every alternative lifestyle from communes to convents (this choice was brief). At times she'd worked at a variety of jobs, mostly shops that sold crystals and herbal remedies. She didn't believe in marriage, but she did believe in child support, so Autumn, Rory, and Daisy had always had a roof over their heads, even though it had been a yurt on more than one occasion. Sophie had seen photos of Sylvia as a young woman, still with the same long hair, but no gray mixed with the blond, and the same lean body, yoga-toned. She'd been stunningly beautiful and was still very attractive. Her clothes ran to tie-dye and batik, but they fit well. A California tan and many beaded bracelets, necklaces, and long earrings completed the picture of Sylvia Proctor at forty-something.

In contrast, the Simon Proctor family could have stepped straight from the Brooks Brothers summer catalog. Father and son were wearing pima cotton tees with the Golden Fleece logo, the sheep suspended by a ribbon that always made Sophie long to set the poor animal free. Uncle Simon was wearing navy blue Bermuda shorts while Forbes was going rogue in madras. Felicity and her mother were in sleeveless linen shifts, lime green for Deirdre and raspberry for Felicity, with strappy sandals to match. Sophie noticed that they had both had recent pedis and tucked her own toes out of sight.

The sun, a fiery ball, was starting to sink into the sea. Sophie looked out at the horizon. A few boats—not the fishermen, who'd long been in port—left plumes of wakes on the flat surface of the Reach. The water was very inviting. She pushed a stray hair back over her ear. It had come loose from the low ponytail she'd gathered at the nape of her neck. After she finished putting the food away and washing the dishes, she'd take a swim. The tide was high and she could go in off the dock. Just thinking about it made her feel cooler. Then she remembered the boathouse and its occupant. Damn. She looked over her shoulder. Will Tarkington or no Will Tarkington, she was going to do as she pleased.

Chapter 3

The notion that bad news never comes during the day, but is conveyed by a middle-of-the-night phone call, is of course a myth. Yet when one picks up the phone at noon, the expectation is to hear a friend's voice, a spouse, someone looking for a volunteer to chair the Girl Scout cookie drive, or increasingly in these economic times, desperate cold calls from small companies or individuals offering carpet cleaning or chimney sweeping. It was with one of these sorts of expectations that Faith picked up the phone at The Pines. Everyone was out and she had been enjoying a few treasured moments alone to sit on the porch and read.

"Hello?"

"Faith? It's Dick. Is Tom there?"

Dick Fairchild, her father-in-law. Faith had given everyone in the family this number when they'd moved over to The Pines, so the surprise was not that he had it, but that he was on the phone at all. Tom's mother, Marian, did the calling. Dick's aversion to Mr. Bell's instrument was well known; Faith had seen him sit and let it ring until someone else in the house answered. Before retirement he'd been a Realtor, and she guessed he'd had enough of phone calls.

Her heart sank. Whatever the news, it was bad.

"Tom is out sailing; he should be back soon."

"How soon? Marian's had a heart attack. I'm at the hospital with her. The EMTs brought her in thirty minutes ago. She is stable now, but in the ICU." The anguish in his words was palpable.

"A heart attack! But she's never had any heart problems! We'll be there as quickly as we can. We can get a plane from Bar Harbor to Boston. What are the doctors saying? Is she conscious?"

Faith knew she needed to sound calmer. She took a deep breath. "I can see the dock from where I am and will know the minute Tom's here. Tell me what happened."

"It's been so darn hot. I thought that was it. We thought that was it." Faith heard the catch in Dick's voice. "She's been short of breath this last week, maybe longer. She didn't tell me about it until yesterday when she thought she might have eaten something that disagreed with her. She had chest pains. *Chest pains!* How could I not have known?"

Very easily, Faith thought to herself. Her mother-in-law would have made the Spartan boy look like a whiner.

"You couldn't have known," she said. "I'm sure she didn't think anything was wrong either." Marian most likely did but wouldn't have wanted to make a fuss.

"This morning the pain was worse," Dick continued. "She wouldn't let me take her to the hospital or even call the doctor. Then it got really bad and, well, I had to get an ambulance."

"I'm going to call the airport and find out when the next plane leaves. It will take about an hour to get there and about an hour in the air, but it will be quicker than driving. We can pick up the car we left in Aleford."

"I haven't phoned anyone else. Craig is up in Vermont and the rest of the gang is over in Europe."

Craig was the baby of the family, behaving like one for too long; but he had finally settled down. He co-owned a ski resort in Vermont, active as a vacation spot in the summer as well.

Betsey, divorced with two college-age boys, was the oldest Fairchild sibling and like her dad had gone into real estate. Marian recently told Faith that empty nester Bets was seeing someone seriously, a fellow Realtor. The two were currently in Provence, maybe checking out the market—what a four bedroom, three and a half bath, kitchen with granite countertops, stainless steel appliances, etc., went for there.

Tom was the next Fairchild to arrive and then Robert, two years younger. He was also abroad, in Spain, on vacation with his partner, Michael. They were sporting goods sales reps, and this was a less busy time of year for them.

Dick had paused before finishing the sentence. "Besides it's Tom she'll want in any . . ." He seemed to run out of steam again.

But Dick didn't have to finish the thought. Of course Marian would want Tom by her side. Anybody would. In addition to his many pastoral calls to those in times of illness, Tom was one of the chaplains at the local VA hospital. It was what he did, and he was very good at it.

"I don't like the idea of your being at the hospital without anyone until we get there. Why don't you call one of your brothers?"

"Maybe in a while. It's early days yet."

Faith understood: calling them, even calling her, was making everything too real. She could picture the hospital waiting room. The hand sanitizer dispensers every few feet, the out-of-date magazines, seating with a view to durability not comfort, the sights and sounds of patients coming—and going. But it *was* real and he shouldn't be alone there.

"Would you like me to call your brothers for you?"

"Okay."

There was a little relief in his voice. And then big relief after Faith spotted Tom and then quickly told Dick, "I can see the dinghy! They're on the way in. Are you using Marian's cell? Never mind, just stay on the line."

"I will."

She sped down the stairs and over the rocks to the dock. Tom, Ben, and Chris Knight, a sailing buddy of Tom's, were within shouting distance. Faith hated to upset Ben, who definitely wasn't used to this sort of crisis, but there was no choice.

"Tom, come as quickly as you can! Your mother's in the hospital and your father is on the phone!"

It seemed only seconds before he was talking to his father, Faith and Ben listening at his side.

He hung up and the first thing he did was hug them both close to him.

"She's going to be all right. We're lucky to live in an area with the best medical care you can get, and the doctors have told Dad there's no immediate danger.

They don't have a diagnosis yet, but she definitely had some kind of heart attack. A major one. Come upstairs, both of you, while I change and pack. Chris told me he could give me a ride to the airport and I'm going to take him up on it. Come to think of it, Ben, go tell him I'll be ready in a few minutes and stow the gear in the boathouse." He gave his son another quick squeeze, then started up the stairs with Faith close behind.

"Tom!" she said. "I'll pack for both of us. I want to come with you. Your mother could want me there, too, and in any case, I can help take care of Dick."

"Of course she'll want you. Eventually. But now you need to stay here with the kids. Explain that they won't be able to see her. I don't even know whether Dad and I can. Will you call both my uncles and tell them what's happened? Once I know what Dad wants, I'll call my sibs. You know Betsey for one will be on the next plane back, and that might upset Mom more than anything."

"Oh, sweetheart, it's so hard to believe."

Marian Fairchild was the picture of health with the stamina of a sixteen-year-old. Faith had never even known her to have a cold.

Tom sat down on the bed and pulled her into his arms, his head bent. She knew he was praying. As she had been since she'd answered the phone.

"You change," she said. "I'll pack your things. And I'll get someone to bring our car to Logan so you won't waste time going home."

One of the things she had grown to appreciate about living in a small town like Aleford was the network of people who would help in times of trouble. There wouldn't be a problem finding someone to drive the Fairchilds' car followed by someone driving another out to the airport. It would easily save several hours.

Less than twenty minutes had passed from the time of the call until Tom kissed her good-bye, told her he would phone when he got there, and drove off in the Knights' Prius with Chris at the wheel. There was a network on Sanpere, too. Faith sat down on the top step of the porch and waited for Ben to come back from the boathouse.

Bad news. Bad news on a sunny, cloudless, perfect Maine day.

"Now that Autumn and Rory have arrived, I'd like to get everyone together after lunch. Pass the word if you will." Paul McAllister paused and smiled at the late risers, who were still lingering over coffee in the kitchen. "I've always wanted to stand in front of a roomful of people and say, 'You may have wondered why I have gathered you all here together'—like Hercule Poirot—but you all know why. So let's get it

out of the way and then we can concentrate on enjoying a bang-up Fourth."

Sophie was standing at the sink finishing the dishes.
Bev had been feeling off-color—the heat again, she'd
said—and Sophie had convinced her to go back to bed
with one of the ancient electric fans The Birches had
in abundance trained on her—fans with lethal-looking
blades and frayed cords that Sophie had seen for sale in
antiques shops with warnings to use for decorative pur-
poses only. She'd put a glass and a pitcher of ice water
on the bedside table, tucking a piece of paper under
one leg to stop the wobble. It wasn't that Bev's room
had been furnished with discards. *All* the furniture in
the house was like this. Bev hadn't wanted anything
more than water—"Never could eat when it was hot.
And my waistline won't suffer."

It was true that Bev was an armful, but it suited her.
Sophie couldn't imagine her any other way than the
small plump woman whose hair had gone from carrot
to pale rust in the years Sophie had known her. Sylvia
had wanted to give Bev some sort of herbal remedy, but
the housekeeper had firmly rejected the offer before
going up to her room. "Took some plain old table salt
and that will do it. And putting my feet up."

Sylvia was one of those remaining in the kitchen,
although she had been up for hours and eaten an early
breakfast. Her children were the attraction. Will

Tarkington, who did seem to be making himself useful in all sorts of ways, Sophie thought grudgingly, had picked Autumn up in Bangor at the airport last night. Her plane from San Francisco had been late. Rory had appeared late, as well. He'd flown from California to Boston several days earlier and driven up. Sylvia was quizzing him now about whose car it was—or was it a rental—and what friends he'd been visiting; so far she'd gleaned very little. It occurred to Sophie that her cousin, who looked like a stereotypical surfer dude with his sun-bleached hair even blonder than she recalled and a deep tan, was showing well-practiced adeptness at humoring his mother while revealing almost nothing.

Uncle Paul's announcement deflected Sylvia's attention from her son.

"I'll go tell Simon before he leaves," she said. "He and Forbes are playing golf at the country club in Blue Hill this morning. Deirdre and Felicity are going, too. Some old school chum of Deirdre's has a house there on Parker Point."

"Thank you, Sylvia. About two o'clock then, in the living room."

And Colonel Mustard with a candlestick, jumped into Sophie's mind. Must be Uncle Paul's Christie reference that had her leaping to the mystery game. In any case, she reflected, Cousin Sylvia seemed to have appointed herself the town crier as well as keeper of tabs on everyone at The Birches's whereabouts.

As for what she would do with herself until the meeting, Sophie wasn't sure. Bev had started to plan lunch, but Sophie had stopped her and emphatically told her she was not to worry, that Sophie would do it. So there was that to organize. She'd take the car and engage in a little hunting and gathering, harder on Sanpere than in New York or London. She had a sudden pang at the thought of the Waitrose around the corner from Ian's flat. All that lovely prepared food, as well as the best ingredients for Londoners who had time to cook. She still had the customer card in her wallet. Well, that was one thing she'd do right now. Throw it away, along with other reminders like her Oyster Card for the Tube.

What mattered was the here and now. Sanpere Island. The Birches. Uncle Paul.

It had been just like him to get right to the point. They *did* all know why they were here, although she would be glad when the specifics were made clearer. Had Aunt Priscilla designed something like the Twelve Labors of Hercules? Except that was penance. No, maybe something like a treasure hunt with hidden clues. There she was again, back in some sort of novel, a mystery novel? One thing was clear. Having the meeting early would make for a much better holiday. Or would it?

Quelling that notion, Sophie took the memo pad that was stuck to the fridge with a lobster magnet to write a shopping list both for today and tomorrow. She loved making lists. Cold cuts and bulkie rolls to make sandwiches for lunches. They had plenty of mustard and other condiments, but she should check anyway; jars had a way of accumulating with only a teaspoon left at the bottom. Tomorrow's picnic would by definition be messy. They'd need more paper goods plus plenty of butter to melt for the lobsters and clams.

Paul and Priscilla, and earlier generations, had hosted the clambake picnic for the entire Point each year. The method for the main course was unvarying. It had originated with the first summer people, the Abenakis, who came down to these shores each year from Canada. Tonight a group would dig a pit well above the high tide mark on the beach, lining it with rocks and driftwood, adding charcoal if there wasn't enough wood. Early in the morning, they'd light it. The rocks had to heat up for at least five hours before the food was layered in between wet rockweed, which would steam it to perfection. A tarp, weighted down with more stones, covered the bake.

The Proctors, and then the McAllisters, always had provided the lobster, clams, and corn, omitting the chicken and sausages some bakes included. The rest of the households on the Point brought variations of chicken and sausage, as well as traditional picnic fare like deviled eggs, potato salad, coleslaw, chips, dips, hot dogs for the kids, and desserts galore. Blueberry pie was a given, as were chocolate chip cookies, but the rest could be anything from coconut layer cake (that family was from the South originally) to Pavlova (a son had married an Aussie).

Sophie found herself getting excited. The Fourth of July was her very favorite Sanpere/Birches tradition. Up early for the pancake breakfast at the Sanpere Village town hall to raise money for the volunteer fire department and ambulance corps, then the parade—a short one, as dictated by the island population, turning around at the top of the hill by the Congregational church to come back through town again. After the parade and games for children in the field by the elementary school, they would head back to The Birches for the clambake that would last until dusk. Will Tarkington was in for a treat. He'd probably never even had a real lobster. A Maine lobster. Knowing him, he'd want grits with it. Grits!

She finished her list and dried the pots and pans from breakfast that were in the dish drainer, hanging each on the pegboard that covered a good part of one wall. Years ago a tidy person had outlined the various kitchenwares with a bright blue marker to indicate where they should go, and no one had ever changed it. No changes. That's what was so special about The Birches. That there had been so few, if any, changes. Sophie knew if she left a sweater or a book one summer, it would be there when she returned—possibly in the same spot. Just like the scrapbook with the ferns she had pressed and labeled as a child and the ones her mother, Simon, and Sylvia had made—Priscilla many years earlier, too. Along with family photo albums, they were all stacked on the bottom shelf of the big bookcase in the living room. Some of the books' pages were crumbling—as were the ferns and other flora— but no one had thrown them away. At least not yet.

This was all so terribly hard, she thought. Why *couldn't* they simply share the house? Allot times, if that became a problem? Draw straws to choose dates? She turned toward the people still sitting at the kitchen table.

"Does anyone need anything from the market? I'm going into Granville for a few things."

"I don't suppose they have quinoa and flaxseed," Sylvia said, walking back into the room. "Rory, I know how much you like the kale salad I make with it. I picked up some kale yesterday from that man who has the little stand across the Reach next to that Mexican restaurant place."

"I'm not sure they have things like that at the market," Sophie said. "But if they haven't left yet, you could go back and ask those going to Blue Hill to stop at the natural foods co-op. And if the farm stand has strawberries out, could you ask them to pick up a few cartons of those, too? They can't miss it. You're right, Sylvia, it's just past El El Frijoles." She smiled. "I'm such a dunce. It took a couple of seasons before I realized what the name meant and got the joke!"

"Glad you reminded me. I love that place!" Rory said. "Skip the salad, Ma, I'm going to head over there and get some of those crab quesadillas for my lunch. I'll bring some back for you, too, sis, unless you're doing the vegan thing again, and in that case I'll score you their black bean dish. Anyone else?"

Sylvia looked daggers at Sophie. As if Rory's defection was Sophie's fault and Sophie's alone.

Autumn had not said a word, her nose buried in an oversize coffee cup that said JAVA HOUND on it. The Birches had what seemed like hundreds of mugs and cups like these. Another instance of what came in never going out. Sophie had used one this morning with the 1950s Tony the Tiger logo. Might be worth checking some of these out on eBay. She caught herself. That is, whoever inherited could.

Autumn had ditched her Raggedy Ann tights and the rest of the outfit for a more conventional summer outfit—cutoffs and flip-flops with a muslin-print long-sleeved shirt that was obviously vintage, something from a flea market. Her hair was long and she'd clipped it up on top of her head like a Gibson Girl. She was one of the most beautiful women Sophie had ever seen, and as usual, she felt as plain as a mud fence next to her. And there were those blue eyes, too. Like big blue marbles or some sort of poetic sapphire orbs. Sophie was sure there had been any number of comparisons from the men her cousin attracted.

Autumn stood up, went over to the sink, turned on a faucet, and rinsed the cup out, handing it to Sophie to dry.

"Thanks, not this time," she answered. "I won't be here for lunch."

"But you'll be back by two?" Her mother's anxiety was not hard to miss. Her voice had gone up an octave and it had already been shrill talking to Rory.

Autumn just looked at her and slipped out the back door without another word.

"Where can she be going? She doesn't have a car!" Sylvia placed a hand on Rory's arm, as if to keep *him* anchored.

Sophie decided it was time to take off herself, after she checked on Bev. She glanced back into the room as she left. Uncle Paul was rubbing his forehead with one finger. A simple gesture, but what was it conveying? Annoyance, forbearance, remembrance? He had been sitting at the table with his coffee beside him and this week's *Ellsworth American* spread out in front of him. Sophie hadn't seen him turn a single page.

Tom called as he was boarding the small commuter plane in Bar Harbor and again when he landed. In between Faith went about the mundanities of everyday life. She did a wash, planned supper, and after the second call set out for the market in Granville to pick up chicken and a few other supplies for the Fourth. That was the thing about news like this. You had to keep on with whatever you had to do, but everything you did took on a surreal air. Standing by the case in the meat department, debating how much white meat versus dark meat to buy, most of her mind was on Marian and the rest of the Fairchilds.

Tom's sibs, and definitely Dick, were all grown-ups—well, maybe not Craig—but Marian was the most grown-up of them all. Faith thought of her mother-in-law as that "central cedar pole" in the Frost poem "The Silken Tent," with her husband and children, the guy wires about her. Faith had long recognized that Marian's solo travels were a respite from this role. What Faith was recognizing now, and recognizing acutely, was what a weakening—or, horrible to even consider, the removal—of this support would mean for the family.

"Hi." A voice to her left penetrated her thoughts. "Are you okay?"

Faith grabbed a package and put it in her cart. "Sorry, just a little distracted."

The young woman looked familiar. Faith quickly subtracted a few years from the pretty face and realized who it was.

"You're Sophie, aren't you? From The Birches? You babysat for my children many summers ago."

"Yes! It doesn't seem that long, but that's what summers here are like—one blends into another. How are you, Mrs. Fairchild?"

In Faith's experience when people asked you this question it was almost always better to say "fine" unless you really wanted them to know, so that's what she replied. And when she asked Sophie in turn, the young woman said the same thing.

And yet, looking each other in the eye, they each immediately knew the other was lying.

For Sophie, one sign was the fact that Mrs. Fairchild had put a family-size package of those red hot dogs, endemic to Maine, in her cart when it was well known that she was a respected caterer and food lover—the hot dogs falling into the comestible category only because they were eaten in a bun. Even more telling was her furrowed face and eyes that threatened to overflow.

Looking at Sophie's expression, Faith thought her former babysitter was bearing the cares of the world on her smooth shoulders, exposed by the bright yellow sundress she was wearing. Knowing what was going on at The Birches, Faith wasn't surprised.

"Is your mother here? And do call me Faith."

Sophie shook her head. "She's in Greece. I'm representing her. What I mean is I'm—"

Faith interrupted her. "We're staying next door at The Pines with Ursula, so we've heard about the conclave." She tried for a smile.

Now Sophie smiled back in a similar fashion and sighed. "I suppose I should tell Uncle Paul to send white smoke up the chimney when he's made his choice. But I'm so glad you're next door. You'll be at the picnic tomorrow, I hope. I'd love to see Benny and Amy— right? They must be so big!"

"Very big, especially Ben—no more 'Benny'—and yes, 'Amy.' We're looking forward to the picnic. That's why I'm getting all this chicken." She looked in her cart and gave a little start. "Oh dear. What is that doing in there?" She put the package of franks back and began selecting the chicken. She was going to get up early and bake it in the oven with her own barbecue sauce, basting it frequently, refrigerate, and then bring it to room temperature, since it would both save time and not heat up the kitchen later. Tomorrow was supposed to be worse than today.

The Point would hear soon enough, so she added, "My husband, Tom, won't be with us. His mother has had a heart attack, and he's on his way to Massachusetts."

"I'm so sorry! Is there anything I can do? I know there are plenty of people at The Pines, but if you want me to help with the kids—if you need to go down yourself, I'd be happy to look after them."

Faith impulsively gave Sophie a hug.

"You are a dear. I always knew that, and I may take you up on the offer, but for now I'm staying here. Ben is working at the Lodge, The Laughing Gull Lodge. He's very proud—it's his first real job. His shift as a dishwasher starts this afternoon. The novelty will wear off soon, I expect. And Amy is in day camp three days a week. She's looking for babysitting or mother's helper-type jobs herself."

"Well, if anyone needs a ride—Ben surely isn't old enough to drive yet is he?—call me. My cell doesn't work anywhere on the island except on the side facing the Swans Island cell towers, but The Birches has advanced into the twenty-first century with a message machine and Wi-Fi. I'll give you my e-mail."

As she scribbled it down on the back of one of her old business cards, Sophie thought Amy wasn't the only one looking for work. Thanks to her uncle's need for Internet access, she'd been checking her e-mail since she arrived, and there hadn't been a response to any of her recent interview requests, nor a reply, except in the negative, for any of the jobs where she'd gotten a foot in the door. She kept telling herself that it was because of the holiday. People started it early. She'd told Forbes that she was casting her net wide, but the net seemed to be rather frayed so far.

Faith turned the card over.

"Very impressive. My sister, Hope Sibley Lewis, has done business with your firm."

Sophie's face reddened. "I'm not actually there anymore. I'm—what do they say in the theater—'resting.' And I've met your sister. She was a guest speaker at a seminar I took in law school. Everyone agreed she was the high point of the term."

"If you decide to break your siesta, I'm sure she would be glad to talk to you," Faith offered. Hope did things like this. But why would Sophie have left a plum job? For a moment Faith was distracted from her worries. Could the young woman have been fired? But for what reason? Maybe Hope would know.

Or was it something else completely?

If Sophie had expected they would have to wait to start the meeting for people to finish lunch or straggle in, she would have been wrong. Two o'clock found all concerned in the living room, ears and eyes wide open, mouths shut—for now.

All concerned. Which was whom? Slipping into a chair, she saw that Will Tarkington was ensconced in one that he'd pulled away from the window and back into the shadows under the stairs. Again she wondered whether Aunt Priscilla had counted her husband's relatives as eligible to inherit.

Bev was also in the room, sitting in a straight-backed chair near the kitchen door. She'd placed a large tray on a table with iced tea, lemonade, glasses, and a basket filled with the kind of cookies she'd always kept the household supplied with—old-fashioned favorites like hermits, oatmeal raisin, peanut butter, and plenty of chocolate chip.

People were chatting, but Sophie knew they were just killing time. Rory and Forbes were drinking beer, Rory a Sam Adams from the bottle, Forbes something imported in one of the German ceramic steins he kept in the freezer.

Paul stood up, and the room went silent. Sophie wished her mother were here, wished she herself weren't.

"I know you all loved Priscilla and I know you all love this place. Priscilla knew it, too. She was not one for drama and she tried every which way to figure out what to do with The Birches without causing it. Whether she succeeded depends on you. She left this letter, which I'll read. The envelope is unopened, but I know what it says." He slit the flap open. "Here goes:

"'My dears,

"'I wish I were in the room with you right now, the living room would be best I told Paul, and I'm sure Bev, my treasure, has supplied you with wonderful things to eat and drink. Every season at The Birches is special to me, but the days around Independence Day are filled with my most golden memories, so that's why I have selected this time for you to gather. It may be because it stretches the furthest back to my very first recollection of Sanpere. And every year after was the same. My grandfather would rouse us early, it almost seemed as if it was still night to me when I was a very *young child. He'd read the Declaration of Independence facing us from atop one of the big granite rocks on the beach as the dawn rose behind him. He had a beautiful voice. I can hear it still. We sang a few patriotic songs, including the national anthem, and afterward there was a race back to the house for blueberry pancakes. I came in first the year I was twelve! Then into town for the parade and back again for the big clambake here on the Point. You'll be doing many of these same things tomorrow.*

"'I know I'm going on and on, but my love for The Birches is what has made it so hard to decide what to do, and so hard to leave this earth, although maybe I am one with the Transcendentalists' Over-Soul now, which always struck me as a place that might be hovering over Penobscot Bay. Grandfather was a great admirer of Emerson, so it could be true. But no more digressions, I promise.

"'First of all, many years ago—and Paul supported me in this—I decided the property could not be shared or divided. That has already been written into my will, as has his life tenancy. Nor can The Birches be sold unless there are no surviving Proctor descendants, an event I sorely hope will never occur.'"

Paul stopped and reached for the glass of lemonade on the table next to his chair, draining it. Immediately Sylvia and Simon leaped up to refill it, grabbing the handle of the pitcher at virtually the same time.

So that's how it's going to be, Sophie thought dismally.

Simon won, replenishing the glass, and Paul thanked them both.

"Now where was I? Yes, the conditions. Can't be sold, can't be divided, can't be shared. In perpetuity. Priscilla felt strongly about this. I'll continue:

" '*I have watched too many families torn apart trying to share a summer place, squabbling over who gets to use it when and even more serious arguments over who pays for what. It costs a great deal to maintain The Birches. There's a fairly new roof, but shingles need replacing all the time. We are part of the Point Family Association, so there are those dues, and other expenses crop up in order to maintain the big dock and the road. Our taxes are high, since we have waterfront. I always enjoy writing that tax check, because it gives back to this island, as do my checks to the volunteer services like the fire department and ambulance corps. I would hope all of you, not just the person*

Paul selects, do this on occasion. Now, this said, it would be more than understandable for any of you to opt out of consideration. Just tell Paul. Old houses are a joy—and a burden.

"'My hope is that whoever takes The Birches on will make it available to the whole family as Paul and I have, but that person needs to understand that he or she is solely responsible for it. I would also hope that no significant changes to the exterior or interior be made. I believe one of the things that makes The Birches special to our family is the lack of change. It really is our history and keeps on being so for each generation. I have loved watching you young people grow up here, and your children as well.'"

Sophie found herself close to tears. She missed Aunt Priscilla as never before. Uncle Paul was reading, but it was his wife's voice Sophie heard, almost as if Priscilla Proctor McAllister were reading it aloud herself.

Daisy got up from the floor where she'd been sitting at her mother's feet and went to get a cookie. Sylvia snatched at her daughter's tee shirt and pulled her back down. "Not now!" she said.

Paul immediately took note.

"Let's have a pause so everyone can refresh glasses and get some of Bev's cookies. I want one myself. I should have warned you that it was a long epistle. Bathroom break, too."

At first no one moved, then everyone did at once. Sophie wanted neither the bathroom nor Bev's treats. She wanted air and went out onto the porch.

"Pressure getting to you?" Will's words dripped with sarcasm but acted like a bucket of cold water. Sophie swallowed the sobs that had threatened. He must have known Priscilla. How could he seem so uncaring, listening to what were some of her last words?

"What is that supposed to mean?" she shot back.

"Just what I said. I imagine a hotshot lawyer like you is pretty competitive. No doubt you'll want to be the winner of this nutty contest."

Ignoring the first part of his sentence, Sophie asked, "Why are you calling it 'nutty'?"

He walked over to the railing and stood next to her. Sophie noticed he was barefoot. That's why she hadn't heard him come up behind her on the porch. His hair was damp; he must have just taken a shower, unless he was hardy enough to swim in these waters, which she doubted. Anyway, he didn't smell like salt, but something else. Something like plain old Ivory soap, a clean smell. Ian had had a wonderfully distinctive smell, his own private label aftershave concocted by Trumpers of Mayfair. She pushed the thought firmly away.

"I should have said 'cruel,' not 'nutty.' Now, don't go nutty yourself. I liked Priscilla—no, I loved her— but she shouldn't have put my uncle in this position. She should have chosen an heir herself, written it in her will with the rest of the stipulations, all to be revealed after his death, leaving him safely out of it." He cocked his head toward the door. "And he's ready to finish. At least for now."

Sophie followed him back into the room. It was stifling after being outside. She hated to admit it, but Will was right.

"Everyone all set?" Paul said. "There's not much more:

> " *'Some of you will think me horrid or worse for leaving this crucial decision to Paul.'* "

Sophie looked over at Will, who seemed as startled as she was. It was as if Priscilla had been eavesdropping on them.

> " *'I have been blessed with two happy marriages and do not intend to jeopardize the present one before shuffling off this mortal coil, but Paul will tell you that the plan is his and his alone. He knew that I was getting more and more worked*

*up about whom to pick. As he has so often done
before, he took charge of my cares and assumed
them himself. What he so lovingly said to me was,
"You'd have to live the time you have left antici-
pating those not chosen's feelings of hurt. The
thought that you had slighted them, loved them
less than the others, would plague you, and you'd
also keep changing your mind. This way your
memory of them stays the way it should, and
you don't have to think about The Birches at
all." ' "*

Paul sat down. "I'm not finished, but my legs are
getting tired. What she wrote is true. You're all dear to
me, but not kin except by marriage. It's not that I don't
care what you think of me, but . . ."

Will emerged from the shadows, deeper now as the
afternoon waned. "But he doesn't. No worries, Uncle.
Better to spell it out. You're not emotionally involved
the way Aunt Priscilla was, so you can be objective."
He looked around the room, and Sophie once again
thought what she had realized before. Will Tarkington
wasn't here to drive his uncle around, do the odd job.
He was here to protect Paul McAllister.

Protect him from all of them.

Casting an affectionate glance at Will, Paul said, "Be
that as it may, let's get to the end of the letter:

" 'I have asked Paul to invite whomever wishes to inherit to come for the Fourth of July and stay for the rest of the month as work and other commitments permit. He will announce the legatee on July thirty-first, or earlier should he choose. It may be that only one of you will want to take The Birches on.

" 'A final note: Paul may also opt to choose no one, although I think that is unlikely and hope the situation will not arise. If it does, however, the house and contents will be put up for sale and the proceeds will go to the Island Community Center to help fund their programs, especially the Food Pantry and Fuel Assistance Fund. That will also be the case should the legatee seek to sell the property him or herself.

" 'From this point on—the date indicated next to my signature below—all decisions regarding the property known as The Birches are Paul McAllister's and Paul McAllister's alone.

" 'My love,

" 'Aunt Priscilla.' "

Paul folded the sheets and put them back in the envelope. "There is a notarized copy of the letter with our lawyer, but I'll leave this here on the table, so you can read it over if you like. Now, I for one am going to take a long walk through the woods to the other side of the Point, and then come back for a martini. Anyone who cares to may join me for either or both."

The room rose as one, but it was Felicity who strode to her uncle's side and assumed center stage.

Looking first toward the ceiling with a rhapsodic look on her face—seeking divine inspiration?—she said solemnly, "Whether I myself or anyone else in my immediate family is bestowed with the honor that guardianship of The Birches would bring, I hope, Uncle Paul, that you will permit my nuptials to take place here in August. As I have told my fiancé, who will be joining us on Saturday or sooner, time and time again: there is no spot on earth that means as much to me, and it's where I want us to plight our troth."

She flashed a triumphant smile, which was almost simultaneously duplicated by her parents and brother.

Advantage Team Simon.

Chapter 4

The Fourth had dawned hotter than any day so far. A scorcher. Faith walked into the kitchen at The Pines for something very cold to drink. The idea of a cup of hot coffee made her gag, and she wasn't at all hungry. The rest of the house seemed still asleep, including her children.

When she'd picked Ben and Tyler up at the Lodge last night both boys had been sweaty and tired, but filled with enthusiasm about the dishwashing job. She listened while they explained in excruciating detail how to run the industrial machine and how you had to sort the silverware into the compartments by type so it would be faster to unload and put away—all things she knew as a professional caterer but pretended not to know as a mom. She hoped they would always be as excited about their jobs. The boys were not going to miss the parade for work after all, as they weren't scheduled for the breakfast shift. In fact, they were going to be *in* the parade, they announced proudly. They'd be marching behind a giant papier-mâché gull, a *Leucophaeus atricilla,* that the Otises had had made. The Lodge had supplied them with high-quality cotton forest-green polo shirts, their elaborate logo—a laughing gull with outstretched wings curved around THE LAUGHING GULL LODGE, SANPERE ISLAND, MAINE— machine embroidered on the pockets. In this heat she'd try to get Ben to wear a lighter tee until the start of the parade—if she could get him to relinquish what was obviously a garment on par with cloth of gold.

Gert Prescott, who had been working at The Pines since her teens, many, many years ago, was squeezing lemons at the counter next to the sink.

"Good morning, Faith. Mrs. Rowe is out taking her walk. There's iced coffee in the fridge, and I'm making a few more gallons of lemonade for the picnic. We're going to need it."

Gert made her iced coffee the way Faith did, freezing coffee in ice cube trays to add to each glass, so the drink didn't get diluted. Faith poured a tall glass for herself with several cubes, adding milk and sugar, which she didn't take in hot coffee but always did in iced.

"Want some?" she asked Gert.

"Thank you no, my teeth are floating now. I guess this heat is because of all that climate change stuff we hear so much about."

"I'm afraid so. I can't remember when people have talked about the weather more. It's the first thing anyone says. I'm ready to declare a moratorium, the way Mark Twain did in one of his books. He thought all the weather descriptions got in the way of the story, so he put them at the end for those who couldn't do without."

Gert laughed. Faith knew she was a reader and would like the reference. "*Huckleberry Finn* was my dad's favorite book. Think he wouldn't have minded rigging up a raft himself and taking off across the Reach and out into Jericho Bay."

Faith finished her coffee. The idea of going to the town's pancake breakfast was not appealing. Nothing on the island was air-conditioned except for a few of the new enormous piles put up along the shore by people from away and one beautifully restored Victorian in Granville by some people from Texas who had not remotely considered a house could be a home without AC. They had become friends of Faith's and had urged her to come sleep there with her family. She wouldn't take them up on it, but maybe she would pay a call.

"If I don't get the kids up for the pancake breakfast, they'll be upset, and Ben is marching in the parade with the group from the Lodge, so he has to get to the gathering spot by the VFW Hall early. I'm thinking I might stay here in case Tom calls again. Pix could drive everyone over."

Faith hadn't heard back from Tom since last night's call saying he was at the hospital and had spoken to the doctor. Marian was getting oxygen and was comfortable. The preliminary diagnosis was something called mitral regurgitation. It was very common, Tom said, and treatable. There were a number of possible procedures. Although it was extremely serious, she wasn't in any immediate danger, so they weren't rushing her into surgery but monitoring her instead—at least overnight and possibly longer. Her vitals were all good. But no matter what was decided, she was going to be in the hospital a while.

Marian had told Dick in no uncertain terms to go home. She didn't want to worry about him, now that Tom was there. Faith was sure her mother-in-law's freezer was well stocked but figured Tom might have taken his father to a local place, The Tinker's Son, as close to an Irish pub as you could get outside Dublin, for shepherd's pie and a pint. Dick had developed a fondness for it, and the family that owned the place.

This was the kind of comfort he needed at the moment. An impersonal, personal place where he wouldn't see anyone in a white coat or have to respond to a family member's well-meant concern.

Tom had said he'd phone this morning before Faith would have to leave for the various Independence Day festivities. He was adamant that she go, saying it would reassure the kids. That argument had swayed her last night, but now she wasn't sure. She'd kept herself from calling earlier; but Tom still hadn't called. Maybe she should try now.

"If your mother-in-law had taken a bad turn in the night, you would have heard," Gert said. "I'll be here until it's time for the picnic and won't leave the phone. Get the kids up now. There's cold juice and some Morning Glory Muffins to tide them over until the breakfast."

"I just wished my cell phone worked here," Faith said.

"I'm not sure everyone on Sanpere would agree with you. Me for one. Don't know why we need those ugly towers when this one has been just fine." She pointed to the wall phone, circa 1967. It still had a dial. The phones in the living room and up in Ursula's bedroom had been replaced with push-button models, but Gert had clung to this one.

Ursula entered through the back door.

"It's going to be one for the record books," she said.

"Let me get you a cold drink," Faith said. "Iced coffee?"

"Perfect and I'll have a muffin. Sit down and have one with me if you haven't eaten already—or have another. It's too early to go to the pancake breakfast yet. Let the kids sleep."

Faith decided to join her. Now that she'd cooled off with the iced coffee, the Morning Glory Muffins suddenly seemed appealing. Gert also called them "Every thing-but-the-Kitchen-Sink" muffins, and today's had ground walnuts, coconut, dried cranberries, and applesauce mixed into the oatmeal and whole wheat flour batter.

Ursula had the look of someone with a tale to tell. She was the kind of gossip Faith loved—eager to share juicy tidbits, but never mean-spirited. She started with what was uppermost in all their minds, however.

"Tom hasn't called yet? You would have told me. Don't read anything into it. Marian is probably sound asleep, which, this being a holiday, they'll allow. Otherwise when you're in the hospital, it's up before the light of day to take your temperature for the ninetieth time."

Faith shook her head. "No, he hasn't—and I'd like to wait here. Maybe Pix, Sam, or one of the others if they've arrived can come get you and the kids for the breakfast." The Miller children seldom missed the Fourth on Sanpere.

Ursula patted Faith's hand. This was the equivalent of a bear hug from this many-generations New Englander, and Faith knew it. It also was a demonstration of how fond Ursula was of Marian. They often met for lunch at the Isabella Stewart Gardner Museum, and Faith thought of these two as latter-day reincarnations of Mrs. Jack—feisty and to thine own selves true.

Gert set a basket of muffins, plates, knives, and butter on the table. She poured herself some coffee and sat down.

"Well?" she said, looking at Ursula.

"Well what?" Ursula gave a mischievous smile.

"What did you pretend we needed from The Birches?"

"I didn't pretend we needed anything. I just thought taking the path through the woods for my morning walk would be nice and shady. And incidentally I saw that Dwayne Hitchcock, hard to miss him, probably on his way to check out our woodpile, and Paul's. See how much he could liberate for winter this time. When I got to the house, I found I was a little tired, so Bev invited me into the kitchen and gave me a glass of her lemonade."

Faith could count on one hand the number of times she had ever heard Ursula Lyman Rowe say she was tired, and four of those had been when she was quite ill.

Gert laughed and lavishly buttered a muffin. Before taking a bite, she said, "Let's compare notes. *I* thought it would be a nice shady walk after dinner last night and Bev gave me lemonade, too. Started to spill the beans on the meeting, but then Sophie—Babs's daughter—walked in. She's a helpful little thing. Bev is feeling the heat terrible, and Sophie has pretty much taken over the kitchen."

"Not so little," Faith said. "I ran into her in the market and she's turned into a beauty—but she has to be six feet tall. She used to babysit for us and I almost didn't recognize her."

Ursula gave Faith a stern look. They were getting off topic and they didn't have much time before *they* would be interrupted, too. Ben and Amy were definitely up from the noise of running water from the upstairs bath and what sounded like "(I'm a) Yankee Doodle Dandy" not sung by James Cagney. Ben had said something about singing while they marched today. This must be it, or he was watching very different movies from his usual anime.

"Sorry!" Faith said and took a bite of her muffin to signify her intent to keep her mouth otherwise occupied.

"Bev told me last night that Paul had gathered every- one together and read them the letter that Priscilla had left," Gert said. "The only person missing was Babs, and that's because she's on some cruise in Greece with whichever number husband she's on. Anyway, Bev thought some of them weren't happy to see her there in the room while it was all going on, but she's never paid any mind to things like that and just plunked her- self down. That nephew or whoever he is of Paul's was there, too."

"But I thought only direct Proctor descendants could inherit the place?" Faith said.

"True," Gert answered. "But Bev thinks he's come up to keep an eye on them all. Wouldn't put it past some of that crew to bump Paul off and forge his signature, leaving the place to him—or her." She gave a laugh.

"I told you when I heard about this 'contest,' I didn't like it," Ursula said, "and the conversation *I* just had with Bev is proof positive." Her tone indicated that as far as she was concerned Gert wasn't joking.

"She didn't get to tell me anything more than who was there," Gert said, looking slightly put out. "And her lemonade needs more sugar syrup."

"It's going to be a very long month for Paul if they all stick around," Ursula continued, sighing. "Bev said he'd barely finished reading the letter, which, by the way, is lying on that big table in the living room where there's usually a jigsaw, before they were all angling to be his best friend. Sticking to him like glue when he went for a walk and then all the rest of the evening. Paul had two martinis, and that's not like him. This whole business could turn him into a dipsomaniac. Priscilla couldn't have thought this through. The letter says that it was all Paul's idea. That he wanted to spare her the aggravation of having to choose. Wanted her not to worry about what they'd think of her—those who didn't get the place—when she was gone."

Faith thought it best not to say what she was thinking, that "gone was gone." Her views on the afterlife were a bit amorphous, and despite being a minister's granddaughter, daughter, and wife, not something she had spent a great deal of time thinking about. Gert, however, was a devout member of one of the island's many evangelical churches, and Faith had no wish to suggest that heaven as a happy, haloed reward might not be a given. As for Ursula, whatever her beliefs, Faith was pretty sure she shared the opinion that it was a bit selfish of Priscilla, wherever she was, to leave Paul with this mess.

"It sounds like junior high. Who gets to be the most popular kid's BFF." Faith had finished her muffin and stood up. She needed to get the kids downstairs, then call over to the Millers' to have someone pick them up for the breakfast and parade. She wasn't leaving the phone.

"What I'd do is send the whole bunch of them away, now that he's read them the letter, and pick a name out of a hat at the end of the month," Gert said.

"He won't do that," Ursula said sadly. "He's too good. This is what Priscilla wanted, so he'll carry out her wishes. He's stuck with them. But I'll mention the hat idea. If he decides to do it and tells them now, it could save a great deal of aggravation—and his liver."

Oh puhleeze, Sophie said to herself when she was awakened at dawn by the sound of someone's voice drifting in the open window from the shore. Upon hearing the words "Life, Liberty, and the pursuit of Happiness," she got out of bed and went through the kitchen into the living room and out onto the porch.

Uncle Simon was reading the Declaration of Independence aloud from the top of the rock on the shore nearest the house. He was wearing the Brooks brick red chinos with a knifepoint crease so beloved by the males of his class—the maid must pack with tissue paper, Sophie thought. Aunt Deirdre had never ironed a garment in her life. In honor of the holiday, he'd paired the pants with a patriotic blue-and-white wide-striped short-sleeved shirt.

Sophie could have told him his efforts both oratori-
cal and sartorial would be wasted, as Uncle Paul never
got up until he could make it to catch the parade on its
return trip back through the village. Over the years,
he had it timed perfectly and never missed. She was
happy to see that she was right. Paul McAllister was
absent, but Aunt Deirdre was there snapping photos
from under a big navy straw hat bedecked with a star-
studded red bandanna around the rim. Cousin Forbes,
garbed the same as Simon, except in Bermuda shorts
that someone with his knobby knees should avoid—
was recording the performance on video. Presumably
for posterity, but no doubt also to show Uncle Paul in
a studied, offhand way later. Sophie could just hear
him—"Oh, might want to have a look at father's reading this morning. The dawn was particularly striking." Felicity, looking a bit less enthusiastic than the
rest of the family, but in a red-white-and-blue-striped
sundress—the colors obviously de rigueur today—
was clutching a cup of coffee and trying to get comfortable on the rock she'd obviously chosen as most
picturesque.

Sophie thought back to her cousin's nuptial announcement yesterday afternoon and realized if this branch of
the Proctors was going to continue to stage these performances, she might have to tell her mother she wasn't

going to be able to stick it out. She had never thought of herself as a cynic, but she was embracing the philosophy wholeheartedly now, having started after Felicity's dramatic words. How long had it taken the girl to memorize the speech? There was little chance that it was Felicity's own work—and what kind of books were her relatives reading these days? The script had been a mélange of contemporary bodice-ripper romances and the kind of three-volume novel beloved by the Victorians. And how much arm-twisting, or Pratesi and La Perla trousseau buying, had Uncle Simon done in order to get his darling daughter to move her wedding to the rock-bound coast of Maine from St. Thomas's at Fifth Avenue and Fifty-Third with a black-tie roof garden reception at The Peninsula two blocks away?

Uncle Paul's response had been typical. Gracious but nonspecific and not what Simon, who had certainly thought this would sew it all up for him, expected. Instead of "Oh gosh, I'll pick you, since your daughter will be getting married here; the rest of you can leave now," Paul had said, "I'm sure that would be lovely, dear. Why don't we sit down with your parents and talk about it later? I was under the impression that you were getting married in December in Manhattan, but Sanpere is a perfect spot for a wedding. Priscilla and I were married here ourselves." A fact, Sophie noted with her newfound cynicism, known to all of them, as the photo of the couple, the lighthouse behind them, was hanging on the wall next to the stairs with the rest of the family photos. Plus Aunt Priscilla often reminisced about what a wonderful day it had been, friends staying for the week following and no honeymoon, as "who would want to leave this spot?"

Looking at Simon now, who was beginning to run out of steam in the steam heat, reading what Sophie always considered a rather boring piece of Americana when compared with something like the Gettysburg Address, she recalled how he had sidled close to Paul, taking his arm, saying, "We knew that and thought it would be a tribute to you both, as well as ensuring these two will have as happy a marriage as you and Aunt Priscilla did."

Paul had detached Simon's hand. "Weddings, birthday parties—I think you have one soon, Sylvia—anything anyone wants is fine. Now I'm off for my walk before the mosquitoes get too bad."

And that had been that. Most of them trooped after him, game for the pests. It had been a worse season than usual for the state bird, and there had been reported sightings of mosquitoes so large they could provide meat for a family of four. Gift shops were selling small replicas of bear traps guaranteed to protect you, which

moved like hot cakes to gullible tourists and flatlanders who hadn't lived in the state long enough to get the
joke—say only about ten years.

Sophie had stayed behind. Much as she would have
loved a walk, mosquitoes or no, she wasn't about to
join the parade. Watching them depart, she was unsur-
prised to see Will following closely behind.

And now here they were again, starting the Fourth
off with a bang, although Uncle Simon's rendition had
become more of a whimper.

"Kinda makes you proud to be an Amurican," a
voice behind her said in an exaggerated drawl.

Sophie was startled but recognized the speaker as
Will. Once again, she noticed, looking at his feet, he
was shoeless. All the better to creep up on people? Or
some sort of Southern thing?

He followed her glance. "Got used to going barefoot when I was a kid. We'd take our shoes off the day
school ended and put them back on the day it began."

"You might want some sort of covering if you plan
on climbing over the rocks on the beach. The barnacles
will tear your toes to ribbons."

"You sound as if you might enjoy the spectacle."

Sophie flushed, suddenly aware that all she was
wearing was a tank top and running shorts with nothing underneath. It had been too hot to sleep in anything

else. She'd been tempted to forgo even these, but the thought of all her relatives in close proximity had made her think again.

"Of course I wouldn't," she said shortly. "I was merely trying to give you a friendly warning."

"Much appreciated." He gestured toward Simon, who was finally winding up the performance. "Are y'all going to be trying to score brownie points like this for the whole month? If so, I just may have to take my uncle on a long sea voyage."

"I have no idea what we *all*,"—Sophie emphasized the pronunciation, finding Will's accent, which seemed to be in play when he was being his most irritating self, grating—"are planning. I can only say what I am planning and that is to get breakfast ready for those not going to the one in town, then head out to it and the parade."

Will was obviously one of those people who didn't understand the notion of personal space. She almost had to push him out of the way to get to the door back into the house.

"Loving the outfit," he said.

Sophie said, "Oooh!" before darting inside. The man was outrageous. Why did he have to be here? It was bad enough to have the family around, but this interloper was making everything worse. Much worse. "Oooh!" she said aloud to herself again for good measure.

"If those are antique cars, I must be an antique, too," Faith said to Ed Ricks, the man standing next to her watching the parade. Tom had called. Nothing had changed, which was good news, and she'd felt relieved enough to leave the house.

"The rules are bent—and you are in no way an antique. If we didn't have all these tricked-out relatively recent models, the parade wouldn't be long enough, even doubled. Besides, I like to see them when they're not burning rubber on the Fishcreek Road."

Faith nodded in agreement. Some benighted soul from away had made a short film about the skids—"tire art"—skipping over the issues of noise, pollution, and the dangerously inebriated states of the drivers. She'd discussed the film last summer with Ed, and they were on the same page. He had elaborated on the drivers' motivations—arrested development, low self-esteem, identification with Burt Reynolds, in a manner appropriate to his profession. Dr. Edwin Ricks was a well-known New York City psychiatrist, often quoted in the *Times.* She hadn't seen him since he'd retired year-round to his summer home on the island last fall and wondered how he'd been faring.

"How did you enjoy island life in the off-season? Any cabin fever?" The winter had been brutal in both Maine and Massachusetts.

"Well, I think I told you that I was planning on catching up on my reading, finally getting the boat in shape to sail it this summer up to St. Andrews, *and* setting up the studio so I could pretend to be a real artist."

"And?"

"Aside from a little reading, none of the above has been accomplished. You have no idea how busy it is here in the winter, especially since I'm a volunteer with the ambulance corps. That has led to some formal and informal work of the kind I thought I'd left behind. I made the mistake of transferring my license to cover Maine a few years ago, and it's been getting a workout."

Faith started to reply but was immediately distracted by the group on foot following the float from the Island Nursing Home, an oversize red-white-and-blue-bedecked replica of the surrey with the fringe on top. The residents participating were all sporting vintage hats and were possibly the original owners.

"Oh look, there's Ben!" she said to Ed. She started to jump up and down but quickly kept herself in check, settling for a subtle wave in her son's direction. He towered over his friend Tyler. It was sometimes a shock to see him looking so much like a grown man. She definitely wasn't used to the sound of his voice on the phone yet. It had settled into a rich, deep baritone. Harder and harder to recall childhood days, except when she looked at photographs and the memories flooded in. She wondered whether the pretty brunette between him and Tyler was Mandy Hitchcock, the driver she'd be entrusting with Ben's life. She sighed. Letting go got harder and harder the older they got. She'd thought the way he walked into his kindergarten class with nary a backward gaze had been tough, but this . . .

Amy had no inhibitions regarding her brother, nor did the Millers, who were all shrieking, "Ben! Ben!" He gave a nod, a faint smile, a British royal family wave, and then faced forward, marching closely behind a young man in a similar shirt and another wearing a chef's hat and a garish Hawaiian shirt with gulls in colors never seen in nature. Faith had heard the chef had worked at a restaurant in Honolulu, and the man beside him in a Lodge shirt must be Ben's boss, Derek Otis. At the judges' stand, a.k.a. the Square Deal Garage's flatbed set up with folding chairs, the group from the Lodge gave a spirited rendition of the George M. Cohan song Faith had heard her son practicing earlier.

She turned back to Ed and picked up the conversation where they had left off. "I'd like to hear about all this. You are providing a valuable service. Tom and I have both thought what the island has needed was a really good full-time shrink. Sorry, that was inappropriate." She covered her mouth. Talk about slips!

"I don't mind. Feel free to call me whatever you want. But you're right about the need. To cope with the drug use, including the time-tested one here—alcohol—depression, and garden-variety dysfunction, requires many more of me. And let's not forget the family feuds! I have gotten to the point where I want to slap those people who don't live here year-round when they talk about Sanpere as a perfect place where all the local families get along, as if it's some sort of Shangri-la."

"Until recently," Faith said, "I would have associated family feuds with the hollers of Kentucky—the Hatfields and the McCoys—but there's one brewing next door to The Pines at The Birches. You may have met Paul McAllister and his late wife, Priscilla. This month Paul has to choose who will inherit the place from among Priscilla's relatives. They've all gathered to, I suppose you could say, audition."

"I met them both briefly years ago. Don't get to that part of the island much, but inheritance is a bone of contention about the size of a mastodon's. No names, but I can tell you stories that would curl your hair if it weren't wavy already."

Thinking how much fun the conversation would be—and a contrast to her tight-lipped husband, who kept the secrets of the confessional, not allowing a single indiscreet morsel drop even with names changed, Faith was about to convey her enthusiasm, when a beeper device on Ed's belt went off.

"Gotta run, talk to you soon," he called, sprinting away. A few minutes later the parade was halted, and not long after that an ambulance, siren blaring, tore off toward the bridge and the nearest hospital on the other side in Blue Hill. A pall was cast on the proceedings until the mistress of ceremonies, who had been describing each float and group, announced over the speaker system that all was well. An "elderly visitor to our island" had succumbed to heatstroke but was doing fine. He was being transported to the hospital as a precaution.

Amy tugged at her mother's elbow. "You don't think that maybe all that is wrong with Granny is the heat, too?" The hopeful look on her face was heartbreaking.

"I'm sure the heat didn't help, but Granny needs to have something in her heart fixed, and then she *will* be better than ever."

Ursula stepped in to reassure Amy, too. "Your grandmother is going to be just fine. We're lucky we aren't back in those times without the advanced medical treatments they have now." She pointed at the Island Historical Society's float, which featured a woman spinning wool, a man with blacksmith's tools, and two children with slates, surrounded by artifacts from the society's small museum illustrating just how hard—and perilous—everyday life had been.

Lowering her voice, Ursula said to Faith, "In this heat, there'll be more dropping before the day is out, which reminds me I want to check on Bev Boynton. I don't see her here, and she never misses the parade. I'll bet she's wearing herself out getting ready for the clambake. Mark said he'd take me back now. See you later."

"I'll go with you. I'd like to get back, too." She'd come with Ursula and her grandson. "Ben is getting a ride to work with Tyler's father. The chef said they'd be done in plenty of time for the fireworks, and I'll pick him up at the Lodge then." No one had clued her in that once she had kids, her whole life would revolve around automobile transportation.

A dark look crossed Ursula's face, and she pointed across the street to the Proctor contingent. Sylvia was shouting at her cousin Simon, and her son was trying unsuccessfully to drag her away.

"Now that's what I call fireworks," Ursula said.

Why was it, Sophie wondered, that the Fourth of July always seemed so much longer than other summer days? Longer in a good way. Other days were filled with less but seemed to go by quickly. Dusk and fire-flies followed close on the heels of morning dew and dragonflies. Maybe it was the sameness.

The clambake was in full swing. People had been coming and going in and out of all the houses on the Point since the parade ended, filling the beach with laughter, enjoying the annual event to the hilt. The pit, so lovingly prepared by Uncle Paul and men from other families—the Usual Suspects, they called themselves—had been the focus for much of the day. The same group had been doing it for years and clearly enjoyed the ritualistic nature of the process, from the preparation, the firing, to the final reveal—the clams opened, lobsters turned a brilliant red, and succulent steamed corn glistening on top.

Bev had produced a seemingly endless number of her baking powder biscuits to sop up the lobster butter, and others had brought specialties ranging from the Potters' secret family recipe coleslaw (mystery ingre-dient revealed years ago as a dash of fennel seed), Ursula Rowe's mustard pickles, a vat of fish chowder kept warm on a camp stove, pies of every variety, and

this year Faith Fairchild's bread puddings. After help-
ings of both, the Point's inhabitants had voted Faith
an unofficial resident welcome back every year. There
were drinks of all kinds, but the most popular was
the one that had been served since the first rusticator
started the clambake tradition—old-fashioned lemonade, with a twist for the grown-ups, the twist provided
by a jigger of gin or vodka. One family brought the
clearly marked insulated beverage dispensers each year
using the recipe that had been handed down—lemony
tart with just enough sugar syrup, summer distilled in
a glass.

The uncharacteristic hot weather had meant adults
who seldom braved the water were diving from the
rocks and long dock. The tide was high, perfect timing.
The Point's children had always gone in and several
teenagers had been appointed to keep an eye on the
smaller swimmers. Sophie realized that one of them,
standing next to Daisy, must be Amy Fairchild. She
looked like her mother—the same thick pale butter-
scotch hair and blue eyes. Sophie was glad Daisy had
found a friend. When the quarrel broke out between
Simon and Sylvia at the parade, she had been down the
street, but Daisy had been right there, and it must have
been both embarrassing and frightening. At least that's
how Sophie would have reacted at that age. Not that

her own mother would ever have behaved this way in public. Whatever scenes Babs made, and she did, were strictly behind closed doors.

The brouhaha had been much discussed at the picnic, though away from the participants. Apparently Sylvia had been planning to read the Declaration of Independence herself and had accused Simon of stealing not just the idea, but also the copy, which she had left in the living room. Rory had pried his mother away before she made good on her threat to punch Simon in the nose. They were at opposite ends of the beach now, Simon surrounded by his family, Sylvia mingling with people from the other houses. It occurred to Sophie that she had never seen Simon and Deirdre with neighbors. They kept to The Birches, Simon's trophy sailboat—the *Fortuna*—and Blue Hill. He didn't have sailing buddies—he could manage the boat alone— and Deirdre didn't go "yard saling" and "antiquing" the way Sylvia did with other summer people. None of them had friends among what Simon called "the Native Population," unlike Paul and Priscilla, who had always been going to a local couple's golden anniversary party or someone's family reunion picnic on the Causeway Beach, the largest on Sanpere. Sophie had tagged along to the Hamiltons' reunion with them one summer and there had been kin from as far away as

China. The roots of the island's first settlers after the Abenakis had spread far and wide.

She was feeling a bit sick, and it wasn't the heat nor the food—she'd managed two lobsters. It was the ongoing spectacle that was her own perverse family reunion. If today's performances continued, as she suspected they would, she'd do a Huck Finn herself, but forgo the raft and light out for the Territory. Her mother would either have to come back or agree that their branch had been duly represented by Sophie's presence for, what—a few days more? Definitely a week, tops.

The long afternoon light made the scene in front of her look dramatic. There had already been too much drama, Sophie thought. She decided to get something cold to drink from one of the coolers and join one of the groups. One of the ones with whom she shared no blood ties whatsoever.

Pix Miller came over to where Ursula and Faith were sitting. Ursula had given in and allowed Faith to get a beach chair for her instead of perching on a rock. Faith was wishing she'd fetched one for herself as well. The Rowes and Millers were big on sticking to their venerable customs, eschewing any seat not created by nature, but this was one Faith thought she could break—before she broke something else.

"It's been a little too warm, but another wonderful Fourth," Ursula said.

"And it's not over yet. We still have the fireworks," Pix agreed. "We'll need to take two cars. Gert said she was heading home soon to go with her family, since Bev doesn't feel like going. But we'll need room for Ben, or you will, Faith. You are going, aren't you? It's going to be a clear night. No fog like the last few years."

"Tom said that there's no point in my staying by the phone. Marian is even making them go to Norwell's fireworks. She thinks everyone is making a big to-do out of nothing. I think Dick's worried she'll walk out."

Ursula took Faith's hand. Twice in one day! This was highly emotional behavior for her.

"She knows what she has to face, and it was bad luck that it had to happen on a holiday. She's right to send them off. What she needs now is rest and no worries. How did Tom's sister and brothers take the news?"

"She won't let anyone get in touch with them until Betsey and Robert are back from Europe next week."

Ursula said, "They'll be upset, but she's right. Why spoil their vacations when they can't do anything unless one of them has suddenly become a cardiologist?"

"Mother!" Pix looked horrified. "If I thought that's what you'd do, I would never go farther than the Boston Common."

Faith agreed with her friend and decided to do her own hand patting. "Don't worry, I'd get in touch with you."

Ursula had the last word, as usual. "And how would you know, my dear? The good reverend would never divulge anything unless I told him he could."

Faith decided to change the subject. "When are Arnie and Claire coming?"

Pix's brother, Arnold Rowe, was an orthopedic surgeon. He and his wife lived in New Mexico. They didn't have any children. Both of them loved the island and managed to spend several weeks each summer at The Pines.

"I'm supposed to have his boat in the water a week from today, so I imagine they'll come the night before. That reminds me I'd better call Billings."

"I can do that, Mother, and I'd think Arnie could make arrangements with the boatyard himself." Pix adored her brother, but she had told Faith often that distance had made him into a crown prince, and his visits elicited behavior from both her mother and Gert Prescott that had never been bestowed on Pix herself, who lived year-round in both places almost at her mother's doorstep.

The Millers' golden retrievers, Henry and Arthur—they had sadly lost Dustin, or Dusty, in January—arrived and happily shook a combination of salt water and sand over everyone. It went with the day but did cause the group to decide to go back to the house and get ready for the trip into Granville and the evening's pyrotechnics.

Faith loved fireworks, especially the ones here, shot high into the sky from one of the tiny islands—little more than a sandbar at high tide—in Granville's harbor. The fish pier was crowded, and as she made her way to her favorite spot off to one side near the end, she kept stopping and getting stopped. It didn't feel as though they had been on Sanpere all that long, although Ben had been a toddler their first summer, but events of all sorts had woven them into the basic fabric of the island.

She missed Tom. That was partly why she wasn't feeling as excited as usual. The other part was the fact that both kids had deserted her. Oh, they asked first. Ben wanted to watch with Tyler and other friends. He also asked if he could spend the night at the Hamiltons'. Tyler and he didn't have to work the breakfast shift, and Mandy would pick them up for the lunch one. Faith had said yes. He was fifteen, after all, and she clearly recalled how little time she'd spent with her own parents at that age. Still, agreeing had been hard. She'd been tempted to ask him to wait and watch some of the show with Amy and her—or they could go to where he would be watching up on Church Street, high above the harbor. But she'd smiled and refrained from hugging him in public. "Love you, have fun." She'd been rewarded, "Thanks, Mom. Love you too."

And then Amy had come running up with her friend Daisy from The Birches, asking if she could watch the fireworks from the deck behind the new, slightly upscale Granville restaurant overlooking the water. "Daisy's mom knows the people who own it. You could come, too."

But somehow it didn't feel right. She didn't know the new owners of the restaurant—or Daisy's family except by sight. She'd given her daughter a hug—still allowed— and sent her off, too. After the fireworks, the restaurant was serving them all desserts and Amy wanted to stay for it. Daisy's mother would drop her off at The Pines.

The harbor was filled with boats—the preferred way of viewing for many, and that was where the Millers were with Ursula, as well. Faith was sorry now that she had refused that invitation. She'd thought she'd be with the kids, and there wasn't room for all of them. Chris Knight and his wife, Kathy, had invited her to join them on their boat as well. Maybe she'd do this sort of thing with Tom next year as their children, make that teens, would now be making their own plans for the foreseeable future. The Knights were known for their shipboard cuisine and often tied on to another boat for a truly movable feast.

It was dead low tide and kids were running on the shore of the cove next to the pier with sparklers and occasionally a brilliant shower of something larger soared up.

The first rocket hit the sky, exploding into a huge golden chrysanthemum eliciting the traditional involuntary "aaah" from the crowd before the jewel-like droplets sank into the night water. And so it continued. Bursts of color, some sizzling noisily in random directions high overhead and the aftermath—loud bangs. Strobes so bright you could make out Isle au Haut, in the distance, six miles away. Faith watched the next aerial display—one of the ones that looked liked a succession of neon galaxies—and suddenly decided she wanted to go home. She wanted to give Tom a call. She needed to talk to him, hear his voice. She slipped through the mass of people who were looking skyward, enjoying the man-made stars invented by the Chinese so many centuries ago.

"Leaving before the grand finale?" It was Steve Johnson, the harbormaster. He was definitely a candidate for one of those calendars featuring the hotties of various occupations. During the long bleak Aleford winters, especially on bad hair days, Faith cheered herself up thinking back to his ego-boosting flirting. "I thought we could take a moonlit swim in the quarry over on Green Island."

"And end up a Popsicle," Faith said, turning to give his wife, Roberta, who was laughing, a hug. She hadn't seen her yet this summer.

Promising dinner soon with the Johnsons, she managed to get back to her car unnoticed by any more friends.

Back at Ursula's she reached Tom and was glad she'd called. He was feeling the same need to talk, even though there still wasn't any news. Despite Marian's urging, neither he nor Dick had felt like going to the town's celebration. They were watching TV, having picked up subs, also, confusingly, called "grinders" in New England. (After she'd moved to Aleford as a bride, Faith had been extremely puzzled by her husband's suggestion, "How about a grinder?" coyly parrying, "Don't you mean a quickie, sweetheart?")

There was still no one at The Pines when she finished her conversation. After trying to read, Faith decided to take a walk. She grabbed a flashlight and set out through the birch grove. There was a way to get to the beach at the other side.

The air was refreshing now and she could hear faint echoes of the island fireworks as well as those from the towns across the Reach. It was a beautiful night and she was feeling reassured about Marian. All would be well.

Sophie had set out for the Granville fireworks on her own before any of the family could ask her for a ride. Uncle Paul was going with the neighbors he and Priscilla had always joined, a tradition she hoped was bringing him some comfort—and a break. She'd found a spot away from the thickest part of the crowd and let out the breath she seemed to have been holding all day. She loved fireworks.

A voice shattered her calm reverie. "I love fireworks. We always go out to Tybee Island for the Fourth. Get a dozen or so of Lucile's fish po' boys from Sting Ray's and eat on a big ole blanket spread out on the beach. You can see the pier where they set them off pretty much from anywhere. Got to watch the tide, though."

Now what was going on? Sophie thought. Had Will been swigging some Southern Comfort? This new, gentler version of the man was almost as disconcerting as his other persona.

"Um." She searched for a reply. "I love fireworks, too. Especially here. But all the fish sandwiches they were selling for the scholarship fund are long gone I'm afraid."

Will was wearing what seemed to be his uniform—gimme cap, faded jeans, and well-laundered tee shirts with the logos obscured. Nothing had come from Brooks, J.Crew, or any sort of Republic. His shirt looked soft, and Sophie had a sudden impulse to touch it, feel it between her fingers. She shoved her hands in the pockets of her crop pants—after this morning's encounter she'd deliberately avoided shorts all day.

The show started with a shower of gold, and for the next fifteen minutes, Sophie stood transfixed, staring into the heavens and giving into the cries of delight she'd planned to suppress. The crowd pressed in and she was aware how close she was to Will. At one point his hand brushed across hers, lingering briefly, and she felt something akin to what was happening in the sky.

Except this is so not happening, she told herself.

And it wasn't.

"See you," he said just before the grand finale was over, giving her a cocky grin as he walked away.

Sophie didn't turn around until she was sure he was out of sight and then she made her way back to her car, hoping she wouldn't bump into him—or anyone else from The Pines.

The house was empty and Sophie decided to walk down to the beach, the end away from the boathouse.

She was restless—and felt like smashing something, preferably something in Will Tarkington's face.

"She's dead."

The words reached Faith and she quickened her steps, running down the path through the thick stand of birches that had grown up over the years between Ursula's house and the Proctor one. Her flashlight bounced off the slender white trunks, sending splinters of light across the scene in front of her. The sky was pitch-dark with no hint of the Independence Day fireworks display that had filled it an hour earlier.

One figure prone on the ground; another crouched low over it. Faith trained the beam on them. One figure very still; the other almost motionless, her hands at the body's throat.

"She's dead." The repetition was uttered in the same voice. Devoid of emotion, the two words a declaration of fact. As if observing the weather: "It's cold." "It's raining." "It's hot."

"It's Bev and she's dead." A catch in the voice. The start of a cry?

The person who was alive was Sophie Maxwell.

"I killed her."

Chapter 5

A nd then Sophie screamed.

Faith knelt down and held her close. She struggled for words of comfort, but the sight of the body on the ground next to them and Sophie's hysterical cries left her speechless. A light rain, almost a mist, was starting to fall. Earlier she had greeted the report of a break in the weather with relief. Now she knew she had to act quickly before the storm worsened.

Faith let Sophie go and leaned over the lifeless form to feel for a pulse both at the wrist and neck. Nothing. From Sophie's outbursts, she'd assumed that had been her initial response, too, but Faith needed to make sure. Sure that the housekeeper was beyond all attempts to resuscitate her.

Sophie's screams turned to moans. "I *knew* she wasn't feeling well. It wasn't the heat! I should have made her go to the medical center. Driven her. Should have taken over everything. She was up at five baking biscuits! *Biscuits!*"

"You couldn't have known this would happen," Faith said, but further reassurances would have to wait. They had to get help immediately and one of them had to stay with the body. Obviously that was not going to be Sophie. Was she even going to be able to call 911 in the state she was in?

"Sophie." She pulled the girl to her feet and gave her a slight push toward Ursula's house, which was the closest. "Go call 911. And Earl Dickinson. His number is near the top on the list by the phone. If any of the Millers are there, tell them to come at once. Can you do that?"

Sophie nodded and started down the path, stumbling over the roots. Faith called after her, "Earl is Sergeant Dickinson with the state police and lives on the island. Tell him I'm staying here with Bev until someone comes."

Except she wasn't Bev anymore.

The rain was coming down harder, but it wasn't yet the storm predicted. Faith knew the ambulance corps would be here soon—volunteers who lived nearby would make it before the ambulance, which was garaged in Sanpere Village by the fire station.

She sat back on her heels and thought about what Sophie had said. Could this have been prevented if the woman had sought medical attention? She looked over at the body. Bev had been carrying a lot of extra weight, and although Faith didn't know the woman's exact age, she was pretty sure she'd been in her seventies at least. It was more than likely she'd had a heart condition, not helped by the kind of food she cooked. As for assuming more of Bev's work, from what Gert had said, since she arrived Sophie had been doing most of the meal preparations, and other household chores, without help from any of the other occupants of The Birches. This was no doubt an attack waiting to happen. Sophie had nothing to feel guilty about.

The air was cooling rapidly. The woman in front of her wouldn't be feeling anything, but Faith wished she could cover her with something. She didn't have anything to put over the body, not even a jacket. In any case, she'd been witness to enough crime scenes to know not to touch anything.

Crime? She felt some relief that this wasn't one. This was a death due to natural causes—Tom would have no cause to be upset that she'd become caught up in murder again. He had been taking an increasingly dim view of her involvements for years, but the almost fatal end for them both during their anniversary trip to Italy had been the last *paglia*—straw.

The trees were keeping most of the rain from the body, which was facedown on the path, pointed toward The Pines. The right arm was bent at the elbow and mostly under the substantial torso. Faith imagined Bev—what was her last name?—walking in the woods to get a breath of air as Faith herself, and apparently Sophie, had been doing. Her mind formed a vivid picture of Bev falling forward, clutching at the pain in her chest, grabbing her heart. From all appearances, it had been a quick death. The body lay straight, no obvious spasms or attempts to crawl for aid. In the beam of the flashlight, the silver in Bev's hair, which she wore short, glistened. The left hand was by her side. Her fingers, nails short and well tended, were long and surprisingly thin. No wedding band. No ring of any kind. An old-fashioned Timex was strapped to her wrist. The only incongruity was what she was wearing—a long night-gown peeped out from below the kind of chenille robe Faith had only seen in vintage clothing stores lately. She was wearing shoes—sturdy Enna Jetticks—but no socks. The impulse to go outside must have come as she was about to go to bed. Maybe the room had been extremely stuffy? But from the little she knew about her, Faith wouldn't have imagined Bev as the type of woman to go outdoors in her nightclothes.

She turned the flashlight off to save the batteries and hoped it wouldn't be much longer before someone came. Earl might still be on duty in Granville. The "fireworks" didn't end with the official show and the Fourth was always a headache for Earl, he'd told her, with drinking, fights, and explosions gone awry. Faith had a sudden fear that the ambulance might be off the island on a run with a casualty from one of these kinds of Independence celebrations. She made herself more comfortable, leaning against one of the larger birches.

Again she reflected, the woman hadn't been some-one Faith knew much about. Just part of The Birches, a fixture. She was always there in the background the few times Faith had visited the McAllisters. She had a sense Bev had been with them for many years. Like Gert Prescott and Ursula—these women who kept their employer's lives running smoothly over time. Ursula called Gert "a member of the family," but she wasn't. She was the help and had a family of her own. Did Bev?

She heard someone running along the path from the direction of The Pines, and soon Sophie appeared. She was breathless, but Faith was glad to see that she wasn't screaming, although when she spoke her words rushed out in a frantic torrent.

"Ursula came home. Pix dropped her off but was gone before I could stop her. I left a message for Sergeant Dickinson. The ambulance is on the way to Blue Hill with someone who may have lost an eye setting off a Roman candle in the quarry and the closest ambulance volunteer wasn't answering the page, but someone will be here soon. Ursula called a neighbor, and they're driving over to tell Uncle Paul." Spent, she slumped down next to Faith and buried her face in her hands. Faith patted her back.

Sophie's voice was muffled, but Faith could still hear her. "I should have insisted yesterday that she go to the doctor. If not here, then off island."

"And do you think she would have listened?"

Sophie lifted her head. Her eyes were brimming, and even in the dark Faith could make out the tormented expression on her face.

"Maybe not—and I know you're trying to make me feel better, which is very kind of you—but I feel responsible." She stopped speaking. Someone was coming from the direction of The Birches. Someone with a bright lantern.

The two women jumped to their feet and soon were caught in a wide pool of light, caught with the body at their feet.

"Sweet Jesus! What happened?" Will Tarkington said, bending over the dead woman.

The fifth of July is inevitably a letdown. With the Fourth on a Thursday this year, it also meant a very long weekend with guests who had begun to smell ever so slightly of spoiled fish—or in some cases were already reeking like the proverbial three-day-old ones.

The mood at The Birches was somber. Sophie had not been able to sleep, so she got up and did what she thought Bev would have done—bake and bake some more. Muffins, biscuits, scones, and pancake batter ready to pour. She boiled eggs for egg salad and made a long list of food they didn't need. The fridge and pantry were well stocked, but she felt impelled to prepare for all eventualities.

Last night Will and the ambulance corps volunteers who were with him had quickly taken charge. He'd been having dessert at the Harbor Café, open late after the fireworks, with one of them, an Ed Ricks, when Ricks had been beeped. Sophie had found herself literally pushed out of the way and had gone back to The Birches with Faith Fairchild. Faith had insisted that Sophie not be alone. Ursula was there with Paul, and they had the sad task of definitively confirming the news Ursula had already brought.

Sophie was taking a batch of blueberry muffins from the oven when her uncle walked in. He was wearing the same clothes as the night before and she knew he hadn't been to bed. She walked over and put her arms around him. He allowed his head to drop onto her shoulder and held her for a moment.

"I've just been on the phone with the state police." He sat down at the table, and she quickly poured him a cup of coffee, putting it before him. She doubted he'd want anything to eat just yet. She hadn't wanted anything, either.

"What did they tell you?" She joined him with a cup herself.

"It's all pretty straightforward—if you call losing someone you've loved straightforward. Bev has been with us since shortly after Priscilla and I got married. Was married herself, young. Lost her husband in Vietnam and said she never wanted anyone else. They didn't have any children, much to her regret, but she was close to her nieces and nephews. They're taking care of"—he choked up—". . . things."

Sophie kept quiet and moved closer. Paul took out a large red bandanna handkerchief—he bought them by the dozen—blew his nose and continued.

"She knew she wasn't doing well. She'd been seeing a doctor down in Massachusetts and he'd been against her coming up here. Wanted her to have heart surgery, but she was either too nervous or too stubborn. Anyway, that's what her niece said. When she got here, she went to the Island Medical Center to get her blood pressure checked out and make sure she could get some prescriptions transferred. That's why it's straightforward. She was under the care, even for a brief time, of a Maine doctor, so the medical examiner can sign off and they can issue a death certificate."

This should be making me feel better, Sophie thought, but it doesn't. She still should have known something more serious than the extreme heat was wrong. Would it have saved Bev if she, or maybe Bev's friend Gert Prescott, had insisted she see the doctor again? Get checked into the hospital, or even go back to Massachusetts to that doctor?

Paul was echoing her thoughts. "I knew she wasn't feeling well and should have done something about it. Will feels the same. She'd been coming to Georgia with us for years. But it was a hard call. Bev kind of believed she was in charge of us, not the other way around. She was the one taking care of everybody."

"What happens now? I mean, where will she go? I mean . . ." Sophie's voice trailed off.

"We talked about things like this. Arrangements. The three of us when Priscilla was alive. People our age do. Bev was one of the lucky ones in that her husband's body was recovered and sent back here. He was buried, and then later his parents were interred in the same cemetery. All Bev's family is there as well. She and her husband had been high school sweethearts and known each other all their lives—his tragically short. She'll be next to him at last. The funeral home on the island is taking care of everything. I feel kind of useless. She didn't want a service, just something simple graveside. Will is going to take me down for it."

"If you think it's appropriate, I'd like to come too," Sophie said.

"As would we." Simon strode into the kitchen. "Bev was like a member of the family."

Sophie had to work hard to control the impulse she had to dump her coffee over her uncle's smug, smoothly shaven face. He smelled of Tom Ford Noir and it was making her slightly sick.

"Very kind of you," Paul said, "but when her family"—was it Sophie's imagination or did Paul emphasize the word?—"lets us know the arrangements, Will and I are going to go alone. Probably fly from Bar Harbor."

Simon put a hand on Paul's shoulder. "Of course— and I will drive you to the airport. Is the coffee fresh, Sophie?"

Tempted as she was to reply that it had been sitting for days, Sophie stood up and said, "Yes. There's also muffins and other things. And pancakes."

"Two poached eggs, runny, and wheat toast."

"Same for me," Deirdre said, entering the room. Apparently the Proctors were watching their waistlines, or had overindulged at the clambake. "How *are* you, Uncle Paul dear?"

"Actually I'm feeling a bit tired and think I'll lie down. Sophie, save two muffins for me, and if you have some of that good bacon, it would go down a treat with some scrambled eggs later. That's a good girl."

"I'm going over to the farmers' market in Granville in a few minutes and I'll pick up some more bacon, eggs too, from the Sunset Acres people. And a whole lot of their goat cheese from Anne Bossi. I know your favorite is her brie."

The minute Paul left and they were alone with Sophie, her aunt and uncle began to quiz her about Bev. What was she doing in the woods? What was Sophie doing in the woods? Had Bev been alive when Sophie found her? And on and on. Sophie poached their eggs and toasted their bread at warp speed. Putting their plates in front of them, she gave a quick summary of what had and hadn't happened last night, before grabbing her purse and exiting as quickly as she could.

"Whoa, what's the rush?"

She'd run straight into Will's arms outside at the foot of the stairs and quickly backed up. He seemed to be laughing at her, but when she looked at his face more closely she could tell the smile was one of surprise. The look in his eyes told her he had had as sleepless a night as she had and was also grieving for Bev. She realized he must have known Bev as well or even better than the rest of them, from time spent in Savannah with Paul and Priscilla.

"How are you?" he asked. "I stayed with the ambulance corps. I'm a trained EMT and they got another call while we were there. When I got back to the house, it was very late and you had gone to bed. It must have been a terrible shock for you to find her."

Again, she noted, he had a thing—a Southern thing?—with personal space. He was so close she could tell he'd just brushed his teeth.

"It was horrible," she admitted. "I just wish I had known how ill she was and gotten her medical care before this happened."

"I feel the same. Bev was very good at keeping secrets, especially about herself. I'm not sure it would have helped, in any case, from what Paul told me the doctor here said this morning. He'd been able to reach her doctor at home. She needed an immediate valve repair and he'd been strongly opposed to her coming to Maine. Wanted her in the hospital for the surgery." He nodded his head in the direction of the house. "What's going on in there?"

"Uncle Paul has gone to lie down and I hope sleep. Simon and Deirdre are eating breakfast. No one else is up. I'm heading out to Granville. There's a farmers' market there every Friday morning during the summer and early fall."

"I saw Daisy on the beach with the little girl who lives at The Pines," Will told her. "And Rory's car is gone and it was gone when I came back last night. Maybe he's made some new friends Down East."

Will's dislike of the Californian was evident. What is this about? Sophie wondered. "The little girl is Amy Fairchild. Her mother, Faith, is the woman who was with me last night. Their cottage is being worked on, so they are staying with Ursula until they can move back in. I used to babysit for Amy and her brother, Ben, back in the day."

"Very sweet. My babysitters tended to be elderly females with chin whiskers. Come on, I'll drive you to Granville. We should take your car, it's bigger. I like farmers' markets, although I'll bet at this time of year it will be slim pickings. If what I hear is true, tomatoes don't ripen until the end of August and you can't grow peaches, period. Not like our peaches, anyway."

Sophie hesitated. But the idea of someone else driving and also some company, even Will's, decided her.

"Just let me get my basket," she said.

She returned with a copious willow market basket.

"Now all you need is a little red cape," Will said.

It was on the tip of her tongue to reply "No need to look for a big bad wolf," but instead she settled into the passenger's seat and tried to relax.

The farmers' market was packed. The ball field across from what had been the Granville elementary school through high school until the state stepped in and said it had to combine with Sanpere Village, raising the combined graduating class to twenty-five, was filled with parked high-end SUVs, the occasional BMW and Mercedes, and Subarus—the unofficial Maine state car—both new and old. Outside the former schools on the blacktop, the lines at each stand were lengthy. Sophie immediately got in the Sunset Acres one.

"Is this the only place you're going?" Will asked.

"I was hoping to get some veggies—chard, early lettuce, anything any of them have—but it will take too long and I want to get back to start lunch. I thought I'd get a few of Bob Bowen's whole chickens here as well as the bacon, eggs, and cheese."

"I'll pick up the vegetables while you go get the rest."

Sophie was stunned. She couldn't imagine any man she knew, most especially Ian, offering to stand in such a long queue. Ian. When would the slightest thought of him stop hurting?

"Are you sure?"

In answer, he gave her a little shove, placing his hand on the small of her back. It felt warm, and there was that tingle again. She quickly gave him her order and he went off to the shortest of the produce lines.

On the way to Bob and Anne's stand Sophie passed Sylvia. Her cousin grabbed her arm excitedly. She had a large canvas bag slung over her shoulder. Sophie thought she remembered its use as a kind of Snugli for Daisy.

"The Community Center has what they're calling a 'General Store' in the old school's basement. People donate usable items, and you wouldn't believe what I scored! An Arabia pitcher from Finland and a lot of antique Nippon and even Limoges. They have no idea what the things are worth. I'm going to make a killing on eBay."

And donate the profits to the Center? Yeah right, Sophie said to herself, feeling slightly sickened. Sylvia was currently living in a beautiful home in Mill Valley, provided by Daisy's father in Silicon Valley. And her cousin's clothes might look Bohemian, but Sophie had seen some of the labels, and Sylvia wasn't tie-dyeing her wardrobe in her bathtub.

"Sorry, I have to go. The lines are so long."

"Ridiculous." Sylvia tossed her head. "Daisy and I are heading to the new place for their lobster rolls. Hear

they are fabulous and well worth the money. Later."
And she drifted off in a cloud of patchouli.

"The guy is a total ass . . . I mean jerk!" Ben said
angrily.

"Who are you talking about? What's going on?"
Faith was bewildered. One minute they were having a
nice visit with Mandy Hitchcock and the moment she
was out the door, Ben had exploded.

Faith had invited her in when she dropped Ben off,
wanting to meet the girl who would be driving her precious son, and she also felt they should offer gas money.
Mandy had refused, saying she lived on Little Sanpere,
too, just down the road. Faith had liked her and been
struck by what a difference less than three years in age
made between teenage girls and teenage boys. Mandy
was on the brink of womanhood and Ben was still tee-
tering toward snips, snails, and puppy dog tails.

"That guy next door. Daisy's brother, Rory whatev'.
Thinks he's God's gift. He came to lunch today with a
group of people and the chef was getting really PO'd.
Their burgers were too rare, then overdone. Who
orders burgers in a seafood place? They were eating
at the tables on the deck and getting rowdy. The bar-
tender couldn't keep up with the drinks orders. Mr.
Otis came out, but ended up joining them."

"So, it was all right then?" Faith still felt a bit clueless.

"No, it was *not* all right! He was like hitting on Mandy, who was their server, and he's way older than she is. Wanted her to go to some party with him."

So that was it. Oh dear, Faith thought. Poor Ben.

"I'm sure Mandy handled it. She seems like a very level-headed girl."

"That's not the point, Mom!"

Faith was suddenly very tired. The deep sadness she'd been feeling after finding Bev Boynton plus the news that Marian might need complicated heart surgery was leaving her drained. She just didn't have the energy to cope with adolescent angst at the moment.

Fortunately Amy reverted to something akin to eight-year-old brattiness and sang out, "Ben's in love! Ben's in love!" which resulted in his swift exit from the room and a slammed back door.

When Tom had called earlier, he'd told her what she'd already assumed—that he'd be staying down in Massachusetts for the foreseeable future. He was due to participate in a retreat the denomination was running for parish ministers toward the end of the month— God Camp, Faith called it, since the locale was at a conference center high up in the Berkshire mountains. After they'd talked today, she had been tempted to pack up the kids and head home to Aleford, but Ben, as well as Amy, would be heartbroken. Thinking back to Ben's outburst a few minutes ago, she realized he'd be furious, too. She might have taken Sophie Maxwell up on her offer, leaving for just a few days, but not after what Sophie had been through last night.

Sophie was probably also very busy taking over for Bev. Faith doubted the others were pitching in much. This thought was just what she needed to get her out of her funk. She'd go buy some fresh crab from Kathy Gray and make up a few dozen crab cakes that Sophie could serve or freeze. If Kathy's husband, Robbie, was home from fishing and had lobster, she'd do a risotto, as well. That with a big salad from Ursula's garden and several of Gert's pies left from the picnic would serve The Birches for dinner tonight. She'd also make a smoked turkey puff pastry (see recipe, page 239) that Sophie could pop in the oven and then cut up bite-size for hors d'oeuvres, or larger as a main course. Besides the turkey, there was cheese and either mustard or an onion/garlic jam between the two pastry sheets. When on Sanpere, Faith bought Pepperidge Farm ready-made dough to make life simple. I should have thought of providing food earlier, she chided herself.

She hadn't known Bev Boynton, but these offerings would be the equivalent of funeral baked meats—food in time of sorrow was a necessity, just as it was in celebration. The celebration yesterday seemed like months ago. She called to Amy, who was upstairs. The summer had already been topsy-turvy because of the delay of the addition to the cottage—and work had stopped for the holiday. Now the summer was starting to feel like an endlessly spinning whirligig.

It was cooler today, thank goodness, Sophie reflected as she finished putting together a massive amount of smoked chicken with steamed vegetables, including the rainbow chard chopped fine and penne pasta she'd found to cook in the pantry, dressed with her own vinaigrette. She put the bowl in the fridge and would bring the dish to room temperature for dinner. It felt good to have accomplished this, and she began to assemble more ingredients. She'd always liked to cook, much to her mother's surprise. "Oh, Sophie, this is why one has people, or failing that, Balducci's in Westport."

She was about to start on some gazpacho and other cold soups to have in reserve when Uncle Simon and Aunt Deirdre came waltzing into the kitchen. Well, not literally, but Sophie thought there was a pronounced glide to their matching steps as they came through the door from the living room where Paul was. Sophie had brought him some lemonade and offered food, but he said he wasn't hungry.

She looked at her relatives and braced herself. Their habitual cat-that-ate-the-canary looks were broader than usual. They'd pulled something off, and Sophie was certain it had to do with the competition. Forbes and Felicity were sailing but had made sure to stay in the running by inviting Paul to come along as they were leaving. Sophie had seen him smile and refuse. "Not today, children," he'd said.

"We've just been telling Uncle Paul that we can't continue to impose on you for all these meals. We've hired a caterer from off island to supply lunches and dinners until Bev can be replaced," Simon announced.

Sophie started to speak but stopped immediately. What she had been about to say was that Bev could *never* be replaced. As for the meals, there was no reason why they all couldn't pitch in until Paul himself decided what he wanted to do. Apparently, since Simon had only mentioned lunch and dinner—she thought in annoyance—they were happy to have Sophie continue supplying them with breakfast.

"I already made dinner for tonight," she said.

"And I made it for the next two nights." Faith Fairchild had quietly entered the kitchen while Simon was speaking. "Such a lovely gesture, but as soon as word gets around the island you'll have more food than you know what to do with—I'm surprised the casserole brigade hasn't shown up by now. I'm Faith Fairchild, by the way. We met yesterday at the clambake and also a few summers ago. I'm staying with Ursula Rowe at The Pines."

"You are a peach, Faith." Paul McAllister had walked in, hearing her voice. He went over and gave her a quick kiss. "And she's right." He turned to address his niece and nephew. "Thoughtful of you, but I think we'll pass on any catering for now. Gert Prescott has said she'll find me someone to pinch-hit for the summer. I'm not sure yet where I'll be this winter."

"With mother and me in Savannah, Uncle Paul," Will Tarkington said firmly. His entry was making the kitchen feel like Grand Central Station. Who was going to walk through the door next? Sophie thought somewhat giddily.

It was Sylvia.

"Has anyone seen my children? Oh, what's going on? What have I missed?"

"Nothing," Paul reassured her. "We're just getting all the meals arranged. And I believe Daisy is on the porch reading. I haven't seen Rory or Autumn today."

"Meals! Of course! Now I can do a stir-fry for tonight with farro and mustard greens. And fish. We should be able to get some nice haddock."

"That won't be necessary," Simon said in a clipped voice. "It appears we're in no need of victuals. Now if you'll excuse me I have a call to make." He left in high dudgeon closely followed by his wife, who was grumbling what sounded like, "Try to do a nice thing!"

Faith turned toward Sylvia. "Amy would love to have Daisy come over for the rest of the day. They had a fun time on the beach earlier. We could bring her back after our dinner."

"How nice," Sylvia said. "Yes, why don't you do that? Where was it Simon said she was?"

Sophie raised an eyebrow. Faith gave her a smile and said, "I'll go out the front and get her, shall I?"

Sylvia didn't answer her, instead asking, "Are you sure no one has seen Rory or Autumn today?"

Faith stopped. "My son is working at The Laughing Gull Lodge and said your son had been there for lunch."

"Why on earth would he go there?" Sylvia ran her hand through her long hair and left. Sophie heard her car start up. Was she going to scour the island for her offspring?

As suddenly as the room had been packed full of people, it emptied. Only Sophie and Will remained.

"Nice relatives," he said and left, too.

The dance at the Legion Hall the Saturday night closest to the Fourth was another long-standing Sanpere custom and a cherished one. Some of the dances remained the same as when the tradition had begun—an old-fashioned line dance, Lady of the Lake, as well as a few square dances. Freeman Hamilton had been calling them, he was quick to tell anyone who asked, "Since Hector was a pup." The Melodic Mariners, who had also graced the small stage at the hall for almost as long, were amazingly versatile, capable of segueing from "Louie, Louie" to "The Blue Danube" seamlessly. For Freeman's dances, however, a trio took over—Dorothy, a plump woman Freeman's own age with raven tresses Faith suspected had been enhanced thanks to the hair color aisle at the Rite Aid in Ellsworth, on guitar; a young man on fiddle; and an even younger one on flat-backed mandolin. These last two had replaced the other trio members now presumably making St. Peter tap his toes with their renditions of "Red Wing" and "Soldier's Joy." The change, which she had noted last summer, had initially brought a lump to Faith's throat, but time had passed, and she was happy to know an island institution—and its musical heritage—was being continued.

Another thing that was standing the test of time was the mix of ages, even a fair mix of people from the island and people from away. The giant mirrored disco ball was sending tiny rainbows over fishermen, shipyard workers, and summer people alike. The musicians were bathed in blue lights that had been rigged up directly overhead and always reminded Faith of *The Blue Angel* with Marlene Dietrich. The Mariners' chanteuse was dressed not dissimilarly from Dietrich in spike heels, short skirt, and, in this instance, a tiny tee that spelled out HOT in red sequins. She had a big voice, though, and was getting everyone up and on the dance floor.

Faith was content to watch, enjoying the range of abilities and sights, like one of the Sanfords with his four-year-old granddaughter standing on his shoes as he jitterbugged. Amy and Daisy had joined a group of girls that included Amy's island day camp friends. They were casting studied nonchalant looks at their male counterparts on the opposite side of the hall. Pix had warned Faith that female adolescence was a bumpier ride for mothers than male, and Faith had been hoping Amy would prolong her entry. She was glad Daisy was next door and she *did* seem like a little girl, although the two were the same age. There was something waifish about Daisy, and she was certainly quiet around adults, although she and Amy chattered nonstop whenever Faith had observed them away from everyone else.

Daisy's older brother, Rory, came in with a group, and they immediately started dancing wildly, but with such enthusiasm that they had everyone laughing.

Ben hadn't wanted Faith to drive him, but he didn't have a choice when Mandy called to say she had to work. He was looking glum and his expression darkened, Faith noticed, when Rory grabbed his cousin Sophie, pulling her into the group. He could really dance and so could Sophie. They looked like *Dancing with the Stars*, 1950s version.

The Millers arrived as the band switched to "The Twist." Faith could see the delight on Sam's and Pix's faces—Mark, his wife Becca, Samantha, and Dan were all with them. The whole group started gyrating; Sam sang out to Faith, "Come on baby!" and she soon found herself twisting 'round and 'round.

The group around Rory and Sophie was getting down, too, but taking the suggestive lyrics a little more to the limit. Ben stalked out the door to the parking lot, followed by Tyler.

"I think we're going to head back," Faith shouted to Pix.

"Oh no, don't go yet! It's early and I'm sure your kids want to stay longer," she said.

The music stopped and the band announced they were taking a short break. Ben had not returned, and Faith decided maybe he needed time with Tyler and other friends outside. In any case, he wouldn't appreciate his mother coming in search of him. Oh these perilous shores.

Amy came running over with Daisy.

"We *have* to buy some raffle tickets! First prize is a ham!"

Faith laughed. First prize had been an enormous canned ham for as long as she could remember. She gave Amy five dollars for the tickets and some extra for punch and cookies. Looking at Daisy, she added a bit more. "Treat your friend," she said.

Sophie was coming toward them, a worried look on her face.

"Daisy, is your mother here?" she asked.

Daisy shook her head. "She dropped me off and said she'd be back later. Can I go get something to eat with Amy now?"

"Of course, let me give you the money."

"Amy's mom gave us some."

"Well, here's a little more and you can treat Amy another time," Sophie said, handing Daisy some bills.

The girls left and Sophie sat down on an empty chair between Faith and Samantha.

"I don't know what to do," she said. "Apparently Sylvia's child rearing comes under the heading of 'Born Free.' Daisy's only twelve and even though the dance is a safe place, I'm not comfortable with her being left here like this. And I can't really say anything."

Faith felt exactly the same. "No, you can't. Maybe she spoke to Rory and told him to keep an eye on Daisy."

"Aside from the fact that my dear cousin has possibly the most roving eye at the dance, he's also feeling no pain. He seems to have made friends with the owner of the Lodge—that's him next to the blonde."

What was Ben's boss doing here? Faith wondered. The Lodge was open for dinner tonight, wasn't it? Mandy had said she had to work. And you couldn't run a successful business, especially on what had to be a busy Saturday night, by remote control.

Samantha Miller was looking uncomfortable as well, Faith saw. She must know Daisy—and the rest of that family—since she'd always gone back and forth between the Millers' cottage and The Birches.

"**Do you** want to get some punch, too, Sophie?" Samantha asked. "Bring some back for anyone?"

"Great," Pix said. "All that twisting has made me thirsty. They have trays; so get some for all of us—and cookies. Lots of cookies."

Halfway across the momentarily deserted dance floor, Samantha said, "I need to tell you something."

"What's up?" Sophie asked. Samantha had been a summer friend. They were about the same age and when young had been together constantly.

"It's about your cousin."

"Oh, Rory's okay. Just very California and maybe a teensy bit stuck on himself."

"No, not Rory. Autumn. I was at the party after the fireworks at the new restaurant and she was there, too. I think she's using."

"As in drugs?"

Samantha nodded. "She stretched her arms up at some bubbles someone was blowing and she has track marks on her arms. She has so many tattoos that they are hard to see, but they're there."

"Oh God." Sophie sat down hard on an empty folding chair. "She does always seem to wear long sleeves. She had the tats last time I saw her—unicorns, lots of swirls, but she has a ton more now."

"Maybe she's stopped. The track marks could be old. I just wanted you to know. To keep an eye on her, especially because of Daisy."

Sophie was having trouble taking it in. "She's always been dreamy—and shy. I can't remember having a real conversation with her even when we were younger. I always thought it was just the way she was."

"Another California thing? Like crystals? We are such East Coast bigots," Samantha said. "If she is using, she won't have a problem finding what she needs here. New England, especially Maine, is now the heroin capital of the United States. It's cheaper than prescription drugs like OxyContin." She gave Sophie a hug. "My sibs have to leave but I'm here for two more weeks. Call me. Let's go out to Isle au Haut with bikes or something else like that. Pretend we're not grown-ups."

"I wish," Sophie said ruefully and followed Samantha over to the refreshments table. As they approached it, they were aware of raised voices coming through the window from the parking lot. Then it got quiet, too quiet before several cars started up. Sergeant Earl Dickinson walked in and headed straight for Faith and the Millers.

"Forget the drinks," Samantha said. "Something's wrong."

They got back to the group in time to hear him say, "Guys get foolish. Don't worry. Just take him home and get him cleaned up."

"But Ben has never done anything like this! I can't believe he'd start a fight, especially with someone older," Faith said. She grabbed her purse and went out with Earl.

Pix explained. "Ben took a swing at Rory Proctor, who proceeded to laugh and blocked the punch with one hand while pushing Ben against the building with the other, giving him a bloody nose."

"Poor Ben," Sophie said. "He must be mortified. Rory can be a bit much. I'll speak to him."

"I'm sure he and all the others he came with are gone. Best let it lie. But could you take Amy back? I doubt Ben wants his little sister to see him. She'll hear about it, and that's bad enough."

"Absolutely. I'll take Daisy, too. If Sylvia comes, please tell her. If she notices, that is."

Sophie had felt overwhelmed by her relatives before. Now she wished she could go back to that simpler sensation. This was more like drowning.

A peaceful scene greeted her after Sophie dropped Amy off and then settled Daisy upstairs in the front bedroom at The Birches with a cup of cocoa. Uncle

Paul and Will were playing Scrabble in a small room that served as a study, a converted oil lamp providing the only light. The Proctors had grudgingly given in to Edison's wattage, but retained the old fixtures. Sophie had a sudden longing to go back to when the house had been bathed in that softer, earlier glow.

"Who's winning?" she asked.

"Neck and neck, as usual," Will said.

"There! That's forty-six for me. 'Sequoia'. Nice word. Thank you for leaving that double word all ready for an *s*. And I get the score for 'players.'"

Sophie could see they both played a mean game. She'd never achieved a score as high as either had now and there were still plenty of tiles left.

"Are you hungry? I could make some sandwiches."

"Thank you, sweetheart. Will and I have been raiding the fridge all evening. You left it well stocked. I wouldn't say no to a little brandy, though. Will?"

"Got to keep my edge. You go ahead."

Sophie returned with a snifter of Rémy Martin, his favorite, for her uncle.

"If you don't want anything else, then, I'm going to turn in."

She gave Paul a kiss on the cheek and almost gave one to Will also. I *must* be tired, she thought.

In her room off the kitchen, she quickly got ready

for bed. The house was quiet. She assumed Daisy was asleep, and no one else seemed to be home. Her laptop was on a small table from the upstairs hall that she'd added to the room. She should check her e-mail, she told herself, but as soon as the MacBook Air came to life, she went straight to Google and typed "Will Tarkington."

For the next forty minutes she typed every possibility: "William Tarkington," "Willard," "Wilfred," "Willy," "Willie," even "Bill" and its permutations. She tried "Wilhelm," "Wilmer," and "Wilton" after checking a baby name site. She turned up a dentist in Salt Lake City and an eighty-four-year-old in Toronto on Facebook. Then she began to narrow a search to Savannah and finally all of Georgia for Tarkingtons. Nothing fit.

Will Tarkington didn't exist.

Chapter 6

"Arnie and Claire are coming early," Ursula announced. Faith and she were sitting on the back porch of The Pines shelling peas. They hadn't had the traditional salmon and peas on the Fourth, so they were having it now for Sunday dinner at the Millers' cottage later. "They'll be here Tuesday and he said he has a surprise for us."

"No hints?" Faith said.

She was happy to have a comforting, culinary task as she was in need of a pleasant distraction.

Tom had called last night and again this morning. Nothing had changed. Marian was still resting comfortably and they would find out tomorrow when her surgery would be performed. Faith was less worried about her mother-in-law—she was in good hands—than she was about her son. She hadn't told Tom about the fight. There was nothing he could do about it from so far away and she didn't want to worry him. But she did wish he were here to both have a talk with Ben and also reassure Faith that it wasn't a big deal. Or was it? Fortunately Ben's boss had just pulled out of the parking lot, so he didn't see his employee try to engage a customer, who also appeared to be the boss's new friend, in fisticuffs. Faith didn't want Ben fired, but she did want him to quit. If Mandy was provoking this sort of behavior after only two days, what was next? Pistols at dawn? Ben had been unequivocal about staying. After repeating "You don't get it, Mom!" several times in ever increasing volume, he had stomped off, presumably to bed. To his room, anyway. Faith was sure the fight involved the girl in some way. She tuned back in to what Ursula was saying.

"No hints. At my age, I don't like surprises, even pleasant ones, but I'm sure he means well. He sounded awfully tickled with himself."

They continued shelling the peas in companionable silence. Faith glanced at Ursula's hands. Her mention of age had startled Faith, as Ursula was not one to comment on the depredations, or anything else, that accompanied her advancing years. Yes, the veins were prominent, the skin loose, and there were liver spots—why were they called that?—but her fingers worked deftly, and Faith knew her friend's grip was still strong.

"Gert told me about the fracas at the dance last night. If you want to talk about it, fine. If not, fine too," Ursula said.

"I figured it would be all over the island by this morning, no make that last night—minutes after it happened. Sanpere doesn't have a grapevine, it has a superconductor. I want him to leave the job and work at the day camp, but he won't hear of it."

Ursula nodded. "I'd feel the same way, but Ben has to decide for himself. I'm not telling you something you don't already know. The whole thing was unfortunate timing, I suspect, and probably misinterpretation on Ben's part. Gert said it was about Mandy going to someone's house for a party off island with Rory. He isn't a bad person and I've always felt sorry for all three of Sylvia's children. Never a stable father around, or stable father figures even. And Sylvia believes children do best bringing themselves up, doing what they want to do."

"I've always thought parents like that used the philosophy to do what *they* wanted," Faith said.

Ursula agreed. "Exactly—and she wants them all here to convince Paul that she—and eventually they—would be the best bet for The Birches. I'm not saying she doesn't love the place—she does—but how could she possibly take care of it?"

Faith put the last empty pod on top of the heap for the compost pile.

"Ed Ricks was telling me he has tales about this sort of thing—who gets the house, the land—that would make my hair curl."

"I'm sure he does, and I have a few, too. Arnie made it very simple for me years ago by saying he didn't want The Pines, just wanted to be able to come and stay for a while each summer. I've set the whole thing up so that Pix and Sam will inherit it and he'll get a monetary equivalent. I know they love their cottage, but with three children and who knows how many grandchildren in the future, they can easily fill both places. What are you and Tom doing?"

"Our house here is the only one we own. Occupying a parsonage is a plus and a minus. You don't have to worry about the upkeep—the church sees to that—but you also don't have any equity. That's another reason we decided to add onto the house here this summer, and put in a furnace. It will increase its value." Faith had resisted all Tom's earlier attempts to convince her to make it a year-round dwelling, preferring to think of winter vacations spent in places with turquoise water and white sandy beaches. She'd given in to the logic of doing it while they were adding the room. "Everything we have, except for a few special charitable bequests, is divided evenly between Ben and Amy. My sister Hope and Tom's brother Robert are our executors. Hope and her husband are the children's guardians."

Ursula stood up. "That all sounds very well thought out and I just wish Priscilla had done the same. Now, that's enough talk about real estate. Ben will calm down. It's unlikely he and Rory will cross paths again. Right now we have a more important topic to discuss. Mint in the peas or just plain with butter?"

Later at the Millers', Pix had seemed puzzled at the change in her brother's plans. "They always have all their arrangements carved in stone, and as for a surprise, this is it so far as I'm concerned. He's coming early. Remember it's Arnie we're talking about. When he got his first Filofax, a five-year one, he promptly scheduled all his teeth cleanings."

Ben was at work, but Amy was there with her ears flapping, so Faith couldn't get the Millers' take on the night before and whether she should insist Ben leave the job at the Lodge. Although, she reflected, the Lodge wasn't the problem. They had been scrupulous so far about his hours as an underage employee. And Mandy had seemed like a sensible girl. Faith had the feeling that with her mother working off island and her father not up for dad, or husband, of the year according to Seth, Mandy had had to grow up fast. Too fast?

When she was helping Pix cut the rich devil's food layer cake that Mark's wife, Becca, had made—unlike his mother, Mark's wife loved to cook and Pix loved her all the more for it—Faith asked Pix what she thought Faith should do about Ben. Pix, her guide in all matters offspring, was succinct. "Nothing."

Well, that's one less thing to worry about, Faith told herself and helped herself to a large slice of cake. Chocolate was the universal panacea, and soon she found herself laughing with the Millers about their recent discovery during repairs to the house's foundation. The backhoe unearthed not only several bicycles and a tricycle, but also the major parts of a chassis from a 1936 Buick sedan under their front garden.

"Must have been one of the island scrap metal dumps," Sam said. "I'm hoping to get that beauty put back together and on the road."

"Yeah, Dad, and give up your Miata. Right," Dan said.

"I can have both. Now, what I want is more cake—and I'll eat it, too."

His daughter took his plate. "Better watch out. If you keep this up, you'll have another kind of tire to think about."

"Sharper than a serpent's tooth!" Sam said, grabbing her for a big hug.

Faith sat basking in it all, wishing Tom was there. Wishing Ben was there. And especially wishing she truly believed she had one less thing to worry about.

They'd managed to survive the holiday weekend without someone killing anybody. But the atmosphere had been poisonous, especially after the altercation at the parade between Sylvia and Simon.

It wasn't murder, but there had been a death, Sophie reminded herself as she sat on the dock looking out toward the Camden Hills. Bev's passing seemed to have left hardly a ripple on the surface of most lives at The Birches. She knew from her uncle that Durgens Funeral Home in Granville had taken care of all the arrangements. "Arrangements." Such a euphemism. Bev wasn't some posies stuck in a vase. Although Paul had said she had been cremated, so she was in a container of some sort. An urn? Sophie was very, very tired, and her thoughts were straying far and wide. In the old days, women would wash the body and wrap it in a winding cloth before it went into a simple wooden box to become one with the earth. That's what she wanted, Sophie decided. She didn't have a will. Didn't have anything to leave, but she was going to draw one up for herself with these instructions.

"Penny for your thoughts." It was Will. Once more, she had had no idea he was there.

"You should copyright that line. Very nice."

He took a shiny coin from his jeans pocket and handed it to her. "I never make offers I can't keep."

She took the penny. It was warm. "I was just thinking how quickly everyone seems to have forgotten that Bev is gone."

A shadow crossed Will's face and he said quietly, "Not everybody."

Sophie felt her throat close and knew she was about to cry.

"Is this a private party or can anyone join?" Rory called.

Without waiting for an answer, he plunked himself down next to Sophie, pulled his flip-flops off, and let his feet dangle over the water. He had an insulated bag over his shoulder, which he unzipped. "The best brew New England has to offer. Good old Sam Adams Summer Ale. Sorry I don't have any fancy hors d'oeuvres, but Pringles are the extent of my skill in that department." He handed them each a bottle and opened the chips.

Sophie had to smile. Rory was, well, Rory. His white-blond hair was combed straight back and curled at the neck. His tan made his eyes look bluer. He was smiling a smile you just had to return. Yes, her cousin was definitely a heartbreaker. The beer was ice cold and she was glad he had joined them. "Thanks," she said.

"Me too," Will said. "And Pringles happen to be my favorite. You can keep your caviar and foie gras."

"Never had any. Mom is pretty harsh about stuff like that, so don't know what I'm missing. Anyhow, besides Pringles and Sophie here what else do you like, Will?"

"Rory!" Sophie jumped up. He was going too far.

"Hey, I'm just messing with you." He turned to Will. "Always been pretty easy to get a rise out of my big cousin."

Will looked appraisingly at Sophie. "That so?"

Sophie sat back down, but she was beginning to feel like some sort of display in a department store window. Available for comment by any and all passersby.

Will took a swig of beer. "I like old cars, new trucks, redeye gravy, and pretty much anything J. D. Salinger ever wrote."

"I had to read that book in school. *The Catcher in the Rye.* Boooring. But seriously, Sophie, old Forbes and Uncle Simon have you marrying the Southern dude here before the leaves fall."

"Talk sense—and proper English," Sophie said.

"I overheard them when I was making my way down here. They were on the front porch. Wasn't in the mood for what the market is doing or who's competing in the America's Cup, so maybe I *was* walking pretty close to the house and behind a few bushes."

"What were they saying?" Will's voice had lost all its Southern softness and was as sharp as an ax.

"That Uncle Paul wanted the two of you to get together, and if that happened, he'd have no trouble deciding who would inherit The Birches. Mom will go ape shit when I tell her. She's already picking out the color she wants to repaint the shutters. You know how she feels about the place. I'm supposed to be in Malibu now, although the natives here are turning out to be pretty friendly. But I knew if I didn't show she'd be on me about it forever. You have no idea what she can be like."

Sophie thought she did. "Please don't repeat this to your mother, or anyone else. I don't know where they could have gotten the idea. It's absurd! I don't even know Will." She thought back to her Google search and added, "Don't know him at all!" for emphasis.

"No biggie. Now who wants another beer?"

"I'll take a rain check," Will said and, getting up, headed toward the boathouse.

"I hope it wasn't something I said." Rory grinned.

The heat had broken, but it was still stifling in the kitchen at The Laughing Gull Lodge. The Otises might have put a lot of money into the place, but they'd skimped on air-conditioning for the staff, Ben thought.

Mandy had picked him up early this morning. They were both working through the lunch shift. He'd tossed and turned last night thinking about what to say, or not say, to her. Instead of waiting at the house, he'd walked out to the main road to meet her. He didn't want his mother barging in with "Keep an eye on my little boy." He knew he wasn't being fair. His mother didn't do stuff like that. Maybe sometimes, but not often and not lately. What she *would* nag at him about was quitting the job, and there was no way he was going to do that. Mandy had been totally cool. After he got in the car, all she had said was "Hi, you okay?" He'd nodded and then they talked about work.

Ben finished putting the last load from breakfast into the dishwasher and went to wait in the other part of the kitchen where it was cooler. He filled his water bottle from the tap. The Lodge had a deep well and the water was ice cold and fresh. The bandanna he wore as a sweatband was soaked. He took it off and reached into his back pocket for another.

Mandy was setting tables for lunch, indoors and out. The other servers hadn't arrived yet. Only the chef was there, and he was in a foul mood. The server who doubled as sous chef was late.

"Can I help? I'm pretty decent at chopping stuff," Ben offered.

Chef Zach was outstanding in the kitchen and Ben figured he was a good judge because his mother was, too. Zach Hale had arrived before the Lodge opened in order to make contact with local providers, especially the fishermen and farmers. He was adding his signature Hawaiian twist to the menu, each night offering a different Poke, bite-size raw fish "cured" in soy with a variety of spices, as an appetizer or side dish. Duck with Chinese five-spice powder was a menu staple, as was Poi. One of the local organic farms was growing taro. Mai tais had become the drink of choice from the cocktail menu. But no Spam much to his regret, he'd told Ben and Tyler. "I might sneak some in, and I'll bet no one notices. They'll think it's some classy French pâté." Until then Ben hadn't known Spam was like the Hawaiian national food. He only knew it from Monty Python.

Yet, despite the popularity of the tropical island dishes, Ben noticed that the entrée most ordered was the chef's take on butter poached lobster ravioli. Chef

Zach coated the raviolis with a velvety nape of citrus beurre blanc—minced shallots, white wine, lemon juice, heavy cream, and a ton of unsalted butter. The first day, Ben and Tyler had been amazed at how much food got wasted. People, especially skinny women, would leave whole plates almost untouched. But the lobster ravioli ones were almost licked clean. The chef had given them a sample, and it was one of the best things Ben had ever eaten. Not that he'd tell his mother.

"I need fresh lime juice for the halibut I'll be poaching as today's lunch special, so you could get that ready. I may have to fire that guy's ass if he doesn't start showing up on time."

Mandy walked in. "The tables are all set, Chef. What do you want me to do now?"

"See if you can find Derek. He hasn't been in this morning, and I need to speak to him about this week's Sysco order."

Mandy looked upset. "Uh, I think he said something last night about maybe not being in until after lunch. But I'll go look," she added hurriedly.

"You do that. Dream job. Oh yes, that's what he and his parents said. Becoming more like a nightmare."

Ben quickly finished squeezing the limes. "Let me do those onions, Chef. My mom has taught me knife skills and you can get going on something else."

If the chef quit, the Lodge would definitely suffer and who knows what could happen. He didn't want to be out of a job. What his mother didn't get was that it wasn't a question of Mandy keeping an eye on Ben, but Ben having to keep an eye on her.

By Monday, Gert Prescott had found someone to take Bev Boynton's place, but Marge Foster wasn't able to be full time. She'd take care of the house, make lunch, and leave dinner. "Can handle the baking, too. Nothing fancy, but muffins, biscuits, cookies, bread— people like my anadama. Crumbles, especially if you can get me some rhubarb."

Sophie thought this sounded like more than a full-time job. She told her uncle she could do the marketing from the lists Mrs. Foster supplied, and she'd also see to breakfast for as long as she was there.

"I'm sure some of the others will pitch in, too," Paul said. "Will is a dab hand at waffles. But, Sophie, I'm hoping you'll be staying the whole summer. Your mother said you were between jobs and had the time free."

Sophie wasn't so sure about people pitching in, no matter how adept at waffles. She silently exchanged a few words with her mother in absentia. Free the whole summer! Then the look on Uncle Paul's face stopped what she had been going to say—that she would only be here a week or so more at most. She couldn't let him down.

"I'll most certainly stay as long as you need me." She gave him a quick hug.

He hugged her back. "That could mean a very long time, my dear."

Sylvia—with Daisy trailing behind—walked onto the porch where Sophie and Paul were sitting. She immediately hugged them both.

"Such a bittersweet time!" Sylvia said. "We all need to bond. Now what should we do today? I know! How about the trail out to Barred Island?"

"I'm afraid the tide is wrong just now. Perhaps later when it's low. Don't want to get stranded. Simon and Forbes have kindly invited me for a sail. Mrs. Foster is packing us a lunch," Paul said.

There was no mistaking the sour look that crossed Sylvia's face and he hastily added, "The walk and a picnic for your birthday? It's Wednesday, isn't it?"

At that moment Simon and his entire family came out onto the porch from the house. Once again, Simon and Forbes could have posed for an ad, this time one for what the well-dressed yachtsman might wear. Felicity and Deirdre were similarly attired, and it appeared the whole family would be going sailing. Or bonding.

"What's Wednesday?" Deirdre asked.

When the pause made it apparent that Sylvia wasn't going to answer, perhaps because her teeth were so tightly clenched, Sophie did. "It's Sylvia's birthday and we're talking about what to do to celebrate."

"Celebrate? Aren't we a little past that sort of thing? Balloons, party hats?" Deirdre's voice hinted that whatever Sylvia's approaching number, any notice would not only be inappropriate, but absurd.

Paul jumped in to soothe the ruffled feathers. "Oh, one is never too old, or too young, for a birthday celebration. Come, Sylvia, how would you like to mark the happy occasion?"

Sylvia's mouth opened and closed, then opened again. "I want to see puffins."

"Birds? I never knew you were an ornithologist," Simon said. "Besides, we'd have to go quite far, and I'm not sure they are still around."

"I called Robertson Sea Tours and Adventures out of Millbridge. That's not far at all. Captain Robertson said there were still plenty of puffins on Petit Manan, which is where he goes. Other seabirds, too."

Simon was intent on raining on Sylvia's parade, probably remembering what she had tried to do at Thursday's parade, Sophie thought.

"Petit Manan is a National Wildlife Refuge," Simon said. "Only the Coast Guard manning the lighthouse and vetted individuals studying the birds from places like The College of the Atlantic are allowed to land. Sorry, Sylvia."

"I know that!" she spat back. "I don't intend to pet one, I just want to see them."

Paul was beginning to look distressed and Sophie decided it was time to stop all this one-upmanship. "It will be a beautiful ride and we'll certainly see birds of some sort plus seals, maybe dolphins. I'll organize a birthday lunch, shall I?" she said.

"And I'll call the tour office to make reservations." Will Tarkington had been sitting off to one side reading a book. Sophie hadn't noticed him. The porch wrapped around the house, and she couldn't help but think that he had stationed himself perfectly to observe without being easily observed.

"That's settled then," Paul said. "We'll all be onboard. Now, if we're going to catch the wind, perhaps Forbes and Felicity can check on the lunch while I get another jacket?"

"Room for me to tag along? I've never sailed these coastal waters, and from what I hear, they have Georgia's beat. Not that I believe that," Will said, his accent noticeably thicker.

"Sure," said Simon. "The more the merrier." Sophie didn't think her uncle was looking at all merry.

Advantage Team Will—or whoever he was?

———

"Okay, make my hair curl," Faith said. She'd run into Ed Ricks at the bank. He suggested they get iced coffee to go from the new coffee roasting place and sit by the millpond behind it. The young women had scavenged some lawn furniture from the dump, painted it, put it out, and now "meet you at the millpond" was a popular invitation.

Faith was tempted to tell Ed about Ben's altercation Saturday night. He didn't treat adolescents, but she was sure he could give her some insights. Pix's suggestion was hard to follow. Faith wasn't used to doing "nothing." Yet it didn't seem fair to ask Ed. Enough people seemed to be taking advantage of his expertise without Faith adding to his load.

"What was the worst family feud?" she said.

"Hmm, there are a lot of contenders. And I'm eliminating the ones where everyone stops talking to each other. Those are pretty mild, but hurtful. Very hurtful."

"And punitive. Like the whole Amish shunning thing," Faith said.

"Exactly, especially when it's parents and children. Adult children, that is. Siblings not talking doesn't have the same sting."

Faith could not think of anything her children would ever do that would cause her to stop speaking to them.

An image of Ben's angry face flashed into mind and she repeated to herself, nothing they could do . . . She might yell, but she'd communicate.

"I suppose the winner would have to be the two Rogers brothers, mainly because it lasted so long and was so public they might as well have taken space in the *Bangor Daily News* for updates," Ed said. "They were flatlanders, originally from someplace near Chicago. Understand, we're not talking about kids here. Grown men in their forties. Their parents bought a whole point jutting out into Toothacker Bay sometime in the 1950s."

He paused.

"With you so far." Faith smiled. "I know what a flatlander is and wonder why Sanperers use that term when it's not mountainous here, but back to the story. Oh, and I know the bay and it's named after a family, not an unpleasant dental emergency."

"Back in that day," Ed said, "you could get a whole point of land for next to nothing, but this family wasn't hurting in that department. Some sort of business in the Midwest. They clear-cut for the view—you could do that then, too, although I'm sure you know some people do it now and pay the ridiculously low fine. They built a real nice year-round house smack on the shore—again, no setback regulations. The boys grew up there, every summer. The father died first. Mother lived to a ripe old age. People round here speak highly of her still."

"Even if she was from away."

"Ayuh. She left the whole thing to the two of them, which did cause some comment, as those brothers were chalk and cheese from the moment they got old enough to be possessive about their toys."

What with all the folksy expressions, Ed was certainly going native, Faith thought.

"The mother did have the sense to appoint an estate executor, a lawyer down in Portland, and for years he tried to get those two men to divide the acreage up and the house, too, so many months each or put up a second one—there was plenty of room. But they just wouldn't do it. That stubborn. Each wanted the whole pie. One of them got up at the Island Country Club's Saturday night dinner every week and asked that they pray for him to get it all as part of the blessing. For a while people went along with it, because he was a darn good golfer and a lot of members wanted him as a partner for the Presidents Cup. Then it got ridiculous. The other son was doing much the same thing. Took out ads for a whole summer in the *Island Crier* asking anyone who had observed 'moral turpitude' on his brother's part to let him know. Think the plan was to get him arrested for something. And yes, they duked it out. Everyone got used to seeing the two of them with black eyes, crooked noses."

"I shouldn't be laughing," Faith said, laughing, "but it *is* funny."

"It became less funny when one of them was in a bad car accident and it turned out the brakes had been tampered with, and the other one came down with some sort of virulent food poisoning."

"No, not funny." Faith thought of The Birches and Ursula's comment. "What happened?"

"They stuck to their guns, that they were waiting for the other one to die. The will was set up so the survivor got the whole place. Meanwhile, they began to run out of money. Taxes are high on that amount of waterfront, and they had to keep the place up. The irony is that they both stopped trying to come to the house and rented it out. Even that wasn't enough income. Eventually the lawyer got it in lieu of payment owed for his services."

"There's a lesson here," Faith said.

"Yup. Only have one kid."

She frowned at Ed. "No, the lesson is decide who gets what and put it in notarized writing *before* you go yonder."

"Yonder? Is that some sort of religious term? Sorry, it really isn't all that funny. You're right. Both of those men had been coming to the island all their lives and loved it. Neither ever married that I heard of, so all their emotions were focused on the place. Both were close to their parents, and that was a part of it, too. It was a kind of shrine. Every once in a while, one of them rents a place, shows up at the Harbor Café, and cries on any shoulder available. They're old men now."

"I guess it also points out how hard you have to work to make sure your kids get along, at least somewhat civilly," Faith said. "Pix is always telling me you're never finished raising your kids. Maybe these parents quit too soon."

"That's an interesting thought. I'm not seeing these people professionally, but I am advising some friends here who have a small cottage about how they should leave it. It's a blended family, which adds more complications. Real estate has increased in value on the island, even with the economic slump. In this case, what's happening is childhood rivalries are getting played out all over again. Who does Daddy or Mommy love most?"

Faith thought back to a ski vacation the Fairchilds had taken en famille several years ago to celebrate Dick's seventieth birthday. Ed had just described the week perfectly. She still gave a slight shudder when she thought about it. Some of it was because she had also found a corpse and almost ended up one herself. She forced her thoughts to more cheerful ones. Like the iced coffee.

"You notice they make their ice cubes from their espresso? All they need is someone to bake some treats and they would be an even bigger success."

"They could have frozen anything for their ice cubes and I wouldn't have noticed. I very much admire a palate—and talent—like yours."

"As soon as we can move back to our cottage and Tom returns, come for dinner."

"I'd like that very much. And Faith, next time you talk to Tom, please tell him I'm thinking about him and his whole family. But also tell that husband of yours he's a very lucky man."

Faith felt her face flush. Must be the caffeine.

She supposed she should bake some kind of birthday cake for Sylvia, Sophie thought, yawning as she opened her eyes. Cupcakes, since it was a picnic. Before he'd gone off sailing yesterday, Will had called Captain Robertson and made the reservations. With such a big group, Sophie had suggested they bring snacks and drinks on the boat, saving the picnic for dry land. The boat was good-size, but trying to balance plates while using binoculars and taking pictures would be tricky. They would picnic at the part of the

Petit Manan refuge that was on the mainland. It was a short drive from Millbridge, near Steuben and in the same direction as Sanpere. Wanting to have a short trip back told her something she already knew but hadn't put into words. She did now, softly out loud. "I don't want to go." Saying it made her feel a bit better and she repeated it, "I *don't* want to go."

But she couldn't skip the outing without offending Sylvia, plus she would have to be on hand to see to the food, and all sorts of other things. Sophie pulled the curtain back and looked out the window. Her bed was like a bunk on a ship, built into the wall under the sill. She liked that she could sit up and see what the weather was before actually getting up. The sky was still gray, not even dawn yet. But, despite the yawn, she knew she wouldn't be able to get back to sleep.

She threw some clothes on, went to wash up, and decided to make a list for the picnic. She had a list from Mrs. Foster and maybe she'd head to the larger market in Blue Hill. She could make a dump run on the way. The urge to get away from The Birches and this particular cast of characters was irresistible.

Someone had at least helped by sorting the trash and tying the large Hefty bag of household rubbish shut. Sanpere recycled newspapers, glass, cans, some plastic; and deposit bottles went into an oil drum for the local Scout troops. Sophie lugged it all out to the car and was happy she'd remembered to spread plastic sheeting to protect Babs's pristine cargo hold. As she hefted the black household garbage bag, she noticed that a piece of wire had poked its way out. She balanced the bag on the rear bumper and took a closer look.

It wasn't a wire. It was a syringe needle.

"What are you doing?"

Damn that man! Didn't he ever wear shoes?

"Going to the dump, then the market off island. Not that it's any of your business." Sophie instinctively went on the offensive to keep Will at arm's length. She straightened up and blocked the bag as best she could. She needed to think about what the needle meant, and she didn't want Mr. Nosey Tarkington to see it. Was it Autumn's? Could Samantha have been right? No one in the house was diabetic or anything else that would require shots either self-administered or by someone else. At least she didn't think so.

"I can take this stuff to the dump," Will said. "You should get going to the market." He was making it sound as if she didn't have a choice.

Sophie jutted her chin out and folded her arms in front of her chest.

"The market won't be open yet, but the dump is. Besides, I've just about loaded everything. I can manage fine, thank you."

"Sophie," Will's voice softened. "I don't know what's going on and I'm pretty sure you don't, either. Please don't do anything stupid."

His first words had almost convinced her to tell him what she'd found, but then he'd had to go and spoil everything.

"I will try to remember your possibly well-intentioned advice. Now, if you don't mind I have to be going." She swung the bag into the back of the car where she'd already stowed the recyclables and pulled down the hatch. Tight.

Resisting the temptation to floor it, she drove away. "Stupid!" she muttered. "Call *me* stupid!"

Before reaching Route 17, she pulled onto a dirt road she knew had no houses on it—it led to an old gravel pit—and stopped to think. She hadn't talked much with Autumn—or even seen her. She and Rory were staying in the bunkhouse. Daisy had been begging her mother to let her stay there, too, and last night had finally succeeded. Forbes and Felicity were up in the stifling attic rooms. Simon and Deirdre were in what Sophie knew her mother considered her room. People seemed to be coming and going, upstairs, downstairs, in the house and out of the house all the time.

She thought hard. No, Autumn hadn't been sleeveless even on the hottest days. She had the figure for any sort of swimwear, but she hadn't appeared in a bikini or other bathing suit. She *was* definitely thinner than Sophie remembered. When she'd hugged Autumn the day she had arrived, her ribs had been so well defined Sophie could almost have counted them.

But what to do now? Was there more than one syringe? Sophie got out of the car and went back to the trash. Babs kept a tool kit and a large first aid kit in the car. Sure enough, there were good scissors in the first aid packet. Sophie carefully cut around the syringe and, using paper towels from the roll Babs also kept in the car—really her mother's organizational talents were being wasted; she should have a cabinet post—Sophie removed the syringe and wrapped it well, taping it with the first aid adhesive. The syringe was empty. Impossible to speculate about what it might have contained. She set it aside and spread newspapers on the ground, hoping it was too early for anyone to be passing by on the way to the nature trail that started at the end of the road. She emptied the bag. It was not a pleasant task.

There were no other syringes or anything else of interest except a few crumpled American Spirit cigarette packages. Someone was a smoker. She stuffed it all back, tied the bag shut, and wiped her hands with some of the towels before picking up the syringe again. It looked innocuous wrapped up. Where should she put it?

She closed the rear of the car and got back in, considering her options. For now it could stay in the glove compartment. It would have interesting company. Or not.

The gun was gone.

Marge Foster had left a huge pan of chicken pot-pie with a biscuit crust, plus a salad that only needed dressing, and grapenut pudding with whipped cream for dessert. She was obviously a follower of the stick-to-your-ribs school of cooking. Sophie found it was just what she wanted to eat, although Deirdre, Felicity, and Autumn did not. They picked at some salad and Felicity took one bite of the pudding. Sophie was pretty sure her cousin wanted more from the way Felicity savored the morsel. She'd no doubt sneak down when everyone was in bed to gorge. She was Sophie's suspect for the person who had been leaving empty Ben & Jerry's cartons in the back of the freezer. Sylvia was eating something that looked like silage with raisins from a Tupperware container.

Despite the comfort food, the atmosphere in the room was tense. Conversations were started, veered off course, and petered out. No one wanted coffee. They'd be making an early start in the morning. Afterward—much to her surprise—almost everyone helped Sophie clean up, then people drifted upstairs and out to the bunkhouse. Quiet reigned.

Sylvia's screams pierced the night. Sophie pulled her jeans on and raced up the back stairs. She heard doors and the sound of rapid footsteps. Sylvia was in the hallway, still screaming without pause. Simon, a hand on each of her shoulders, was attempting to quiet her. Deirdre was at his side and had her hand poised to slap Sylvia's face. Will Tarkington emerged from Sylvia's bedroom with what appeared to be some sort of small animal covered in blood.

"It's not real," he said. "Sylvia, stop. It's a Beanie Baby puffin. A joke. Not a funny one."

Sylvia stopped, gulped, and looked closely at the object in Will's hand.

"It was on my pillow," she whispered. Rory and Autumn had joined the group, and Sophie hoped Daisy hadn't heard the commotion. At least she wasn't there.

"A bird in the house—doesn't that mean death?" Rory said. "Better get your crystals out, Ma."

"Shut up," Autumn said. "And anyway it's not a live bird."

Sylvia drew herself up and gathered the shocking-pink-and-turquoise paisley pashmina she had donned against the night air tightly around her. "If the person responsible—and you know who you are—thinks a dead bird, even a fake one, is going to scare me, make me cancel my birthday trip, you—and I *will* find out who—have another thing coming. Now, I'm going to bed for a good night's sleep before my birthday!"

Mouths that had been hanging open closed. Simon, grabbing a chance to show how very, very solicitous he was, put an arm around Paul, murmuring, "I hope this has not upset you too much, Uncle Paul. May I get you something? Cocoa?"

Paul shrugged the arm off. "Takes more than a stupid, tasteless stunt like this to upset me. But I do believe I would like a little something. Will, could you bring me a snifter? I'll be in my room. I'm in the middle of the book *Hour of Peril* by that Stashower fellow, about the first plot to kill Lincoln. How Pinkerton got his start. Good night, all."

Sophie took a deep breath. The screams and the fleeting sight of blood had sent a tidal wave of adrenaline coursing through her veins. Her heart was still beating fast. She turned to go back downstairs. She wouldn't mind a snifter of something herself. At the bottom of the stairs she almost collided with Rory, who was headed toward the back door.

"Good night," she said to him and ducked into her room. The scene that had just unfolded continued to play in her mind and she gave a slight shiver. She kept returning to one image. Will Tarkington emerging from Sylvia's room. After the kitchen was cleaned up, Sophie had seen Will leave by the front door to go down to the boathouse, where he was staying.

How was it that he was first on the scene?

"I think I hear a car," Amy said excitedly. "Yes, they're here!" She'd overheard the talk about Arnie and Claire's surprise. To her a surprise meant something like a puppy, which would be fun. Most likely it was some kind of special outing for the family. Maybe in his boat. She'd discussed all this with her mother and had refused to go to bed until they arrived, despite having to get up very early to go on another sort of boat trip with Daisy's family. Her mother had been invited, too.

Faith was tired. She had stayed close to the phone all day. Early this morning Marian had been scheduled for a diagnostic cardiac catheterization. The results had determined that the first treatment step would be an angioplasty to increase the flow of blood. After that, bypass surgery might be next. Tom had called whenever he had news and once just because he wanted to hear her voice. She wished again that she could be with him. His sibs were due back at the end of the week and she only hoped they would understand that he couldn't tell them without Marian's permission. Families.

At Amy's words, everyone got up and moved onto the porch. Moths clustered on the outside lights, dimming their already low wattage.

Sam Miller rushed to help with the luggage, which Arnie was unloading from the trunk. There was a mountain of it. Faith looked over at Pix, who seemed to be struggling to keep her expression neutral. Faith knew Pix loved her brother and sister-in-law, but in small doses. It looked as if this was going to be a much longer visit than usual.

Claire was paying the driver and still in the car. Everyone moved inside, grabbing a bag or two. Ursula was holding the door wide open. Dropping what he was carrying, Arnold Rowe gave his mother a big hug. If his smile were any broader, it would crack his lips, Faith thought.

"How was the trip?" Ursula said.

Before he could answer, Amy grabbed his arm. "The surprise! What's the surprise?" Arnie picked her up and swung her around. He hadn't done that with her, or any of his nieces and nephews, for years.

"The surprise is that I've packed it in," he said. "I've retired so I can be a stay-at-home dad! Meet my son, Dana Cameron!"

Chapter 7

A boy, who looked to be about nine or ten, walked
in beside Claire, so close he almost seemed an
appendage. His fine dark hair was as glossy as a raven's
wing and the bangs almost covered his eyes. His face
was tanned, and a sprinkling of freckles covered his
nose and cheekbones. He reminded Faith of a wood-
land creature trying for protective coloration.

Arnie's announcement had silenced the room, frozen
everyone in place. Typically, Ursula was the first to
react—and was doing so splendidly. She crouched down,
looking directly in the boy's face, and said, "Welcome to
Maine, to The Pines. I'm Ursula, Arnold's mother, and
your grandmother now. You can decide what you want
to call me. You share a name with one of my favorite
writers, a grown-up also named Dana Cameron."

She straightened up. "Now, I'm sure you three would like something to eat. And before that your parents can show you where you'll be sleeping." She addressed Claire. "Why doesn't Dana start out in the little room off yours and then as he gets to know us, he can choose one of the bigger rooms if he wants?"

Everyone started moving and talking.

"We have chicken salad and I can make some sandwiches," Pix said. "Plenty of cold drinks, and of course Gert left you your favorite, Arnie—a strawberry rhubarb pie." It was her favorite, too, and she quickly quashed the churlish thought that in all these years no one had made one especially for her. She started to head for the kitchen to cut her brother a big slice.

It was left to Amy Fairchild to point out the emperor's clothes, or lack thereof. To voice what everyone was thinking—maybe with the addition of "Arnie's love child?" "Claire's?" "Left in a large basket on their doorstep?"

"But how can he be your son?" Amy said clearly and emphatically. "He's pretty grown and you never brought a baby here. Where did he come from? Did you adopt him?"

Faith said hastily, "I'm sure it's a wonderful story, honey, and we'll hear about it later, but now we need to let the Rowes settle in."

Arnie picked Dana up. He seemed as light as a feather. Still grinning, the proud papa said, "You're absolutely right, Amy. You never did see us with a baby, but we have always wanted one, and yes, we have adopted Dana. We have known him since he was born."

Claire picked up the thread. "Dana is my cousin's little boy, and they lived near us in New Mexico. Sadly she died last winter, and at first Dana went to live with my aunt and uncle, but they are getting on in years. He was spending more and more time with us. When we asked him if he would like to be with us all the time and be *our* little boy he said . . ."

Dana's shyness fell away like a suffocating blanket. "Yes!" he shouted and then embarrassed, ducked his head down on his father's shoulder.

There was a general exodus with Faith hustling Amy into the kitchen before she could ask what had happened to Dana's father—a question Faith had as well—with Pix following to help prepare the food. Ursula sat down on the couch, and Sam joined her, taking her hand.

"Some surprise," he said.

Ursula smiled ruefully. "It just goes to show how little parents know about their own children. All these years we thought Arnie and Claire didn't want children. I'm sorry to say that I even said to Arnold, husband Arnold that is, that I thought they were too involved in their careers and taking those expensive exotic vacations to bother with raising a child."

"Since they never said anything, how could you have known? We certainly didn't, and many's the time I said the same thing to Pix—that it was even a good thing they didn't have kids, because how would they fit them into their schedules?"

"I just wish I could have shared this particular heartbreak. And I wonder why they didn't adopt earlier?"

"I have the feeling that with his newfound expansiveness—never saw him smile like this ever—Arnie will be sharing a lot with us."

Pix came in at the last words and sat down on her mother's other side. She was deeply ashamed at the thought that sprang to mind and tried desperately to push it away—Arnie and his new family would want to be sharing more than their joy. They would want to share The Pines.

Captain Robertson, with help from Sylvia, had regaled them with some puffin facts while getting ready to cast off. So far Sophie had learned that the Atlantic puffin, *Fratercula arctica,* is the only puffin native to the Atlantic Ocean. They are erroneously called "sea parrots" and more accurately "clowns of the sea" for their brightly colored, face-paint beaks. They are particularly attracted to Iceland, but also have colonies in the British Isles, Norway, Greenland, and Newfoundland. Most of North America's puffins are Newfies, but the 5 percent not there lure birders, ecotourists, and just plain people who think the small birds are cute to New Brunswick, Canada, and Maine. She'd been surprised to hear that puffins are still a prized—tasty?—food source in the Faroe Islands. But so far lobster rolls and fried clams dominate on this side of the Atlantic.

Sophie was trying to take this information in while keeping an eye on Daisy, whose mother was so busy being the birthday girl and puffin specialist that her small daughter had almost toppled off the dock twice before they all got on board. Everyone was wearing life jackets now. Simon and his crew had, of course, brought their own, the expensive ones with the CO_2 cartridges that always reminded Sophie of horse collars. The rest of the group was buckled into the puffy orange kind provided by the captain. A moist chilly fog enveloped the harbor, but they had been assured it would burn off by the time they got to the nesting grounds at Petit Manan Island.

It had been cold when Sophie had gotten up before dawn to make sure those who wanted breakfast would have it, plus pack up the food for the boat and the picnic.

Maybe she should forget about the law altogether and go into the catering business. Working for someone like Faith Fairchild suddenly had great appeal. No more nights sleeping in her office. No more power suits. And especially no more people like Ian Kendall. She didn't kid herself that the food business wasn't without stress, but at least there would be great stuff to eat. Even if one had to make it oneself.

The engine sprang to life and they were off on the hour-plus journey to the island. Sophie looked around at her fellow voyagers. They'd had to take three cars to accommodate all of them. She was glad Sylvia had agreed to include Faith and Amy. Daisy needed someone her age, and after last night's dead puffin skit, Sophie needed someone sane like Faith around. As she surveyed the group, she noticed Uncle Paul was looking cold. She'd brought a duffle with extra warm clothes, as well as two fleece throws. She took one of these over to him, and he didn't complain as she wrapped it around him.

"I have Thermoses of hot coffee, peppermint tea, and cocoa," she said loudly over the steady put-put of the engine.

"Maybe later," Paul said. "For now, I'm enjoying the sea air—and the company. This was a good idea of yours, Sylvia."

Sylvia was sitting next to him in pride of place and shot a self-satisfied look at the rest of them. "I'm Number One" was virtually etched on her forehead.

They had been late leaving Sanpere, but since they were the only ones on this tour because of their numbers, Captain Robertson had said he could wait. Rory had been missing. Really missing, not simply sleeping in or dawdling. Daisy had appeared early in the kitchen, followed a bit later by Autumn. When Sophie had asked whether Rory was awake, Autumn buried her face in the oversize coffee cup she favored while Daisy piped up, "He's not in the bunkhouse. Wasn't all night. His bed hasn't been slept in. Although it's kinda hard to tell. He doesn't make it much."

They had decided to leave without him—much to his mother's distress—when his car pulled up. He leaped out with a balloon bouquet and a package of party hats. Sophie was amused. So there, Deirdre.

"Give me the hats and I'll put them in with the picnic things, but let's leave the balloons here with the flowers for later," Sophie had said while Sylvia beamed at everyone. Could any mother ever have a better son?

None of the stores on the island offered the elaborate floral arrangement and party hats covered with glitter that Rory had brought. Where had he bought them? Sophie was guessing Bangor, maybe Ellsworth. He must have taken off right after his mother's gruesome discovery last night. What he did with his time was his business, yet she wondered how many nights he'd been tucked up in his bunk and how many somewhere else.

Too many things to think about. She flashed back to the scene yesterday by the car. Will had said that Sophie—and he—didn't know what was going on. Maybe she should have pushed him to explain further instead of getting angry. She turned to look at him. He was behind the captain, sitting on the bench diagonally across from her. Autumn was next to him. Was it Sophie's imagination or was Autumn, usually someone who kept a distance, sitting very close to the Southerner? Maybe she was cold.

"I have extra jackets and other things if anyone needs them," Sophie said, almost shouting.

Autumn shook her head, but Rory, who was only wearing a hoodie with the name of a Santa Cruz surf supply store on it, said, "Got a down parka in there? And maybe ski pants." He was wearing shorts. At least he'd grabbed Docksiders before they left, shedding his ubiquitous flip-flops.

Sophie gave him the other throw and a denim L.L.Bean jacket lined with flannel she'd found on a hook in the hallway. She recalled seeing it there last summer—and the summer before and the summer . . .

"Thank you for thinking of this—and everything else, Sophie." Paul almost had to shout as well. Sophie smiled back at him. Nice to be appreciated. She looked past Captain Robertson out the windshield at the water. The fog was starting to clear. She almost missed her Uncle Simon's frown at Paul's words and it thrust her back where she didn't want to be. In the bosom of her family. A family that was fast resembling a nest of vipers. Time for Babs to come to Sanpere. Sophie resolved to call her mother as soon as she could get a signal. Passing through Ellsworth and Blue Hill would give her a chance, and since she'd been one of the drivers, she'd insist on stopping. She needed to go to the big market, Tradewinds, again, anyway.

Faith Fairchild had seated both girls next to her, and the three were talking. Sophie couldn't hear what they were saying, but from the way Faith was pointing, it was probably about the birds that were starting to loom into view. Should she try to get some time alone with Faith and tell her about the syringe? And the Beanie puffin? She could hear Aunt Priscilla's voice warning her not to air dirty laundry in public, but Sophie thought this was getting way beyond soiled linens.

Autumn and Will had their heads bent together, almost touching, talking about who knows what. Sophie had noted from her own experience he wasn't big on keeping a distance, but they were starting to look like Velcro. Not that she cared.

She looked at her watch. They'd only been on the water seven minutes.

Over the years Faith Sibley Fairchild had come to love Sanpere, more than Aleford, but never as much as Manhattan. No place on earth came close to her visceral connection to the Big Apple. Still, despite being happy to spend the summer in Maine, there were aspects less appealing. Bundled up as if she were headed for a winter Alpine trek rather than a July boat ride under what she hoped would soon be sunny skies, she felt a strong twinge of "what is wrong with this picture?"

There was more than the temperature wrong. She looked at her fellow seafarers. Sophie's face showed a mix of sad and mad with a touch of having sucked on a lemon. Paul was exhibiting a determinedly bland countenance. Next to him, Rory was sound asleep. Faith sensed he hadn't had much last night. He'd been very hail-fellow-well-met when he'd arrived at The Birches just in time to come with them this morning. But beneath that, it was obvious he'd had a rugged night.

It was hard to see Autumn's and Will Tarkington's faces, as they were leaning toward each other, engaged in conversation. Not so the rest. First there was Simon Proctor and his crew. Faith had come across the family over the years, usually at the kind of party she and Tom avoided. The Proctors were properly dressed for the voyage—for a nor'easter, should one suddenly blow up—in matching foul-weather gear that Faith recognized as top of the line from Hamilton Marine. She had no doubt that when they stripped it off for the picnic there would be Lily Pulitzers or maybe Vineyard Vines beneath for the women and top-to-toe Brooks for the men.

Other than the two little girls, Sylvia was the only one wreathed in a smile, having the time of her life. She'd tucked one of the flowers from her birthday bouquet, a red carnation, under the scarf that kept her flowing locks in place.

The fog was starting to lift. Faith got her camera out as they passed pilings with several cormorants perched on each plinth, their elegant crooked necks silhouetted against the still overcast morning. Ebony statues. She took a few shots and some of the passengers as well so Sylvia would have a record of her birthday.

Faith had never seen an actual puffin and was starting to get excited. She wished Tom were with her, and Ben, too. He was scheduled to work the lunch shift into the evening. Mandy was picking him up. Faith would have to start getting used to the fact that Ben was independent—pulling away, as he should be, she reminded herself yet again—from his family.

The two girls were giggling about something. She put an arm around her daughter and pulled her in for a little hug. Bless Amy for saying what had been on most of their minds last night. Faith thought back to her conversations with both Ursula and Ed Ricks about inheritance. Would Dana's arrival in the Rowe family change what would happen to The Pines after Ursula's death? And what about The Birches? Faith didn't envy Paul's position. She looked at each possible heir before gazing back at the cormorants, "sea ravens" they were called. From her long-ago degree in English she recalled that the cormorant was the disguise Satan used in Milton's *Paradise Lost*.

More birds had joined the flock on the pilings and she could hear their cries as they landed. Not "Nevermore," but a noise like a pig grunting. A pig in some pain.

No, she didn't envy Paul McAllister at all.

The kitchen at the Lodge was always warm, but today it was bearable. The servers had to wear the green polo shirts and khaki pants, but the kitchen crew could wear what they liked, except sandals or other open shoes. This meant Ben had donned a much lighter shirt and thin river pants to come to work.

Mandy had been quiet on the way to pick up Tyler, and once he was in the car, the conversation was mostly between the two guys. Ben thought Mandy looked tired. And she must have felt chilly. She was wearing a turtleneck and over it a sweatshirt with the Lodge logo.

She'd smiled, as she always did when he got in, but it wasn't her usual smile. More like a worried one. As soon as he got to the Lodge he started working fast. He wanted to get the breakfast dishes washed plus the pots done so he could help her set the tables for lunch.

"What's the rush, bro?" Tyler asked.

"Thought we could give Mandy and the others a hand."

Tyler eyed him keenly and nodded. "Excellent idea."

Ben felt himself turn red. He did *not* have a crush on Mandy. He just liked her, liked her a lot. As a friend. She was eighteen! Three years older, well, two and a half.

But since they'd met he'd been getting a strong vibe that she needed looking after. Okay, it sounded kind of lame when he thought about it, but there was just something about the way she was acting . . .

Saturday night he had been sure she didn't want to go off with Rory Proctor. He could tell from the way she was standing, pulling back, putting some distance between them. But the asshole kept at it—the way he had when she'd been his server at the Lodge—telling her what a great party she'd be missing and walking closer and closer. Ben hadn't even realized he'd swung at the guy until Rory pushed him against the wall. He could still hear Rory's laughter. Don't think about it, he told himself. It was a dumb thing to do. No, it wasn't. Yes, it was. No . . .

He started the last load in the dishwasher.

"Ben, go see if you can find Derek. He's not in his office or anywhere in the Lodge, but his car is out back. Check the grounds. Even the beach." The annoyance in Zach Hale's voice was clear.

"Yes, Chef," Ben said.

"Tell him I need his signature on these orders like yesterday."

"Will do." Ben slipped off the clear vinyl dishwasher's apron he was wearing and hung it up to dry.

"Don't worry, we're almost done. I'll help Mandy," Tyler said softly, adding, "think the big boss is in T-R-O-U-B-L-E."

As Ben searched the rec hall, the gardens, and other areas nearest to the Lodge with no success, he realized he really hadn't seen much of the boss since he'd started working here. Chef Zach seemed to be running things—and not just in the kitchen. Maybe this was the deal? Only if it was, why was the chef so pissed off at Derek all the time? Ben had long ago stopped calling his employer Mr. Otis or anything but Derek in his mind. The guy seemed pretty young to have the responsibility of a business like The Laughing Gull Lodge, but then Ben remembered his mother had started her successful catering business when she was way younger than Derek.

He'd have to go down to the beach. Maybe Derek was checking the kayaks they had for the guests. There were a couple of large Old Town canoes, too. The Lodge also owned a yacht, but so far Derek hadn't gotten around to hiring someone to take people out on day sails. It was still in storage down at Billings Marine.

Today was what everybody always called "a Perfect Maine Day," Ben thought. Blue sky, no clouds, warm but not too warm. He'd didn't mind an occasional foggy or rainy day, though. Except some summers when they'd had almost nothing but. Guess that's why the ones like today were called perfect. No flaws. Mandy's face was like that. Smooth, like some kind of polished stone. Faint pink. Rose quartz. He laughed at himself. Good thing Tyler couldn't overhear these thoughts.

A steep gravel drive led to the beach, which was one of the prettiest and largest on the island—a long curve that ended in a tumble of granite boulders and ledges leading up to the woods on either end. There were only a handful of public beaches on the island. Used to be more, Freeman Hamilton had told Ben, until rich people started buying up all the waterfront natives couldn't afford to keep because of the hike in the taxes. These beaches had been spots where families had had reunions, Fourth of July and Labor Day picnics for generations. Now they were off-limits with chains across the road and big NO TRESPASSING signs. Up until a court case in the 1980s, you couldn't own a beach in Maine, Freeman had explained, but people had still limited themselves to the public ones where there was no question of access. "To avoid a ruckus," Freeman said.

Ben wished he'd grabbed his cap. The sun was blinding. He put his hand on his forehead and looked up and down the full length of the beach and out at the water. Maybe Derek had gone kayaking. The water was flat; no breeze disturbed the surface and no paddle. The beach was empty as well. It was just after the turn of the tide and it had been a high one. Easy to spot anyone walking on it. He turned to go back and report his lack of success.

Then he saw two legs sticking out motionless from behind one of the largest rocks. He closed his eyes briefly. The sensible thing would be to run to the Lodge for help. Call 911. He ran without giving it any more thought. Ran to where the body was.

It *was* Derek. And he was breathing. Snoring, in fact. Ben felt himself go limp. He called out to his employer, "Hey, Mr. Otis. The chef wants to speak to you."

Derek Otis sat up. He didn't seem to take in where he was for a moment. As he got closer, Ben wished he could cover his mouth and nose. At some point, Derek had tossed his cookies and much much more from his stomach.

"Bob," Derek said.

"It's Ben, sir, and the chef . . ."

"Ben, run up to the Lodge and get me a cold can of Coke, no, better make it two, and in the top drawer of my desk there's some Tylenol. Bring me the bottle." He stretched out again.

"What should I tell the chef, that you'll be coming soon?"

"Whatever. Now hop to it."

Ben hopped.

Happily Chef Zach wasn't in the kitchen. Tyler looked questioningly at him when he grabbed the Cokes from the bar fridge. Ben mouthed "Later" and went into the office. The Tylenol was in the top drawer just where Derek Otis had said it would be—along with a whole bunch of other pill bottles. Prescription pill bottles.

Captain Robertson—and Sylvia—was picking up Puffins 101 where they left off.

"Males and females are identical, and since it is breeding season they both display the same distinctive beaks," Robertson said.

"Not like other birds where the male gets to sport the better accessories." Sylvia almost sounded like she was chirping. "And they make their nesting burrows together. Equal partners."

The captain was nodding. "The female produces only one egg and they take turns keeping it warm tucked under a wing until it hatches into a puffling, as the chicks are called. Know for sure my wife, Kandi, would have liked me to take over during the nine months before our kids were born. Especially the first and last parts."

Everyone laughed. The mood was ebullient as the group trained binoculars and cameras on the little birds covering the cliffs on the island and even closer to the boat in the water. The Petit Manan lighthouse, the second tallest in Maine, jutted into the cloudless blue sky.

Amy and Daisy were taking turns with the binoculars Faith had brought; she was content to watch the scene from afar. The lighthouse looked like a version of the Washington Monument, and it struck an incongruous man-made note in the midst of the birds—not only the puffins, but also several types of gulls, razorbills, terns, eider ducks and black guillemots. She'd learned to reliably identify all of them from Pix, especially the guillemots, with the striking white patch on their glossy dark wings. Sylvia's remark about accessories was apt. When the guillemots were in flight, their ruby red legs were revealed, the perfect touch of color for the outfit. The air was filled with a cacophony of bird cries, the gulls dominating. Laughing Gull Lodge. She hoped Ben's day was going well—and that he was keeping his temper. Soon she'd have two teens. She was so not ready for it.

For now she was glad that Amy had made a friend who was not racing into adulthood—much less than Amy, in fact. When the Fairchilds moved back to their cottage, Daisy could come spend time at that house. Faith hadn't had a chance to get over and check on the progress since she and Tom had last been there. Over a week ago, she realized, sighing inwardly. This had not been what she had blithely hoped would be an easy, uneventful summer. She wondered if it would be too rude to take the girls back to the island and skip the picnic. She had had enough of the Proctor family's obvious friction, dissipated for the moment by the entertaining birds and the captain's commentary, liberally sprinkled with jokes and what she assumed was a Maine accent even thicker than his normal one? No, she couldn't cut out early. Sylvia, the birthday "girl," was Daisy's mother. Faith would have to stay.

Sophie's first thought was that the Beanie puffin had looked larger and more like a puffin than the real ones bobbing about in the water. Forbes handed her his binoculars and there they were! Chubby and more adorable than any reproductions. The bright sun made their beaks into works of art. Their little triangular eyes did indeed make them look like clowns. Sad clowns. She would never have pegged Autumn as a bird lover, but when she wasn't glued to a pair of binoculars she was asking the captain questions and squealing with delight at the sight of more fauna. She also seemed to be adept at spotting schools of dolphin and seals popping up in the water that Sophie was just a second too late to see. If they had been there at all, of course.

Her cousin was leaning against Will Tarkington and had grabbed his Bulldog gimme cap earlier, which she was wearing backward now. Her golden hair streamed down her back, and Sophie had to admit that Autumn would look gorgeous no matter what the cap or how she wore it. She was still bundled up in several layers of clothing. She had gotten so thin, she must feel the cold more than other people. Sophie had peeled off her sweatshirt and was enjoying the feel of the sun on her bare arms.

Warmth. She closed her eyes and indulged in the memory of lying in Ian's arms. That warmth, the feeling of not knowing where she left off and he began. The sense of security. Entwined together forever. Except, she opened her eyes, that's not what had happened.

How long were they going to stay out by the island? she wondered. She wished she wasn't driving the car that held the most people. Otherwise, she'd make some sort of excuse—the food shopping—and leave her clan to fend for themselves at the birthday picnic. There were crab rolls in one cooler, Sylvia's kale salad and other veggie offerings in another, plus a third one with cold drinks and dozens of the cupcakes Sophie and Marge Foster had made. Faith Fairchild had brought a container filled with deviled eggs and another of dilled new potato salad (see recipe, page 237) for those who didn't care for crab, to go along with it, or just to fill in the cracks. There was plenty of food. And plenty of people to pass it around. Could she switch cars with someone?

Captain Robertson was telling everyone to take final photos. They'd be heading back by way of an osprey nest on a tiny island and the cormorant nesting grounds on a larger one. It couldn't be too soon for Sophie, and she closed her eyes to try to doze. Really, someone should tell Will and Autumn to get a room. She was almost in his lap. Not that Sophie cared. It just struck her as extremely inappropriate, especially in front of children like Daisy and Amy. The two were giggling again, heads together, and Sophie was sure it was about the ridiculous behavior occurring in front of them.

"Who owns that big house? Some billionaire?" Sylvia's question woke Sophie. She *had* fallen asleep.

The captain slowed the boat to an idle. "Now, this is an interesting story. The whole island's owned by one family, bought originally in the 1920s. The house started small and got added onto. There are some other structures you can't see, too. After a while there were a bunch of family coming—a colony—kids having kids and so forth. A lot of group decisions being made. They figured out some thirty years ago that the only way they could hold on to what they had and let everyone who wanted to use it was to form a family association. Think there were some lawyers in the family, which saved dough. You buy in, pay your yearly dues, and if you want out, you have to sell your share to a family member. The property can't go on the open market. I provide the lobsters for their annual meeting, and it's some shindig."

The awkward silence that greeted his answer may have surprised him—or not. In any case, he gunned the engine and they took off. The pier and float where they would be tying up was in sight in minutes.

A family association. That would be the perfect solution. Could she get her mother to agree? Sophie wasn't sure. Babs was all about control. And so was Simon. Sylvia. Forbes, Felicity, Deirdre, too.

As she stepped onto the float and started toward the ramp going up to the pier and parking lot, Faith was glad she'd come along after all. She had a sudden urge to fill the cottage with puffin pot holders, puffin coasters and place mats, little carved puffins . . . These delightful, intrepid creatures would be returning to the sea and their journey to colder waters in August, but maybe she could come back with the whole family before then. Captain Robertson had told them about the decrease in the colony's population due to a marked decline in their major food supply—herring— displaced by the increase in the ocean's temperature. Better try to come back soon, she thought.

It all depended on how Marian was. Her mother-in-law was never far from her thoughts. There had been no change in the diagnosis. She was free of pain and apparently threatening to "get out of Dodge." Tom thought that bypass surgery would likely be scheduled soon, and Faith resolved to take Pix up on her offer to keep the kids for a few days so she could be at the hospital. She was so intent on the plan—what food she could leave Pix to feed everyone, clothes to pack, tactful admonitions of a widely varying nature for each of her offspring—that she didn't realize she had missed something major until she heard a splash and a yell. Closely followed by even louder yelling and another splash.

Sylvia Proctor was in the water flapping about and her shouts had to be reaching all the way to Bar Harbor. The captain had immediately gone in after her, pulled her toward the float and hoisted her up out of the frigid water into Will Tarkington's waiting grasp.

Wet and sputtering with fury, Sylvia cried, "Who was it? Who pushed me?"

Only the two girls had gone up the ramp and they were scampering back again, Faith noticed. Daisy made straight for her mother and flung her arms around her. Sylvia shoved her away and repeated her question. "Which of you pushed me off!"

Paul walked over and put his jacket around her shoulders. "The deck is very slippery, Sylvia. Nobody pushed you."

The captain reappeared with what looked like a horse blanket and some towels from the boat, handing them to Sylvia.

"Don't worry. No bait smell. My wife is very particular. Now let's get you to the house and dried off good. It's just up the road."

Sylvia burst into tears. "It's my *birthday*! Things like this aren't supposed to happen!"

Somehow it was Will who organized the rest of them to go set up the picnic while he went to wait for Sylvia and drive her there.

Autumn followed him to the car and got in the passenger's seat, her moves as graceful as a gazelle.

Sophie pulled into the parking lot at Tradewinds in Blue Hill. Some of her passengers headed across the street to the Dunkin' Donuts, still a novelty in these parts—blessedly franchise-free—while the rest went into the store for whatever they craved not currently supplied at The Birches. Rory had already told her he'd be loading a case of beer.

The picnic had gone smoothly, with everyone on best behavior, gamely wearing the party hats and lustily singing "Happy Birthday to You" to Sylvia while she blew out the single candle Sophie had placed on one of the cupcakes. "Fairy cakes," that was what the British called them. Why were all these memories, unbidden, flooding back today? Another semantic one. "Scatter cushions"—so much nicer, gentler than "throw pillows," although Sophie had a strong urge to throw a pillow or something else right now. What was going on? Her emotions seemed to be ricocheting not just below the surface, but out into the afternoon air.

They'd all brought small presents for Sylvia, and she had pounced on them with the glee of a kindergartener. Deirdre's gift—a beauty book for women over fifty—was nasty, but Sylvia had turned it around, remarking that Deirdre could borrow it for herself until Sylvia reached the milestone. Autumn and Rory had given her a lovely silver necklace from Sanpere's Pearson Gallery. Daisy had strung tiny origami peace cranes she'd made on a silk cord for another necklace. Sylvia had probably hoped Paul's gift was the deed to The Birches when he handed her an envelope. Her face fell noticeably when it proved to be a card with a gift certificate for the Harbor Café.

Autumn, as usual, hadn't eaten much of anything. She spent the time feeding Will strawberries and then the two of them went off to see if they could spot any puffins that might have drifted inland. They left with Uncle Paul before the others, having first offered to help pack up—a request Sophie firmly refused. Wasn't she the maid of all work around here?

Pulling her cell from her purse, she walked to the side of the market across from the All Paws Pet Wash. Someone was washing an Irish wolfhound, and every inch of space was taken up by the dog and owner. Sophie started to laugh at the scene and immediately felt better. She keyed in her mother's cell. At this point, Sophie didn't care what time it was wherever Babs might be or what her mother might be doing. She needed to talk to her and she needed her to come to Sanpere so Sophie could leave. Her mother wanted her to find a job, right? So let her come back and let Sophie get on with her own life.

There was also the little matter of the pistol Babs was packing. Sophie didn't intend to mention it was missing, but she did want to know why her mother had felt the need to pack heat in one of the safest towns in Connecticut—and was the gun the reason she had been so insistent Sophie take the big Lexus?

Babs had set up something like twenty rings so she could take her time answering. Sophie waited patiently. But there was no answer, just Babs's crisp voice. "I'm not available. Leave me a message with your name, time, and date. Speak clearly. If I can't understand you, I can't call you back."

Typical Babs. "It's your daughter. Sophie. That's S-O-P-H-I-E. I'm in the Tradewinds parking lot, and it's July tenth, three forty-six P.M. I'll call you again. You need to make plans to come to Sanpere ASAP. I mean it, Mother. Love you."

Sophie hung up. She *did* love her mother, and without those last two words, she knew Babs would be too annoyed to take the message seriously. She'd try again after the marketing. And then, if there was still no answer, she'd drive to the spot that had cell service on the other side of Sanpere.

She had to get off the island.

Faith was tired and ready for an early night. Ben had called when his shift was over and asked if he could stay at Tyler's. They were working the breakfast-into-lunch shift tomorrow and Mandy wasn't. One of the Hamiltons would drive them over. Faith offered to pick them up, but Ben said it was okay. She started to tell him not to stay up too late and also that she could drop off clean clothes, but clamped her mouth shut. Damn, this was hard.

Ursula had been eager to hear about the day and said if there were another outing she'd join them. She had seen the colony on Matinicus Rock a number of times and was a supporter of the Puffin Project, which was repopulating some of the other islands in the Gulf of Maine with the birds, but she had never been out to Petit Manan.

"I'm going to turn in," she said. "I'm rereading all of Dorothy Sayers's Lord Peter Wimseys this summer and *Gaudy Night* is calling me."

Amy looked puzzled as she gave Ursula, whom she regarded as another grandmother, a kiss.

"You explain, Faith. See you both in the morning. Let's invite Daisy over and take her on the Settlement Quarry walk for more birding. Two osprey nests there this summer."

She left the room, and as Faith was starting to explain who Dorothy Sayers was and what the word "gaudy" meant in this case—never too early for this sort of education—all the while thinking she might soon qualify as an ornithologist and couldn't they go to Nervous Nellie's Jams & Jellies in Bonneville to bird-watch and get samples of their delicious wares instead? Amy said something. Something Faith had to ask her daughter to repeat. She did.

"Daisy thinks someone is trying to kill her mother."

Chapter 8

Without hesitation, Faith replied firmly, "Sweet-heart, *nobody* is trying to kill, or hurt, Daisy's mother. What happened was an unfortunate accident. I began watching my step closely when I noticed the dock looked slippery, and I was wearing boat shoes. Daisy's mother had sandals on." Leather sandals that looked like something a Roman gladiator might have worn with thin ties crisscrossing above her ankles. The soles were flat and it was easy to see how her feet had gone out from under her sending her into the drink.

Amy shook her head. "Maybe today was an accident, but there was a dead bird on her pillow the other night. It was supposed to scare her to death, Daisy says, *and* her mom has been having a lot of stomachaches. Her mom says someone is putting something in her food. She's only eating stuff she makes herself now."

Faith moved closer and put her arm around her daughter's shoulders. They were sitting on the comfy, overstuffed couch in front of the big window overlooking the Reach in The Pines's living room. Faith was sure this particular piece of furniture had been host to many tête-à-têtes of all sorts, but perhaps none so odd as this discussion. Outside, the porch light illuminated the path, and beyond that the scene was completely dark.

It was very quiet. The windows were open, yet the usual nocturnal sounds of buzzing insects and peepers were eerily absent. The dead calm presaging a storm?

"There was no dead bird," Faith said. "It was a puffin Beanie Baby."

Gert had relayed the incident in all its gory and nongory details that morning, having taken an early walk through the birch grove to say hi to her friend Marge Foster—at least that's what she said. Faith thought it more likely part of the continuing investigation into what was happening at The Birches.

"It was a practical joke in very bad taste." And, Faith realized, an easy one to pull off. Almost every gift shop on the island sold the Beanie puffins, as well as lobsters, gulls, and crabs.

"As for the possibility of food poisoning . . . ," Faith tried to think how to delicately phrase what all the roughage Sylvia routinely consumed might be doing to her digestive system. "I think it's just some tummy troubles and maybe Daisy's mom needs to change her diet a little. A few days on clear liquids and soft foods."

"Like maybe mushed-up bananas and vanilla ice cream?"

"Exactly." Amy was the Fairchild most interested in food preparation and also shared her mother's willingness to try anything. It amused Faith to watch Amy make lunch for herself. A recent sandwich contained roasted peppers, rosemary ham, and honey chèvre with baby spinach leaves, plucked from the garden, on Tinder Hearth bread—baked across the bridge in Brooksville in a wood-fired oven and happily sold at the Granville Market. Amy was good at sharing, and they had ended up making another sandwich to consume together as well. Faith's number one rule for judging a person was whether he or she would share food. "If you wanted it, you should have ordered it" or "I might have a teeny cold" and other spurious excuses were dead giveaways to the persona lurking below the surface. Faith had helped her sister, Hope, avoid what would have been a disastrous marriage when she and Tom had joined the newly enamored couple for a meet-and-greet dinner at New York's Le Bernardin and the would-be groom proved to be a food miser. Didn't even give an excuse, just said no. As did Hope the next day.

"Would you like me to have a talk with Daisy? I have to go check on the cottage tomorrow. Maybe she could come with us?"

"Great! I want to show her where I really live and we'll walk down to the big beach to look for stuff. But, Mom, I think it would be better if I talked to her. She might think you were just trying to make her feel good, but she'll *believe* me."

Out of the mouths of babes, Faith thought. But Amy wasn't one anymore. Her little girl, who seemed to have grown several inches since they got to Sanpere, was becoming a savvy young woman.

Way too fast.

Her mother hadn't answered Sophie's phone the second time she tried in Blue Hill or later when she drove over to a spot directly facing the cell towers on Swans Island. She left another message with instructions to call The Birches, not the cell, and resigned herself to at least another week on Sanpere.

Marge Foster arrived as Sophie was setting out breakfast for everyone. So far only Daisy was up, and they were making pancakes in shapes from the batter Sophie had prepared. Sophie was not surprised to learn that Daisy had never made pancakes—had only eaten them a few times. Her mom, she told Sophie solemnly, believed that white flour, all sugar, and all milk except soy milk were poisonous to the body. Sophie was beginning to fantasize about scooping the girl up for a very long, very normal kid-friendly vacation. Someplace like Harry Potter World.

The phone rang and it was Amy, asking for Daisy. She wanted to know if her friend could spend the day with them. Sophie got on to talk with Faith while Daisy raced upstairs to ask her mother.

"Why don't you come along, too?" Faith said. "You can help me decide what color to paint the walls of the room we're adding. I'll bet you're good at this sort of thing and I have a stack of chips. One minute I'm sure it's going to be Ocean Beach, and the next Blanched Almond seems perfect, although it could be that I'm being swayed by the name."

"I'll drop by later. Marge Foster and I are stripping all the beds and changing the sheets this morning."

Daisy came back into the kitchen more slowly than she had left. Her little face was scrunched in a frown. "My mother isn't in her room or the bathroom. I knocked on the door, and it was Felicity. I looked on the porch and in the backyard, too. She's not anywhere. So I guess I can't go."

Sophie told Faith, who said there was plenty of time before they would leave and to have Sylvia call as soon as she turned up.

When Sophie relayed the information to Daisy, her face shone again and they got busy making pancakes to keep warm in the oven. Marge and Sophie exchanged glances over the child's head. They were definitely on the same page.

Then everyone seemed to arrive at once. Rory devoured a stack of pancakes, and seeing his mother wasn't around, made a quick exit. Autumn toyed with a single serving and followed his example. The pancakes had disappeared in no time. Sophie made more batter and for a while the Proctors seemed like one big happy family—maybe not the Waltons, but kinfolk enjoying a summer vacation breakfast. Uncle Paul had arrived last, save Sylvia, and plans were being finalized for a picnic sail to North Haven when Sylvia appeared. Daisy immediately began asking for permission to go off with the Fairchilds, but her mother wasn't listening. Instead her attention was focused on the group finishing breakfast around the kitchen table.

"A sail to North Haven? Sounds like great fun. Daisy will love it, won't you, pumpkin?"

"*Mom,* I was just telling you I want to go to Amy's house. Her real house, not The Pines where she's staying until it's ready."

Sylvia patted "pumpkin" on the head and said, "Another time. Today is family time."

Daisy didn't say a word, but tears gathered in her startling blue eyes and one made its way down her cheek.

"Now, I need a bite to eat. Up at dawn. The rocks were beckoning to me, calling me to the sea, and I've had a long walk on the beach."

Sylvia was clutching two Tupperware containers. One, Sophie knew, contained some sort of coffee substitute—could acorn be right?—and the other a cereal concoction, the ingredients anyone's guess. Sylvia had taken to keeping her foodstuffs in her room, despite Marge Foster's warning about mice. Sylvia had replied that mice were not what she was concerned about and she'd take her chances with the rodents.

"No can do, Sylvia," Simon said smoothly. "Too many even for the good ship *Fortuna.* We're four plus Paul and Will."

"But, Daddy," Felicity said, "I'm playing tennis with the McDonald twins and Bitsy Biddle Bower in Blue Hill! I told you last night!"

Sophie turned away to hide her grin, both for what sounded like the start of a "Peter Piper" tongue twister and Felicity's emphasis on the name McDonald. The McDonald twins could easily be Calvin Klein underwear models. Totally built and all the rest just right, too. Apparently Felicity might be engaged to be married, but she could still look. The McDonald family had multiple homes, and the twins wouldn't be in Blue Hill long, Sophie was sure. They came to sail with their "old man" and to help host the family Fourth celebrations that culminated with a catered soiree during the fireworks that would not be out of place in the Hamptons. In fact, Sophie had heard, it had been catered this year by a Hamptons outfit. Felicity had been there with the rest of her family and was oh so sorry Sophie had not been invited. Besides their social and familial obligations, the twins did have some sort of hedge fund–type jobs in Manhattan.

Simon patted his daughter's shoulder, not her head. "Sorry, sweet pea, you can go another time."

All these vegetative endearments were getting ridiculous, Sophie thought—and annoying.

"You young folks go have fun. It's a splendid day for it," Paul said. "Will and I have plenty to do here. Maybe take the car for a spin to Castine."

"Not the plan at all" was written all over Simon's face, though he recovered quickly, Sophie observed. The mercurial swiftness of her uncle's devious mind was kind of scary. He was on to Plan B before Paul had finished speaking.

"Now, I don't think that's necessary. Sylvia, why *don't* you join us and then Felicity can keep her tennis date. We can always squeeze little Daisy in."

Little Daisy spoke up. "I want to be with my friend. I don't want to go sailing."

Her mother looked shocked. Sophie had the feeling it was the first time the child had spoken back to her mother. Rory needed to start giving his baby sister lessons in the care and management of Mother.

Sophie said hastily, "I'm going over to the Fairchilds' cottage to help Faith pick out paint colors later, so I can bring Daisy back. Now, what would everyone like for lunch? Egg salad sandwiches? Or I have sliced ham. Ham and pickle?" She was reverting to Brit talk again. At least she hadn't said egg mayonnaise.

An hour later, the washer was churning away and everyone had departed for his or her various destinations. Rory had not shown up again, and for once, his mother hadn't appeared to notice, so intent was she on joining the voyagers. Autumn's whereabouts didn't seem to concern her as much.

Felicity had looked the very model of a modern major tennis player in crisp whites, the flirty skirt short enough to reveal white lace panties that were definitely not from Foot Locker. Sophie wondered whether all was proceeding smoothly toward the altar. She hadn't heard mention of Barclay, Felicity's fiancé, since the dramatic announcement of the new wedding locale. He was supposed to have arrived last weekend. Well, it was no never mind to her.

The Fairchilds had picked Daisy up, and Marge had left, too. The woman had already made the picnic lunch with some left behind for any landlubbers, done the housework, and prepared baked haddock with cracker crumb topping, scalloped new potatoes, and green beans that just needed steaming for dinner. There were still plenty of pies and other desserts in the fridge as well. Sophie thought she had certainly done more than her half-time day's work.

While she was waiting to switch the wash to the dryer, Sophie decided to check her e-mail. Babs might have contacted her. But there was nothing save two more "Sorry, we don't have any openings at this times," several offers for Canadian prescription drugs, and a perky E-Save the Date from a Wharton classmate about her destination wedding in Fiji.

She pushed back the chair, got up, and thought about what to do next. The house was in order. They'd changed all the beds and all she had to do was fold the wash when it was dry. There used to be long clotheslines in the backyard and Sophie remembered the smell of the fresh linen, something a dryer sheet could never duplicate. Also how Priscilla had made it fun to hang the wash up with the old-fashioned wooden clothespins that Sophie also used for making dolls. That would be a good thing to do with Daisy, although maybe she was a bit old for it. Her cousin would soon enter her teens, Sophie reminded herself.

Being at the computer brought back her futile search for information about Will Tarkington. She'd watched the *Fortuna* leave the mooring and start to tack up the Reach. Will wouldn't be back for hours. Time for another kind of search?

Feeling as if she should be wearing a trench coat and carrying a magnifying glass in her pocket, Sophie headed for the boathouse.

She stepped outside the kitchen door. Uncle Paul had been right. It was a great day to be on the water, or anywhere else. The heat had not returned and the threatened storm had passed well to the east of them. A walk was just what she needed after her busy morning.

There was no reason she shouldn't be going into her own boathouse, well they didn't exactly know whose boathouse yet, but it was still the whole family's, Sophie told herself, brushing away the clandestine feeling that had swept over her the moment she started to slide the double door open.

The interior was dim. There weren't many windows and those needed a good cleaning. It smelled a little musty, but it wasn't an unpleasant odor. More like a combination of dried salt, ropes—or rather lines— and canvas cloth. She moved inside, not sure what she was looking for amid the canoes that had been retired in favor of kayaks, oars, paddles, mooring balls, pot buoys, fishing gear, a stack of boat cushions, and almost a mountain of life vests in assorted sizes. She hadn't been in here for a long time. Hadn't been on Sanpere at all, and as she watched the sun make its way through the old panes, picking up dust motes as it lit up the long tool bench against one wall, she was filled with an emotion the strength of which shocked her. She didn't want anyone else to have The Birches. Paul *had* to pick Babs. If not, a part of her own being would be lost to Sophie forever.

Will was camped out against the rear of the large shed. All that was lacking was a tent over the tidy arrangement of a cot with sleeping bag, battery-powered lantern on an upended lobster trap that also held a stack of books, mosquito repellent, and an ancient Boy Scout canteen. She opened it and sniffed. Scotch. The Scouts were definitely loosening up. A large duffle bag presumably holding some of his wardrobe was tucked under the cot, along with a pair of running shoes, Teva sandals, and dark brown leather dress shoes. Now why would he need those here? Sophie straightened up and looked around for some sort of place where he could hang other clothes. Dress shoes said dress suit to her. Nearby, nails held some outerwear, including the jacket he had had on yesterday, the one he had draped over Autumn.

In a dark corner, she discovered a men's garment bag hanging from a hook and unzipped it. Bingo: a suit. She wasn't expecting Armani and it wasn't. She wasn't expecting Paul Stuart, either—and it was. She started to go through the pockets. Men left all sorts of things in them. Receipts, business cards. Could be he had a dress wallet, say one with a duplicate license with his name and address?

"May I help you?"

Sophie froze. Shit, shit, shit!

"Sudden need to cross-dress?" Will's voice was icy cold.

He was standing so near to her she could feel his breath on her face as he reached across and closed the bag. She removed her hands just in time to escape being caught in the zipper.

He repeated his question. "What are you doing here, Sophie?"

His tone brought all her pent-up ire to the surface and she fell back upon a tried-and-true lawyer's trick: answer a question with a question.

"What are *you* doing here? Why aren't you sailing?"

He wasn't falling for it—and he hadn't moved away. His nearness was distracting. Didn't the man have any manners at all? She couldn't get out of the corner without shoving him and it was going to have to come to that.

Pushing past him, she said, "I'm going kayaking and I wanted a particular paddle."

"Other than the fifty or so under the front porch." His voice sounded amused now. But she wasn't buying it.

"Yes, it's one I always use. Oh, there it is!" She grabbed a paddle that was leaning against the wall by the open door that she had stupidly not slid closed.

He followed her out, clicking shut the padlock that was seldom locked, and grabbed her arm. She started to pull away, but he tightened his grip and she stood still.

"First of all, I came back in the Zodiac for a spare gas can that Simon left here and wants on board. I'm going back out to meet them in Buck's Harbor at the marina. And next, that's a child's paddle and we both know you're no child, Sophie Maxwell."

He tilted her chin up and brought his face down close to hers. She closed her eyes. Waiting.

And then he was gone. Strolling toward the dock.

"Have a good afternoon," he called over his shoulder.

Driving with the two girls down the main road that led from the dirt roads to the Point, Faith saw Mandy Hitchcock in front of a small house Faith had passed often. Although sporadic attempts had been made to plant flowers in the tire planter Mainers had been using well before recycling was in and although the grass was kept mown, it was a losing battle. The lawn was home to spare parts for many other items besides cars and the cement walk was cracked beyond repair. The front door looked painted shut, and weeds had sprung up along the lintel. On other trips, Faith had seen a very large man in one of the lawn chairs. He seemed to be uninterested in the traffic that passed and that may have been because of the ever-present pile of empty cans next to him. Faith had never slowed to see what they were, but she doubted they were soft drinks, even Moxie. The man was there now. Mandy's father?

"Hey, it's Mandy, slow down, Mom! I want to say hi," Amy said.

Faith started to slow, but seeing the look on the man's face, she kept going. Mandy's back was to them.

Faith couldn't see her expression, but his was beyond livid.

"Another time, hon. We need to get going. After we check on our house and I talk to Seth, Pix said to come over."

Faith was relieved to see Seth and his crew at the cottage. She pulled in and parked next to his pickup. Down East was prone to vanity plates and bumper stickers. Seth had one on his rear bumper that was her favorite: SAVE A HOT DOG EAT A LOBSTER.

Leaving Amy to play hostess, Faith walked into the new space now connected to the rest of the house.

"Should be able to move back next week," Seth said.

Faith mentally added one more week, happy they would be in their own place before the end of July.

"It looks great," she said. "I wasn't sure those light fixtures from IKEA would work—they seemed so big when we unpacked them, but somehow suspended from the ceiling they look smaller."

"Ayuh. Have to get down to that place—if my truck will let me cross the state border, that is."

"Or the bridge," Faith teased. Although Seth made frequent trips to Ellsworth and even Bangor, he rarely ventured farther. "No time," he'd told her, adding, "if I'm going to go someplace, I want to *go* someplace. Costa Rica, maybe. The rain forest."

"Sophie Maxwell is coming to help me pick out the color for the walls and then there's nothing else I have to decide, right?"

Seth nodded. "Babs's daughter? Well, I recall the days I used to caddy at the country club here on the island when Babs would stroll by in her short shorts headed for the tennis courts. Wanted to be her summer fling somethin' fierce, but she went for one of the Snowden boys instead. Saw her last summer and she's still got it. Also a husband, more's the misery. Number five or six, but who's countin'?"

Faith laughed and thought she'd go out to wait for Sophie by the garage so she didn't miss the house. Seth stopped her with his next words.

"Ben doing okay at the Lodge?" There was something in his tone of voice that suggested more than idle chitchat.

"Yes, why do you ask? What have you heard?" Seth had been at the dance and she assumed he already knew about Ben's little altercation. It must be something else.

"Nothing much, except his boss seems to believe in delegating authority. I hear the chef is running the show since Derek's not around much. Partying pretty hardy."

"At the Lodge itself?"

"He's not that stupid. A few places on island, mostly off."

"Ben hasn't mentioned anything about Derek." Which, Faith thought, she should have picked up on earlier. Plenty about Chef Zach and the staff; nothing about his employer.

"Well, he wouldn't, would he? Not at his age. He and Tyler—Mandy, too—are good kids. I don't think you should worry."

Sophie walked into the room.

"Worry about what? Hi, you must be Seth Marshall. I've heard a lot about you from my mother. She had a big crush on you."

Seth looked over at Faith and pulled a comically mournful expression. "Just goes to show you . . . well, that ship has sailed. You look like your ma, Sophie, but if I may say so even prettier."

"You may and thank you very much. Now, what are we worrying about?"

Faith answered, frowning, "Apparently Ben has an absentee boss, absent purely for personal pleasure. And sorry, Seth, I *am* worried. I wish Ben would quit."

"My cousin Rory has been hanging out with Derek," Sophie said. "I can ask him what's going on. A bonfire and some beers or heavier stuff. Rory doesn't do drugs. He has this whole surfer Zen thing going. More important, I've never seen him high, except at the thought of a perfect wave. But I also doubt he'd stay away from people who were, if it was a good enough party."

"I'll ask around, too," Seth offered.

"I suppose that's all we can do for now," Faith said. "I know the island isn't paradise and there's always been drugs of all kinds, but there was a big article in the Bangor paper recently about heroin. How it's almost getting cheaper than buying cigarettes and definitely much less than all those pain pills."

Sophie appeared startled by Faith's words but didn't say anything. Faith resolved to bring the subject up when they were alone. With Samantha, too, who was staying another week. Samantha had grown up summering on the island and had friends from both now increasingly distinct groups—natives and people from away.

"I shouldn't have said anything," Seth said. "Was trying to give you a little heads-up, but in my usual dumb-ass way, blew it."

Faith assured him, "No, I would have been more upset if I found out you knew something about Ben's workplace and *didn't* tell me. Now, Sophie and I have to make a serious paint choice."

After considering beige hues with a tinge of rose and almost going for Fennel Seed, the two women came to a decision: Moccasin, one shade lighter than Blanched Almond. When Seth intoned "Is that your final answer?" they chorused back "Yes!" and went to get the two girls, who were in the woods behind the house. For a few moments, Faith had forgotten all about the fact that her son could be working for not just a party animal, but also a possible druggie.

Ben had never kept anything from Tyler, who was not only a summer friend, but also his best friend, period. Tyler had come to Aleford many times and Ben had taken the bus up during ski season to go to Sugarloaf with Tyler's family. So, as soon as he had a chance, he told him about the pills in Derek's desk drawer, as well as finding their boss dead drunk on the beach, a scene that grew more revolting in the telling.

Tyler wasn't surprised. "Dude definitely has some problems. Just hope he doesn't run this place into the ground before the summer ends. It's a good job. Pays way better than other places on the island."

"Think we should tell Mandy?"

"She probably knows, but yeah, I think we should during break. She just came in. Said she could drive us home."

Ben thought about the party Rory had been urging Mandy to go to and got mad all over again. He went into the dining room, where she was setting tables, to ask her if she wanted to walk with them on the beach later. The three of them always headed there during their breaks instead of joining the other staff grabbing smokes by the rec hall.

"Hey," he called out. "Tyler said you could take us home. Thanks."

He was surprised at the panicked look she gave him. Maybe it wasn't convenient for her to give them a ride?

It was hot inside the room. The AC had been turned off after breakfast and wasn't back on yet. Mandy had taken off the Lodge turtleneck and sweatshirt she had been wearing the other day, too, and was in a tank top. As he approached she frantically pulled the turtleneck over her head and Ben stopped, momentarily frozen in his tracks.

Mandy's neck was severely bruised. And from the marks, it wasn't hard to tell what had done it—two hands.

"Mandy! Who did this to you?"

She pulled the neck up high to her chin and the sleeves down, but not before Ben noticed there were bruises on her arms as well. "It's nothing, Ben. I'm handling it. *Please* don't tell anyone. I mean it. Not even Tyler. Especially Tyler."

"But, Mandy—" Ben made no attempt to disguise the anguish in his voice. "I can't just sit by and let someone hurt you!"

She gave him a slight smile. "Oh, he's not going to hurt me again. Don't you worry about that. He's not going to hurt anyone again."

Ben had to be satisfied with that and the hug she gave him, murmuring, "It will be all right. I swear."

Then he went back into the kitchen sick with secrets.

When Faith arrived at the Millers' cottage, the two girls headed straight for the beach, which had more sand than most on Sanpere.

As soon as they left, Faith and Pix both started talking at once.

"You go first," Pix said. "Mother told me that Marian is doing well and the surgery is scheduled for tomorrow. That's wonderful news. Now, how's Seth coming along? When does he think you can move back?"

"He said a week, so . . ."

"That means two." The friends were used to finishing each other's sentences and Faith laughed.

"Everything looks great and Sophie helped me pick out the wall color. Sort of like a whole milk latte. It's called Moccasin and it does remind me a little of a light beige brushed leather one. I love picking out paint. Wish we could do something about the parsonage walls."

As a new bride, she was able to get the vestry to approve new paint for the yellowed walls, but only an extremely neutral palette.

She wanted to tell Pix about what Seth had said and see whether her friend still thought Ben should work at the Lodge, but first she had to find out how the new addition to the family was going.

"How is Dana settling in? It must have been terrible for him to lose his mother like that. Was she sick long?"

"I haven't really had much time to talk to Arnie—or Claire. They've been on the go since they came."

"How long are they staying?"

A shadow crossed her friend's face and she quickly banished it with a smile. "Until Labor Day weekend. Arnie wants to take Dana to the Blue Hill Fair. They've been reading *Charlotte's Web* together. Isn't that wonderful?"

"Pix! It's me! Or I, whatever. Talk! This has got to be hard for you. Arnie and Claire never spend that much time here. I know he said he'd retired, but what about her work?" Claire was a financial adviser with a firm that had offices in Santa Fe, Tucson, and Albuquerque.

"She's arranged to telecommute once her vacation is over."

"From The Pines! Ursula still has a dial phone, or a push- button one, anyway. Don't tell me the house is going to be wired for the Internet! I just can't see it."

"It's not, but both libraries on the island—in Granville and Sanpere Village—have Wi-Fi. You can even get it sitting outside. I think it's great that they want him to experience summer here."

Pix was sounding very firm. Very noble, Faith thought. Yet, thinking back to her conversation with Ursula about inheritance, Faith also realized that the game had most likely changed. Arnie had a son, and fathers want to hand down what they treasure, even if they had relinquished said treasure for some years.

Ben hadn't called and left word with the Millers, which meant he must be getting a ride with Mandy, but Faith still wanted to get to The Pines and be there when he arrived. Not that she was going to quiz him about anything, say, his boss. She just needed to see him. She'd get the girls and head back.

Pix said good-bye to her friend and went into the kitchen. She was the type of cook that relied heavily on things that said "Helper" on the box. In Maine she could always grill some haddock or halibut, boil lobster, and there were clams and mussels almost on their doorstep. They always put in a garden over Memorial Day weekend and it was starting to yield now. Life was simpler on the island.

But not anymore.

As they drove by the Hitchcocks' house, Faith noticed that Dwayne was still slumped in his lawn chair. She was continuing past when she noticed he was under a ratty-looking afghan that was pulled up to his extremely thick neck. It seemed odd on a warm summer day. His bulk wouldn't call for a blanket except in the dead of winter. She slowed the car and tried to see more of his face. His head was bent at an angle toward his left shoulder and his long, greasy hair had fallen over his eyes. She drove a few feet farther, pulled the car over, and stopped.

"I want to make sure Mandy's dad is okay," Faith said to the girls. "He's been sitting in the sun a long time. He probably fell asleep and didn't realize how long it's been."

"He might have sunstroke like that man on the Fourth of July," Amy said.

"You two stay here and I'll check."

Faith walked back and crossed the lawn. Dwayne Hitchcock wasn't moving. Flies were buzzing about his head and he wasn't responding to the annoyance. She put a hand on his shoulder and shook him gently.

"Mr. Hitchcock? Dwayne?"

Even as she spoke she knew he wasn't going to be responding to anything ever again. Mandy's father was dead.

The afghan slid down, exposing a slightly torn wife beater undershirt that was several sizes too small. Also exposed was a rubber tourniquet wrapped tight around his arm. Faith bent down and looked under the chair near his lifeless hand. It was almost touching an empty syringe.

Feeling sick, she looked back at the car. She had to get the girls to The Pines, which was the closer of the two houses, and call 911. But first she'd knock and see if by any chance someone was home.

Giving a little wave to the girls, who were peering out the rear window, indicating they should stay put, Faith went around the back to the kitchen door. It was wide open.

Gingerly she stepped into the room. Someone, Mandy or her mother, had attempted to keep some order, but there were dirty dishes in the sink and the table was littered with beer cans, empty Humpty Dumpty potato chip bags, several whoopie pie containers, and beef jerky wrappers. Dwayne's last lunch?

She knew she shouldn't disturb anything, but this wasn't that sort of a crime scene, and she went to the wall phone, punching in the numbers.

The volunteer dispatcher answered immediately, and Faith described what she had found.

"I have two children with me and will stay in my car until you get here."

"We'd appreciate that."

"And I think you'd better call Earl."

"Already on it."

It seemed only a few moments before the ambulance, which was garaged on the other side of the causeway in Sanpere Village, arrived, siren blaring.

The girls had been subdued, but at the sight of the emergency vehicle, Daisy said, "Wow, I've never heard an ambulance siren up close! They always turned them off when they came for my sister, so she wouldn't freak."

Filing this information away for thought, Faith got out, told the EMTs where she would be, and drove down the road. It was now late afternoon.

At The Birches, they all got out. Daisy went streaking in the back door with Amy. Faith followed more slowly, still dazed by the shocking discovery. She found the entire Proctor clan gathered for cocktails on the front porch. Daisy and Amy were already telling everyone that Mandy's dad had sunstroke and the ambulance was there to take him away.

"And Amy's mom found him," Daisy said. "She thought he didn't look well when we drove by and went to help him!"

"He's carrying a lot of extra weight," Paul said. "Maybe he can get it under control now. Heard he's diabetic, too."

Faith opened her mouth to let them know that Hitchcock was beyond any sort of diet, but decided to keep the news to herself. It would be all over the island soon enough, and she didn't want the girls to be upset. Let them think he died on the way to the hospital.

Instead she said, "How was your sail?" Sophie had mentioned the expedition.

Simon answered, "Best waters on the East Coast, although the wind did give out and we came back much earlier than I thought we would."

Forbes gave him a playful punch on the arm, that ultimate expression of male affection among certain groups. "Now, Dad, you never think we've stayed out long enough."

"Stay and have a drink, Faith," Sophie said. "The sun—or maybe it should be the moon—in Uncle Simon's case, is over the yardarm. Rory made mojitos."

"I'll take a rain check. Ben should be home soon, and even though he works in a kitchen, he's always ravenous. We'll be eating early."

As she drove over to The Pines, Faith thought about Mandy—and her mother. Would this death leave them with heavy or light hearts? One of the ambulance corps volunteers was staying to tell Mandy. They'd already called her mother at work in Ellsworth, and she was on her way. But, she realized, Mandy would have stopped at the sight of the EMT in front of her house, and Ben had likely walked the rest of the way.

But Ben wasn't home yet, and Ursula hadn't heard from him.

"Maybe he had to work late?" she said.

Tom had called, though, and Faith quickly called him back. Marian was definitely being scheduled for surgery the following morning. All his siblings were back and the entire family was camped out at the Norwell house.

"Sis was a little put out with me at first, but Dad set her straight," Tom said.

Knowing Betsey, "a little put out" had to be a major understatement, and Faith was glad Dick Fairchild was running interference. She was also glad they were all together. She just wished she could be there, too.

While she was on the phone, Ben slipped in, mouthed, "Taking a shower," and disappeared upstairs.

Ursula declared it was a good night for a simple kitchen dinner. Faith quickly told her about Dwayne Hitchcock, and Ursula did not express surprise.

"It's wrong to be glad that any mortal soul is gone, but there won't be much weeping over him, definitely not from me—and he won't be skulking around our places."

Before they sat down for dinner, Faith asked Ben how Mandy was taking it.

"Taking what?"

"Wasn't the person from the ambulance corps waiting for her at the house? Mandy's father was taken to the hospital. It looked pretty serious—he may not have made it."

Ben sat down at the table, as if his legs had gone out from under him. His face was pale.

"So, you didn't hear before you walked back?"

"Mandy couldn't give us a ride today. One of the other servers lives in Sedgwick and dropped me off at the church."

"Ben! That's miles! You should have called me from the Lodge."

The color returned to his face. "It was no big deal, Mom."

Amy came into the kitchen. "Yum! Something smells great!"

"It's my corn chowder [see recipe, page 238], and even though the corn isn't ready to pick yet here in Maine, it's still good, summer corn from New Jersey," Ursula said. "And plenty of bacon crumbled in, Ben—I know how much you like it."

Ben and his male friends had some relationship to bacon that escaped Faith. The geekier the guy, the more bacon accoutrements he had. Ben told her his friend Nick had put membership in the Bacon of the Month Club on his holiday wish list.

Ursula's chowder was just the sort of meal Faith needed and she was glad for it. They finished early. Amy and Ursula began work on a new jigsaw while Faith tried to read. Her mind kept wandering to the scene on the Hitchcock front lawn. She hadn't told Tom about it. The list of things she hadn't shared with him so as not to upset him at this difficult time was getting longer and longer.

When the knock on the door came and she could see Earl Dickinson through the glass, she wasn't surprised. As the person who had discovered Dwayne, Faith figured the police would want to take a statement of some sort from her.

"Come in. Would you like some coffee—hot or iced?" she said.

"No, I'm good. Ben around?"

"Ben?" What could Sergeant Dickinson of the Hancock County Sheriff's Department possibly want to talk to her son about?

"We're looking for Mandy Hitchcock."

"She didn't give me a ride today." Ben must have been listening just out of sight on the stairs. He came the rest of the way down into the room.

"When is the last time you saw her, son?"

"She was setting the table for lunch at the Lodge."

"So about ten-thirty, eleven?"

"I guess. I wasn't wearing a watch."

"What's this all about, Earl? What's going on? Doesn't Mandy know about her father yet?"

Earl looked at Faith and motioned her out to the porch, shutting the door firmly behind him.

"It was an overdose, just as you said when you called it in. But it looks like it may not have been accidental."

"Suicide?"

"No, Faith. Homicide. And Mandy's disappeared."

Chapter 9

The big day had finally arrived. Or the big day before *the* big day. Felicity's extremely suitable fiancé, Barclay Smythe-Jones, would be arriving at the Bar Harbor airport at noon.

"Private plane," Felicity announced at breakfast. She wasn't eating, thinking ahead to the dress perhaps and an avoidance of bridal boot camp. She had, however, consumed three large cups of coffee.

"Of course," Sophie murmured, wondering why her cousin seemed to need so much caffeine on what should have been a serenely ebullient occasion. Way too soon for wedding jitters. Or maybe not.

"He may be giving a lift to a friend. We'll all grab a bite on the terrace at the Bar Harbor Inn. Forbes made reservations as soon as we knew when Barks was coming."

"Barks" appeared to be, literally, Felicity's pet name for her intended. Tempted as she was to let out a few "woofs," Sophie merely nodded. "You'll be here for dinner, yes?"

"Of course!" Felicity gave her cousin a scathing look that vanished at the sight of Paul coming through the kitchen door. "Uncle Paul! Good morning! Barclay can't wait to see The Birches and meet you."

Paul gave her a kiss on the cheek, grabbed the newspaper, the brimming mug Sophie handed him, and sat down.

"Okay, so you three will be here. What about the friend?" Sophie persisted. "Is he or she staying in Bar Harbor?" She cracked three eggs into a bowl. Paul would prefer an omelet to pancakes.

The look threatened Felicity's face again, and she smothered it with a smile so broad, her pink gums were revealed—also her clenched teeth. "It's a 'he,' obviously, and yes, if it's not too much trouble, we would like him to join us for dinner. He's staying at the Sanpere Village Inn."

That seemed odd, Sophie thought. Why would a young single guy want to spend his vacation on Sanpere and not in the Hamptons? Maybe he was the best man and wanted to scope out the proper rocky ledge for the toast? She mentally adjusted the dinner menu and decided that they could welcome the bridegroom and friend with lobster, steamers, and coleslaw—a modified version of the Independence Day clambake. She wasn't even going to try to match the pricey, complicated offerings at the Inn in Bar Harbor—tasty as they were. However, it was a celebration of sorts, so she might make a trifle with the strawberries and blueberries in season now. The Granville market sold spongy ladyfingers that would taste fine with real whipped cream, the fresh fruit, and she'd steal a few tablespoons of Uncle Paul's good brandy.

Felicity pronounced a clambake a wonderful idea, with no mention of actually helping, and disappeared, presumably to titivate, although she was already in full makeup with nails done and hair artfully arranged. Her outfit today was not her mother's Oldsmobile but said "hot summer girl"—tight white crop pants and a sheer turquoise linen shirt that stopped at her waist, revealing not only a perfectly tanned midriff, but also a perfectly flat one. Not so the neighbors just above, coyly peeking out from a lacy push-up bra. Sophie hoped Forbes had also booked a room at the Inn for a couple of hours. His sister was definitely planning on making up for her time apart from "Barks."

Sophie began to wash up. Marge Foster had arrived and was preparing baking powder biscuits for dinner. They were the size of a baseball mitt but light as a feather. Try as she might Sophie hadn't been able to duplicate them.

Earlier Will Tarkington had consumed a stack of pancakes with honey instead of maple syrup and left. Glancing out the window over the sink, Sophie saw he was engaged deep in conversation with Autumn in the garden. From the intense expression on his face, whatever they were discussing was serious. Yet, when Autumn turned around, Sophie was surprised to see that her face shone with happiness. She could not recall seeing this emotion on her cousin's face for a long time, certainly not this summer. What could Will have said to provoke this response? Autumn started to walk away toward the bunkhouse, then took a few steps back and pulled Will into her arms for a hug before continuing on.

Sophie scrubbed the cast iron griddle harder. Some of the batter had caked on. She broke a nail. Not that it mattered. Nothing mattered. Except getting the whole Birches mess settled, so she could be history. Maybe she could hitch a ride with Barks and his private plane when he and his friend left. Lord only knew what his name was. It was guaranteed to be one that lent itself to a nickname like Chaz or Biff. Not that she cared what it was. At the moment she didn't care about anything.

Will was walking toward the kitchen door. Hadn't he had enough to eat? She gave the griddle one last rub. Another nail went. Not that she cared.

Amy had been invited to The Birches to take a walk in the Tennis Preserve on the other side of the island with Daisy, her mother, and Paul McAllister. Sylvia had called just after breakfast and said they'd probably go on for lunch somewhere.

When Amy left, Ursula had turned to Faith and said tartly, "Paul's the most popular man on the island now, I'd say. What Sylvia and the rest of them don't take into account is that he's also one of the smartest. He was a close friend of Doctor Tennis, who as you may remember, left a good part of his land for the preserve. Sylvia no doubt thinks that by showing how much she cares about this island treasure and what his friend did, Paul will up and give her The Birches straight out."

"I get the feeling," Faith said, "that taking the two girls is calculated as well. Lets him know that Daisy has a close friend on the island, as well as reminding him of the next generation who will look after The Birches. Sylvia's offspring, not the others."

Gert Prescott was filling a large jar to make sun tea and turned the tap off with an audible *humph*.

"What?" said Ursula.

"You know what. This is getting out of control, if it ever was *in*. The poor man must be exhausted. Being pulled this way and that. Time he went up to see his friends on MDI for a breather. Hightail it out is what I told Marge this morning. The fiancé of that niece who wants to have her wedding at The Birches arrives today, Marge said. Mr. McAllister needs to skedaddle before he has to add a wing on the house."

"I did hear something about Felicity—she's Simon's daughter, so a great-niece—wanting to get married at The Birches just as Priscilla and Paul did," Ursula said.

"See what I mean?" Gert punctuated her words with a snort. "Out of control. And Dwayne Hitchcock dead in his lawn chair, which anyone could have told you was bound to happen, as the man rarely stirred from it. Mandy missing. This whole summer is just plain spleeny."

Both Faith and Ursula nodded in agreement. "Spleeny" was one of those useful Maine words that Faith had come to appreciate years ago. It needed no translation. You knew exactly what the speaker meant.

Faith was trying hard not to worry about her mother-in-law, but had soon realized that worrying was the proper and only thing to do. She'd spoken to Tom both last night and very early this morning. He had called an hour ago to say that they had taken Marian in and he would let Faith know the minute there was news. "She still thinks it's much ado about nothing—her words," he'd said. "And she told the doctor she has plans for next Wednesday—the South Shore Garden Tour—so he'd better have her out by then."

Without saying anything, Ursula had brought her knitting onto the porch where Faith was sitting not reading a book, well within earshot of the phone. Faith told her what Marian had said.

"She just might make it to the tour. The treatment now is very different from even a few years ago. The doctor will want her up and moving around as soon as she's able. Not that she should run a marathon, but a stroll around a garden or two could be what he will order. And Marian is in excellent health except for this, Faith dear. I know you are worried. I am, too. But once they get in there and repair her heart she'll be good as new."

Faith *did* feel reassured. It was true that Marian was in great shape—although, that was the main reason this had been such a shock.

"And," Ursula added, "if you live long enough, you are going to get something. One half of the people I know have had hips, knees, all sorts of parts replaced or repaired and the other half has made it through all kinds of cancer."

Of course, Faith thought to herself, there was that third half who were gone, but she quickly banished the gloomy thought and concentrated on the scene in front of her, straight from a Down East calendar or tourist brochure for the state. The old granite lighthouse stood out more prominently than usual since the tide was low. As the full moon approached, the tides had been extreme. Just now it was as if someone had pulled a plug offshore. The slight clicking sound Ursula's needles were making as she deftly knit yet another pair of mittens for the Sewing Circle Fair in August was calming. Without looking down, Ursula was producing a complicated snowflake pattern. For a moment Faith toyed with the idea of asking Ursula to teach her how to knit, crochet, do crewel, needlepoint—any of the myriad handwork the older woman was never without. Faith could make sweaters for her whole family. And someday in the very far distant future when she was a grandmother herself, she could knit tiny booties. The notion made her laugh out loud.

Ursula raised her eyebrows. "Share the joke?"

"I was just thinking I should learn to knit. Booties for grandchildren. Sweaters for the family now."

Ursula was kind enough not to laugh herself. "A nice thought, Faith dear, but I think the Almighty had other plans for your hands. Stirring and so forth."

Faith knew her friend was thinking of the time she had tried to mend the ripped hem of one of Amy's dresses and sewed it to the skirt Faith herself was wearing.

"You're right. And that's exactly what I'm going to do now to fill the time. I think we need some chocolate. I know I do. How about those cookies that Nan Hamilton makes? The dark chocolate drop cookies rolled in sugar? [See recipe, page 240.] They're Tyler and Ben's favorite."

As she said her son's name, Faith let this particular worry that had been pushed to the back of her mind start to seep forward. This morning Ben had called Brian, the person who had dropped him off the night before, and arranged to meet him at the church. He had refused his mother's offer of a ride that far and had ridden his bike instead. Brian had a pickup and the bike would easily fit in back. Ben had told Faith he would try to arrange the same shifts as Brian until Mandy came back. He'd sounded very definite that she *would* be back.

"Gert didn't say any more about Mandy Hitchcock after I went upstairs, did she?" Faith said.

"Only that Leilah wanted to file a missing person report, but the police told her it was too soon. Mandy's over eighteen, so they can't issue an Amber Alert, either. People are saying it looks like Leilah's suddenly become maternal."

Faith was particularly stunned by the first part of the comment. "Her mother thinks something happened to Mandy? That she may have been abducted?"

"The last place anyone saw her was the Lodge just before noon. She didn't wait the lunch tables and didn't tell anyone she was leaving. That's not like her, according to Gert. She's known Mandy since they came to Sanpere and says the wonder is that the girl didn't leave home years ago, what with her mother gone so much and a no-good, or worse, father. But she also agreed that Mandy wouldn't just take off."

"I wish Ben weren't involved."

"Concentrate on Marian. And make those cookies. We don't know that Ben is involved in this or anything else. It's an island tragedy, and I doubt he has any more to do with it than, well, I do."

The familiar rhythms of measuring, stirring, and baking soothed Faith. The cookies went into the oven, and the house was soon filled with their delectable aroma. But Tom's call to say that Marian had come through her ordeal with flying colors and that they would be able to see her as soon as the anesthesia wore off was the most soothing—delectable, too—of all. She took the last batch of cookies from the oven and brought a plate of them with glasses of lemonade out to the porch to give Ursula the good news.

"Why don't you go off and do something?" Ursula suggested. "You've been tied to the phone for days. They're having a sale at Mainescape, and I could use some more astilbe for the shade garden. Stop in at The Meadow and get something to send to Marian. They have all those nice shea butter soaps and hand lotions. Karen will wrap it up a treat."

She was no knitter, but Faith *had* become something of a gardener and was particularly fond of dependable perennials, and the idea of wandering around the Blue Hill garden center to pick some up as well as heading to the enticing gift shop was very appealing.

"I won't be gone long and my cell will work there," she said. "I can call Tom. And I'll stop at Tradewinds on the way back. We need a few things. Ben finished all the leftover ham and the scalloped potatoes, too. I swear he must have two stomachs these days."

"Go by the stand in Sargentville and get strawberries if they've put any out. You know where it is, next to the Eggemoggin Market and Hair Extraordinaire. We can have them tonight my favorite way—cut up with only a sprinkle of sugar to release the juice."

Armed with a list, Faith set out. She was happier than she had been since she'd answered the phone a scant nine days ago. It seemed much longer . . .

"**Did you** want something?" Sophie's query as Will walked into the kitchen sounded curt even to her and she felt herself flush. "I mean, did you get enough to eat with all those pancakes?" And that sounded wrong, too. As if she was suggesting he'd stuffed his face. She amended her words once again. "I can make some more batter or there are muffins."

Will grabbed a dish towel and started drying what Sophie had put in the rack. "I could probably eat another stack. They were delicious. Buttermilk? But I don't want to spoil my appetite for future meals. This kitchen has been serving up the best food on the island."

"Yes, I did use buttermilk, and it's really just plain Yankee cooking." Now, that sounded snarky, too. Yankee! What was wrong with her?

"Uncle Paul, Sylvia, and Daisy have gone over to the Tennis Preserve and I'm off to Granville to get lobsters and clams for dinner," she said.

Simon had been sitting at the table reading the *Wall Street Journal* on his tablet. He looked up.

"Get some of Granville Seafood's smoked mussels to have first. Plain and the ones in mustard sauce." He didn't reach for his wallet.

"Why don't I run you down?" Will said. "You haven't been in the Triumph—just near it," he added with a mischievous grin.

Before Sophie could answer, Simon, who had not returned to his paper but seemed to be watching the two, said, "The car's too small and, in any case, I've been wanting to chat with you, Will, about an idea I have that concerns your uncle."

"I'm sure it can wait, can't it? The Triumph has a large boot, as the British call it. Sophie seems to be doing all the toting and I'd like to help."

She'd been about to accept, but the image of Will and Autumn on the boat as well as just a short while ago in the garden muddled her initial thoughts of sitting next to the tall Southerner in the undeniably sexy vintage sports car.

"Uncle Simon is right. I wouldn't want to drip anything from the lobster or clams on those precious seats."

Will shrugged and sat down at the table across from Simon. He did not look happy.

"What's on your mind, sir?" He sounded coldly polite. There was a "Frankly I don't give a damn" lurking not far behind the sentence.

There was no mistaking Simon's look of annoyance at the use of "sir," a term Sophie was sure her uncle thought suggested a much older man. Was this yet another move in this high-stakes, winner-takes-all Birches game? Curiosity kept Sophie from leaving and she took the memo pad from the fridge to make another shopping list, one not strictly necessary.

Simon started right in. "It has been a little over a year since we lost Aunt Priscilla, and it was a devastating blow to me. She was the person I was closest to in the family. A much warmer person, I'm sorry to say, than my own mother, Mary, and Daniel, my father, was wrapped up in his work as was typical for men of his generation. None of this changing diapers, hands-on parenting the way it is now."

"As it was for you?" Will didn't hide his skepticism, Sophie noted.

Simon ignored the comment.

"Priscilla is buried with all the other Proctors in Massachusetts, and it well may be that Paul will want to rest with his family in the South."

Simon made it sound like a destination akin to Limbo. It was all Sophie could do to keep from laughing aloud. She was glad she'd stayed.

"There is no memorial to her, or any of the family, on the island and I'd like to surprise Paul with something tasteful, a small granite obelisk perhaps with the names and dates of everyone who has gone before Aunt Priscilla, too. An enduring tribute that could be placed somewhere on the property."

"With plenty of room for those Proctors to follow who will be going to their just reward?"

Completely missing Will's mocking tone, Simon nodded. "Exactly."

"And this would be a gift to Uncle Paul from everyone?"

"Oh no. This would just be from me. And my wife and children, of course. Because of the very special relationship I had with Aunt Priscilla. To commemorate it. I have been in touch with one of the stonecutters on the island who does this sort of work. But I thought I would run it by you, although I am sure Uncle Paul will be very moved."

"I think that's fair to say." Will stood up. "If you'll excuse me, I'm heading over to the Preserve. I want to be sure Uncle Paul isn't getting tired. He may want to leave before the others."

"Don't trouble yourself. I can drive over."

"It's no trouble. You see we have what you might call a very special relationship."

He let the screen door slam behind him and didn't look back to see the expression on Simon's face. He didn't need to, Sophie thought, grabbing her purse to leave, too.

Faith called Tom to tell him she was in Blue Hill with a full complement of those lovely little cell phone bars. He'd seen his mother, and although she was still groggy, she had instructed him to take his father and siblings out to dinner "on her." For some reason she was instructing him using a very bad French accent. He told Faith he'd once seen his mother approaching this condition after several cups of a Patriot's Day punch that she thought was pure fruit juice, but this was something else again—"high as a kite and never funnier." Giddy with relief, the Fairchilds had decided to do what Marian said, and since cuisine française was not at hand, were heading for Italia and the Trattoria San Pietro in their hometown. Thinking of the restaurant's excellent seafood pastas, Faith decided to do something similar for dinner. They needed to celebrate here, too. Linguine with a garlicky clam sauce and plenty of the flat-leafed Italian parsley from Ursula's garden would hit the spot.

With a gift for Marian in mind, she headed first for The Meadow and, with Karen Brandenburg's expert help, assembled an array of self-indulgent soaps, lotions, and bath oils that her mother-in-law would never buy for herself. At the last moment, she added a long peony pink slightly ruffled silk scarf. The Meadow would package it all up beautifully and send it. Impulsively, Faith added the same scarf in blue to give to Ursula. It was that kind of day.

At the garden center, Faith soon filled one of their red wagons with several varieties of astilbe for Ursula and another with an ambitious selection of perennials for herself. She knew she'd have to plant them all, but in their pots they looked so pretty, and the toil that awaited—the sweaty digging while mosquitoes whined in her ears—was not going to deter her from loading up. Several new varieties of daylilies—always her friends, more elegant bell-shaped campanula, Moonbeam Coreopsis—how could she resist the name? She couldn't resist Dragon's Blood Sedum for the same reason, too. Tolkien fans Ben and Amy would appreciate it, plus the flowers were wonderfully crimson, and it would spread. Fill in the holes. Two summers ago she had succeeded in growing delphinium at last. She added another, blue with a white center, and, throwing caution to the winds, decided to try lavender once more. Hidcote, an English lavender, might work. A climate more similar to Maine than that of Provence, the source of her previous failures.

"Looks like you're opening a branch down on the island," a voice behind her said.

Faith turned to see Ed Ricks. "I guess I'm getting carried away, but I can't resist a sale, especially here. What are you looking for?"

"Advice about my climbing hydrangea. It is very peaked. And that's what led me astray. Althea told me I've almost watered it to death, thinking I was saving it."

"Ursula has one climbing up one of the brick chimneys and it's flourishing. I don't think anyone has ever done anything to it. Maybe neglect is the answer."

Ed laughed. "Easier said than done in my case. Too many years dealing with the results for the *Homo sapiens* species. Do you have to get back right away? If not, how about getting something to eat at the De-Li? They're open until three."

Feeling very much off the leash and also very hungry, the idea of sitting outside overlooking Blue Hill's harbor from the front deck of the small deli sounded ideal.

"I'll settle up here and meet you," Faith said.

As she drove the short distance, Faith came to a decision. She couldn't keep worrying about Ben without telling Tom—couldn't keep the fact that she was finding bodies a secret either, for that matter. Ed had his finger on the pulse of the island, and at the moment, she wanted it on hers as well. She was loathe to take advantage of his expertise in his retirement, but he had said the last time they talked to feel free to call on him for anything.

At the restaurant, she ordered an egg salad sandwich—her comfort food. The De-Li's was a delicious deviled egg version that added mustard, vinegar, and celery salt to the traditional ingredients. Taking a tall glass of iced coffee outside, she found Ed waiting for her with iced chai.

"How is your mother-in-law doing?" he said. "I forgot to ask back at Mainescape."

Faith brought him up to date, and their sandwiches arrived. He was having one of their specials—a Black Forest ham panini with Swiss cheese and apple slices.

They were sitting on the same side of the picnic table so they could both have the view. On a day like this, there was constant activity as pleasure boats left and fishing boats put in. Faith took a bite of her sandwich. Ed paused, his partway to his mouth.

"You want to talk about it?" he said.

Faith swallowed and gave a wry smile. "It's that obvious or you're a very good shrink—or some kind of wizard."

"How about all of the above? Faith, you found Dwayne Hitchcock and that must have been terribly upsetting, coming so soon after being on the scene where Bev died, too. Your husband is away, and I know Ursula and her whole family are there for you, but it's not the same."

"You're right. Except I don't want to burden Tom with any of this now. For one thing, what can he do? Besides his mother, he has a clerical obligation starting in a few days and can't get up here until after that." She hesitated. "It's not just the two deaths." She told him about Ben, starting with the fight outside the Legion Hall dance and ending with the visit last night from Earl.

"Has Mandy turned up?" she asked as she finished the tale.

"No. And it's not like her."

"That's what I keep hearing."

"I think you do need to share all this with Tom. Not to get too technical on you, but as we say in the trade, 'You have a lot on your plate.'" He smiled at her.

"And here all these years, I thought my mother coined that phrase when we wanted more cake."

Ed looked serious again. "The good reverend's used to hearing things like this. Yes, tougher when it's his family, but you can't keep dealing with it on your own. And I'm sure one of the first things he'll say is how upset he'd have been if you *hadn't* told him."

This was something Faith had not considered. Were it the other way around, she would have been mad as hell at her spouse for keeping it from her.

"Should I ask Ben to quit his job?"

Ed shook his head. "Not unless you want that to be your battleground this summer. That's the tough one for parents—which battleground to choose. I've heard good things about the chef, and Ben's friend Tyler is there with him. I feel a little sorry for Derek Otis. At his age, running an operation like The Laughing Gull is a lot of responsibility to have dumped in your lap—and I'm pretty sure that's what happened. My sense is his parents got tired of what one might term his aimless pursuit of pleasure and bought the business for him, thinking being an innkeeper would suit his outgoing personality. He was all for it and maybe he'll stick with it. But there's more required than meeting and greeting. I doubt either he or his parents took that into account."

"Ben would be very angry if we insisted he quit, and you're right. It's not the right issue," Faith said. "I'm sure he'd say he hasn't done anything wrong and that we're being overprotective. But I can't shake the feeling that something toxic is going on at the Lodge, and Mandy's disappearance is making it worse. When Earl came last night, he said her father's death wasn't an accident. That it was being treated as a homicide. What made them rule out an unintended overdose so fast?"

Faith was sure Ed knew. He would have responded to the call and come to some conclusions on the spot, plus he would also be privy to the information shared from the sheriff's office. Whether he would share with her was the question.

He did. "It's a small island, so you'll hear eventually. A couple of things jumped out at us right away. Dwayne is no stranger to those of us on the ambulance corps. A neighbor, Leilah, or Mandy—whoever was around— saved his life more than once when he overdosed on alcohol. Determined effort on his part, considering his size. He also had frequent diabetic seizures."

"Seth Marshall told me that Dwayne had some sort of disability and hadn't worked in years," Faith said.

"He was at the paper mill a while back and claimed he broke his wrist on the job. I think they were happy to get rid of him. He probably did it himself during a liquid lunch in the parking lot. He had a motorcycle in those days, and it wasn't long before he was back on it, so it couldn't have been much. Then in recent years he took to the lawn chair. The point of all this is that alcohol was his drug of choice—and food. Occasionally pills when he could get a doctor who didn't know him, or was just plain foolish, to prescribe them. He didn't have the money they cost now from a dealer, so he wasn't that kind of addict. None of us ever picked up rumors that he was doing the hard stuff."

"But I've heard that heroin is easy and relatively cheap to get, all over Maine."

Ed nodded. "True, but even if he had enough cash, Dwayne was phobic about needles. Wouldn't even get a tattoo—and the crowd he ran with when he was younger was covered with them. Each time he was hauled into the hospital, he was a total baby when it came to an IV. And would drop into a dead faint at the sight of a syringe."

"So shooting up would have been the last thing he would have done."

"Well, it was the last thing. Only we're pretty sure he wasn't the one who did it."

Faith thought back to the man she had seen, a mound molded onto what must have been a sturdy lawn chaise, day after day, except in the pouring rain. He often appeared asleep or, now she realized, was passed out. It would have been easy to approach him without disturbing him, but to tie his arm off and send what must have been a megadose into his compromised bloodstream—how would someone have been able to do that? And in broad daylight?

"It must have been someone he knew," she said.

"That's why they're looking for Mandy," Ed said.

After his words, they sat in total silence for a while. The view was no longer a serene one. The contrast with the images in Faith's mind was enormous— the picturesque harbor seemed a mockery, a kind of painted ship upon a painted ocean.

"Leilah was at work. No doubt about it," Ed said softly. "Dwayne used to knock her around, and Earl thinks he may have done the same with Mandy—or worse. Couple of years ago Dwayne began saying Mandy wasn't his."

Faith felt sick. "And no one tried to intervene?" She thought of all those notices, small and poster size, about help lines in the island restrooms and other places.

"Not that I know of. And Mandy would have had to tell someone. The problem with domestic abuse is denial coupled with the way most abusers manipulate their victim. 'I wouldn't have hit you if you hadn't made me.'"

Faith kept trying to find some logic in a terrifyingly illogical situation. "I don't know the girl, but everyone keeps saying how intelligent she is. Wouldn't she have been smarter about it?"

"It"—she found she couldn't say the word. Say aloud what she was thinking: murder. She kept on. "Done it in a less dramatic way. And Mandy would have known about his fear of needles."

"She *is* smart. Given that, maybe planned the whole thing to point suspicion away from her or her mother. I'm just telling you what the thinking is now. Why Earl said it wasn't accidental. We don't have the full post-mortem results, just some preliminary blood work. As expected, Dwayne's blood alcohol level was through the roof, but we've known him to survive higher. And they found traces of heroin, but there may also be something more. He may have been drugged with something else so the fix could be administered without his waking up."

Driving back, despite the end of the conversation with Ed, Faith felt the familiar surge of pleasure as she started up the seventy-five-year-old suspension bridge—that graceful and essential link from Sanpere to the rest of the world. There were those who seldom crossed it heading away from Sanpere and also those arriving who wanted to pull it up after them—preserve the island in amber. She didn't feel either of those emotions. Change was an inevitable part of life. Even all the changes whirling about her this summer. The Birches would pass to someone. She hadn't gone into it with Tom. She also hadn't had a chance to tell him about the other change: Dana Cameron, the newest addition to the Rowe family. She tacked this one in particular onto her lengthening mental list. Both were quickly replaced by the topic uppermost in her mind.

Ben. All Faith could think about was Ben. Ben had a serious crush on this young woman she was sure. He'd started to date—going out in a group mostly—but this was different.

Her son was in love.

At four o'clock Felicity called to say they were leaving Bar Harbor. Simon answered the phone, as he usually did. Sophie, scrubbing potatoes for potato salad, heard him tell his daughter, "Don't make any stops. Come straight to the island," enunciating his words in no uncertain terms.

It appeared they would be dining fashionably late. With summer traffic, it would be at least six before they arrived, possibly later. Then drinks would further delay the main meal. Sophie decided to aim for dinner at eight.

Simon left clutching the tablet that was an extension of his right hand and Will, who had been in the kitchen getting a glass of water, said, "So, what's the plan? And how can I help?"

It was all Sophie could do to keep from throwing her arms around him.

"The bugs will be terrible on the beach, but I think we could set up outside on the porch with plenty of citronella candles."

"There are some sawhorses and an old door out in the shed. We can set them up as a buffet. And let's be ecologically unsound tonight—paper plates, plastic cutlery. Otherwise we'll be doing dishes until midnight or later."

"Great! There's a long tablecloth that Aunt Priscilla used to use for lobster feasts. Checkered oilcloth. I don't think you can buy those anymore. But since we'll be using metal lobster tools, let's skip the plastic and give everyone a real fork. And I'll put the melted butter in the ramekins we have that go over votive candles. Uncle Paul likes his sizzling. We can do one dishwasher load."

Sophie was beginning to look forward to what she had been viewing as a pain-in-the-neck job. "Rory will help with drinks. Maybe he could make a run to the market soon—they have something they call a 'Beer Cave' now—and get ice for the cooler, too. I think he's in the bunkhouse. At least his car is parked outside. Could you go ask him? And if she's there, see if Autumn would come help us get everything ready later?"

Sophie watched Will's face closely as she mentioned Autumn's name. He'd finished his water and walked slowly to the sink, placing the glass on the counter. She moved away, running her hands down her jeans to dry them, and opened the pantry, looking to see what she might transform into gourmet hors d'oeuvres. All she had so far were the smoked mussels.

Will followed, standing just behind her. "I think you should be the one to ask your cousin. Think she'd like to be included."

He put his hand on Sophie's arm, pulling her toward him. She turned, and this time when she let her eyes close, the kiss came. Soft and gentle, like a first kiss should be with all its hope for the future and reminders of long-ago ones, teenage ones. As Will drew her into his embrace, it became more insistent. A kiss that blocked out the memory of any others. He wanted more. More than kisses.

And so did she.

They moved apart. She was holding a jar of olives, and the incongruous sight caused her to burst out laughing.

"Now, that's a sound I've been waiting to hear," Will said. "You're such a serious lady, Sophie Maxwell."

"Not really—" she started to protest.

"No," he cut her off. "Serious is good. I'm a serious man myself, darlin'." He stepped toward her again and Sophie felt a shiver of anticipation.

"I think we should try to have dinner on the porch, Sophie." Uncle Simon was standing in the doorway. Sophie wondered how long he'd been there.

"That's just what Will and I thought," she said coolly. "He's going to get some things to make a large table from the shed. Maybe you could help." It was the closest she had come to being rude to her uncle, and it felt great. She had a feeling Babs would approve.

In fact, she realized, she was probably channeling her mother at the moment.

She also realized she had just kissed a man whose occupation, possibly his name, and all sorts of other things were a mystery to her.

Pix was at The Pines when Faith got back. Her brother and family weren't back from sailing, and she was returning from having driven her mother to a garden club meeting. Apparently an expert on deer resistant plants had been a big draw. Amy was still with the Proctors and Ben was at work. Faith had planned to call Tom the moment she entered the house, but one look at her friend's face put it on a back burner.

"Mother's taking a nap. I think the fact that she can plant spirea, one of her favorite shrubs, up here after thinking the deer would destroy it all these years may have been too much for her," Pix said.

Faith said, "Do you have to run back home? Iced tea—or better yet, gin and tonic? You can tell me more—not that it will help. Our deer eat the marigolds, and even I know they're supposed to hate them. Sort of like my father-in-law and brussels sprouts."

They took their drinks to the Adirondack chairs at the edge of the front lawn overlooking the beach. Faith loved the idea of the furniture. It looked as indigenous to the Maine coast as lupine, but in fact it was all too reminiscent of the pews in First Parish, seats desperately in need of cushioning.

For the second time today Faith looked at a picture-postcard view in silence. This time the gin was helping to lighten her mood.

"You almost never hear the sound of real lawn mowers anymore," Pix said.

Faith was startled. It was not the subject she expected. Nor were the deer-resistant plants.

"And those real ones would be?"

"Hand mowers. The whirr, whirr sound they made. It was what summer sounded liked. Just like the way fall smelled. Burning leaves."

Having never experienced these Proustian madeleine moments on Manhattan's East Side, Faith simply made a murmuring sound in reply.

They sat sipping their drinks. Faith waited for the next tangent. Retired Crayola colors?

The silence continued. Pix broke it.

"I'm a terrible person."

"How so?' Faith knew enough not to contradict what was patently a foolish remark.

"Dana is a love. I've never seen Arnie and Claire so happy. And I *am* happy for them, for the three of them. But everything was set. Sam and I—eventually the children—would take on all this." She waved toward the lighthouse, but Faith knew what she meant. "It was always enough for my brother to arrive, with his boat and strawberry rhubarb pie waiting. I have no idea what he has in mind now. And I can't ask him. Or my mother. Especially not my mother."

"Why not?"

Pix turned to look at her friend. Faith could read the quickly suppressed thought that skimmed across her friend's face—"Well, *she's* not a New Englander."

"I just can't," Pix said.

Faith poured a little more gin in Pix's glass. She was planning to feed her dinner before she drove home.

"Pretty much ninety percent of the time I'm the one coming to you for advice," Faith said. "Starting with the time Ben swallowed a paper clip when he was a year old. Here's my ten percent."

Faith was starting to hear echoes of her conversation with Ed Ricks. "You *have* to talk to your brother. Ursula told me earlier this summer that she has told both of you what her plans for this place are."

Pix took a big swig of her drink.

"Have breakfast at the Harbor Café. Bond over their amazing strawberry pancakes. And then the two of you talk to Ursula. I would be very surprised if she hasn't been thinking about all this since your brother's family arrived."

"Someone's been pouring Moxie on your Wheaties," Pix said.

"You know I would never eat processed cereal—or drink Moxie," Faith replied.

"That's my girl—and since I am clearly staying for dinner, pour me some more gin." Pix stretched her long legs out and leaned back against the slanted back. She made it look as comfortable as an overstuffed armchair.

Uncle Simon had been fuming for almost an hour before Aunt Deirdre suggested they start drinks without the latecomers. She made a point of sitting by Paul and chatting about the wonderful Sanpere garden club lecture she had attended that afternoon. How much she had learned about what plants flourished on the island, what a "superb spot" The Birches was, and how she was itching to put her green thumb to work, enlarging Priscilla's beds in front of the house with some new plants. "But no hosta!" she chortled. "Candy for the deer population I now know!"

Paul thanked her for her offer and agreed that the deer had plenty to eat in the woods surrounding The Birches without providing more fodder.

Finally, after noting a few too many drinks consumed by several of her relatives, especially Deirdre, Sophie had declared dinner served. Felicity, Forbes, and their guests finally arrived at nine with apologies that included an overturned tractor-trailer truck and a lengthy detour through Ellsworth. Their flushed faces indicated the detour might have been to the Irish pub there.

The friend who had "hitched a ride" on the plane was the last on the porch. Tall, the light catching his thick ash-blond hair, he was startlingly good-looking, and followed Felicity's fiancé, who was already making the rounds—"I'm Barclay, but do call me 'Barks.' Everybody does." Barks looped an arm through his friend's, shepherding him straight over to Sophie.

"This is a good buddy of mine from across the pond. Ian Kendall. Sophie, Ian. Ian, Sophie."

Ian.

Chapter 10

"I hope you don't mind. I couldn't leave things as they were. I was a total ass, Sophie. And, well, I've missed you terribly." Ian was standing in front of her and had taken her hand in both of his. Sophie could see the tiny chicken pox scar on one side of his lips that looked like a dimple unless you were close. Very close. Like now.

She seemed to have lost all power of speech. Of movement. Ian's voice made everything he said sound as if he had trained at the Royal Academy of Dramatic Art. Trained so the words would sound completely natural. Natural, sincere, and seductive. Her head was spinning.

"Do you know this guy, Sophie?" Different accent. *Very* different accent. It was Will. He was standing next to Ian. He asked again more insistently, "Do you know him?"

Sophie thought she might faint. It was warm, and the two men, their faces doubled before her eyes, were smothering her.

"I . . ." She tried to get a sentence out and failed.

Forbes's laugh rippled across the porch. "I'd say 'know' would be the operative word here, cuz! Sensed you were pining for your British beau. When Barks mentioned Ian was in town—they work for the same firm—Felicity and I told him to bring him along."

"Especially since Ian has agreed to be Barks's best man." Felicity twinkled, feeding her intended a steamed clam dipped in melted butter and kissing the ensuing drip on his chin, an act so nauseating it jolted Sophie from her trance.

"I imagine Barclay can wipe his own chin," Aunt Deirdre said, moving slowly toward Ian with a hand out in welcome. "I think you'll enjoy your time here. You must take us as you find us here in this place that has been in the family for many generations. It may not be Blenheim, but we like to call it our own castle."

She was doing a veddy credible imitation of Dame Maggie Smith.

"Now," she continued to trill, "what can we get you to drink? Gin and It? I'm afraid no Pimm's."

Ian removed one hand from Sophie's and shook Deirdre's, leaving his other firmly in place. "I can't tell you how much it means to me to be here. Sophie has told me so much about Sanpere Island. Many thanks; whatever you're drinking is fine with me."

Sophie freed her hand and watched as Ian proceeded to enchant her aunt further. Sylvia approached with an outstretched plate of the dried kelp chips she had prepared as her canapé contribution, and he proceeded to charm her, too. Then, without giving the ladies short shrift, Ian tactfully made his way over to Paul McAllister and thanked him for letting him "crash" the family evening get-together. Deirdre had placed a vodka tonic in his hand, and Sophie watched him startle slightly as he took a drink. Throughout the week, she had noted that her aunt's idea of the perfect summer cocktail was a glass of Stoli with a splash of tonic and a wedge of lime. It explained the rather stately, studied way she was moving about the porch.

Sophie had often heard Uncle Paul and Aunt Priscilla speak of spending time in England, where they had close friends both in Yorkshire and London. It wasn't long before Ian and Paul discovered mutual acquaintances—"Different generations," Paul noted with a slightly wistful smile. Ian had brushed that aside and proceeded to regale the older man with what the

McAllisters' friends had been up to, noting that they were "much more interesting than their boring offspring like myself and much naughtier as well."

Sophie had still not moved—only her eyes followed what seemed like a Noël Coward drawing room drama. Will hadn't moved, either. "Sophie," he said softly, bending nearer. "Who is this guy? Why is he here?"

"He's . . . we met in New York. And . . ." She automatically began picking up some of the used plates. "I don't know why he's here," she said finally and looked straight at Will.

"You may not, but I do," he said, and walked down the front stairs toward the boathouse.

Hurricane Cary was not meant to amount to much and had spared the coast from Florida past the Carolinas, considerately moving out to sea. A fickle storm system, it then decided to move back toward land, and soon they were battening down the hatches from Ocean City, Maryland, to Bar Harbor, Maine.

The storm threat to The Pines was falling trees, and branches, near the house. Ursula kept clearing deadwood, but there was always the possibility that the gale force winds would take some down that had seemed firmly rooted.

Gert Prescott arrived for work early, setting out the oil lamps, a battalion of flashlights and emergency candles. She and Faith baked bread and sweets, also preparing soups and dishes like chicken in gravy that could be heated up on the stove. The propane tanks had fortunately just been filled. As one last precaution, Ursula filled the old claw-footed bathtub with water in what she laughingly called the "mistress bath" off her bedroom. Faith, with grave misgivings, drove Ben to work and made him promise to call when his shift was over. Amy wanted to invite Daisy to come stay for the day and an overnight.

"She said they don't lose electricity in California, Mom, and she's scared. She says she's never been in a hurricane and doesn't want to have the house blown away with her in it."

"I think she's seen *The Wizard of Oz* too many times," Faith said, "but I'm happy to have her here, although her mother might want her close in case Daisy gets upset."

Apparently Sylvia did not, and Daisy appeared at the door with her things bundled into a tie-dyed satchel.

It was a typical day-before-a-storm day. Both the market and convenience store in Granville ran out of essentials like batteries, milk, and beer. Rumors were rife. It was going to be another Sandy. Or not. The range of advice was even broader. Cover all the windows with plywood. Or don't. Move inland. Move to higher ground. Or stay put.

And hovering over the island, low on the horizon, was a yellow sky. It flattened out both the land and sea below and promised nothing good.

Tom Fairchild had heard the weather report and called early. He and Faith had talked for almost two hours the night before. Hanging up after midnight, Faith thought she had never missed him—or loved him—so much. This morning when he called after hearing the latest predictions, he started to tell her what to do to get ready for the worst, but she assured him they were well prepared. Not Fairchild-family prepared, which would have meant more than a swimming pool's worth of water, food for weeks, and some sort of underground shelter stocked ages ago; but definitely prepared for the storm. The Millers and Rowes had been through many hurricanes on Sanpere, Faith reminded Tom.

He calmed down, and she was happy that her husband was not as concerned as he might have been, distracted by Marian's doing so well. He had gleefully reported that his mother was up and about. Her doctor had even decided she might be better off in her own bed, possibly discharging her as early as Monday. She'd received Faith's package from The Meadow and had insisted on slathering herself with the Botanic lavender lotion—"Better than all these chemicals."

Promising to call with weather updates, Faith hung up and steeled herself for what she knew was going to be a very long day. Waiting for a storm to hit stretched minutes into hours.

The dinghies and other small craft had been hauled, the larger boats would have to ride it out, and they'd tied down or removed anything that could fly off in the winds—porch furniture, planters. The storm shutters were in place. There was something almost pleasurable in the preparations until Faith remembered why they were doing it.

Unlike the princess and the pea, Sophie had gone to bed early and slept like a rock, blocking thoughts of both swains from her mind. Yet when she awoke at dawn as usual, she was exhausted.

Now she was busy preparing for what they were saying could be a major storm. Will was in and out of the kitchen with a hammer, presumably nailing the plywood shutters over the front windows. When Paul came downstairs, Sophie immediately poured him a mug of coffee. With her uncle up at this hour, she was beginning to think it might indeed be heavy weather.

"I'm going to help Will with the windows," he said. "Send anyone else who comes along out to give us a hand with it, will you? We'll also need to put things away from the lawn and porch. And could you call Marge Foster? I don't want her coming to work. Nothing's going to happen for a while, but I'm sure she has plenty to do at her house. How are we fixed for supplies?"

"We're fine. Yesterday we baked and made things that would keep a while. I'm going to add one more large veggie pasta casserole to the others. I thought you'd want Mrs. Foster to stay put, so I've already called her."

She was rewarded with a broad smile from her uncle as Will came back into the kitchen.

Will and Uncle Paul were clearly enjoying the preparations, Sophie realized. Man versus Nature. Something like that. And afterward Man with Chain Saw to clean up the downed trees and limbs.

"More coffee before you start?" she asked them. "I also have some blueberry lemon muffins that just came out of the oven."

"No coffee. I've had more than I should already, but one of those muffins would be great, thanks," Will said.

She and Will began doing awkward do-si-dos in the kitchen as she took the muffins from the tin and refilled her uncle's mug of coffee. Will kept looking over at her, his mouth half open, as if he wanted to say something. He didn't.

Paul put his cup in the sink.

"Better get to it. We probably have hours to spare, but I never put much trust in the weather reports. Even the marine forecasts. Which reminds me, Will. Be sure we have that Uniden marine radio and anything else you think we might need from the boathouse. You'd better bunk up here tonight."

There was no mistaking the look Will gave Sophie. "I'll be fine down there. It's a solid structure. And I wouldn't want to get in anyone's way."

"Nonsense. Don't want to worry about you. There are still beds free on the third floor, and it won't be too hot there tonight. We'll probably all be in the living room anyway. Besides, I'll need a Scrabble partner."

Sophie took a pencil from the junk drawer. She started to make a to-do list and had just written "check flashlight batteries" when she realized she was alone. She was alone with her thoughts, all the ones that hadn't kept her awake.

Ian. Will. Ian some more.

Last night as Sophie had started to slip away from the increasingly merry group on the porch, the Englishman had blocked her way and said, "I need to talk to you, Sophie. You can't know how badly. The way I behaved has haunted me since you left London. Make time tomorrow? Please?"

She'd tried hard to resist, knowing what she ought to say—words justifiable for a lady who had been treated the way she had, words a lady usually didn't use. Instead, she'd said, "No . . . well, maybe."

The memory of her feeble response was still grating on her. She should have said no. Better still, never. She was glad he was staying at the Sanpere Village Inn with Barks and she wouldn't be running into him. Because of the storm, their paths wouldn't be crossing—not today at least. Will underfoot was bad enough.

Simon Proctor strode into the kitchen. "I'd be very grateful if you could go check on your aunt, Sophie. She seems to have picked up some sort of bug, and I can't find Felicity."

Since Felicity had taken off for a night at the inn with her betrothed, Sophie knew he wouldn't find his daughter for a while.

"What seems to be the matter?" she asked.

"Some sort of stomach upset." Simon clearly did not want to go into details.

As she went up to their bedroom, Sophie thought the aftereffects of what her aunt had imbibed were most likely the cause and stopped to get a large glass of water and Tylenol.

But Deirdre was not just hungover. She was clearly running a fever. She had also thrown up several times throughout the night, continuing into the morning, she reported.

Grabbing the water and analgesic from Sophie, she said, "Where did you get the clams? I'm positive I got a bad one."

"Bad one what?" Sylvia was standing at the doorway and came into the room.

"A clam that was off." Deirdre quaffed the rest of the water and slunk down in the bed, pulling the light blanket almost over her head. "You must not have checked them, Sophie."

Her aunt might be ill, but she was still very much herself.

"I did check. They were from Granville Seafood, where we always get them. You must have picked up a touch of some flu," Sophie said.

Sylvia put her hand on Deirdre's forehead. It was quickly shaken off. "Someone is putting something in our food. I know it!" Sylvia's voice rose. "Someone is deliberately trying to poison us!"

"I'm sure no one is doing anything like that," Sophie said gently. "Why would they?"

"Because of the house, of course. It must be that nephew or whatever he is of Paul's." Sylvia almost spat out the words.

"He *is* Paul's nephew, and he's not in the running," Sophie said, thinking at least one of those things was true. Although, was she sure about both?

Deirdre handed Sophie the empty glass. The command was clear.

"Nonsense, Sylvia. Must you always be so dramatic?"

Sophie fetched her aunt a full glass of water. She was tempted to curtsy. The audience was clearly over. Deirdre was feeling better. But what had been wrong?

Downstairs, Felicity was coming into the kitchen through the back door with Barks, both of them with that dewy-eyed, just-had-great-sex look. Sophie was getting ready to leave with her list in hand, although it would be potluck at the market. As soon as the last batch of muffins was done, she'd go.

"Barks and Ian are moving over here," Felicity said. "I wouldn't be able to sleep a wink tonight thinking about them at that old inn. A stiff breeze would blow the whole place down. Uncle Paul said it was okay, which is good, because they already checked out."

Sophie looked longingly at the cast-iron frying pan drying on the stove top. "Felicity! That's two more people to feed here and two empty rooms at the inn when they count on keeping it full during the summer season."

"Oh pooh, Sophie. I'll help cook. I make great pop-overs if you have the pan. And Barks can have my food anyway. I've been eating way too much. The inn people didn't care. Ian paid for them both for all the nights. They'll fill the rooms and get twice as much. I would think you'd want your honey here under the same roof, too."

"He is *not* my 'honey' or my anything else!" Sophie said.

"Really?" Ian Kendall walked in, took the muffin Sophie had been about to put on the plate with the rest, and took a bite, slowly licking his lips.

Everything was still. The water at the turn of the tide was like a mirror and even the aspens—the leaves said to continuously quiver in sorrow—weren't stirring. The sky had turned from yellow to slate gray, and even those who had dismissed the warn-ings were stocking up now. Too late for essentials, and there had also been a run on pork rinds and Slim Jims.

Faith had had enough. She wanted Ben with her and wanted him now. She called the Lodge and left a mes-sage that she would be picking him up just after the lunch shift.

Pix, Sam, and Samantha, who were moving to The Pines on higher ground, hadn't arrived yet. They had offered to check the Fairchilds' cottage to make sure everything was protected there, although Seth Marshall had called to tell Faith he'd been by.

Ursula was teaching Amy, Daisy, and Dana the names of island birds; field guides and books of photos were spread out on the big round table.

Faith had nothing to do. When the phone rang, she lurched for it in relief, even as she feared what news it might bring. It was that kind of day.

"Faith? Hi. It's Ed Ricks. All set over there for the storm?"

"You know what Ursula and her family are like. They could give a course in hurricane preparedness."

He laughed. "That's what I assumed, but just checking."

"Have you heard any more about Dwayne Hitchcock's autopsy?" Faith said.

"That's the other reason I'm calling. After our conversation yesterday, I thought I'd let you know that Dwayne *was* knocked out before the overdose was administered. He had enough chloral hydrate in his bloodstream to put him to sleep for weeks."

"What about Mandy? Has she come home?"

"No, and once the storm blows over, Earl will be picking up that thread. Right now we're all concentrating on making sure people come through it safe, especially some of our elderly residents. The nursing home has some respite care beds free, and we've moved a few folks there."

So many things to consider, Faith thought. "Is there anything I can do? I could go over there and help out in the kitchen."

"That's kind of you and I'll let them know. I think they're all set. But about Mandy, Faith. Leilah found a note from the girl saying not to worry and that she would be back in time for the start of school, which suggests she's left the island. But no one has a clue where she'd go. Earl seems to think your son knows more than he's saying. Maybe he'll open up to you."

"I'll try, but Ben isn't exactly Mr. Chatty with me these days."

"Don't worry about it. Just thought he might let something drop. I've got to run. You've got my cell, right?"

"Yes, but only the landline works here."

"Take care, Faith."

"You too," she said. Faith hung up and headed straight for the car. Job or no job, Benjamin Fairchild was coming home with her right now.

What kind of people go out for lunch with a major hurricane on the way? Ben thought darkly. The dining room at the Lodge was almost empty. Only a few guests had decided to stay on and brave the storm, eating quickly before leaving for their cottages to pack for a hasty escape if need be.

With a severe staff shortage, the chef had assigned Ben to wait tables despite his inexperience.

"Just don't dump food on anyone or break anything."

But that was exactly what Ben wanted to do. Specifically on Rory Proctor, who had arrived with three men and a woman. Ben recognized Forbes and Felicity Proctor, but not the others. When he went to take their orders, Ben noticed one of the guys had an English accent. He sounded like that movie star his mother thought was so great. Colin something.

It wasn't long before Derek Otis came in and joined them. He'd been helping the maintenance crew put outdoor stuff away, and Ben was sure he was supposed to be in the kitchen further preparing for the storm with Chef Zach. The Lodge had a generator, but the chef had been worried all morning that it wouldn't provide enough power to keep the food on hand from spoiling. Well, Ben had done his part, he thought to himself, picturing the knapsack he'd stashed behind the kitchen's back door.

Addressing the table, he told them that because of the storm they were stopping lunch service early and some things on the menu weren't available. They ordered haddock burgers and fries—the English guy, "Ian" Rory had called him—said it sounded like a fish and chips bunty, whatever that was. Ben just wanted them to eat and leave. The sooner the better.

They all ordered beers, but Ben explained he couldn't serve them, since he was underage and they'd have to wait while he got the chef. It was at this point that Derek had arrived, overhearing Ben's statement.

"The guest is always right, Ben. Go get the drinks. I know your dad is a sky pilot, but that doesn't mean you have to be a wuss."

This produced a general laugh, and Ben left for the cooler in the kitchen, but not before he heard Rory say, "Where's that cute little thing from the last time we were here, Derek? The kind that keeps you coming back to the table for more!"

That was when Ben seriously started thinking about spilling things.

He went to the cooler and began to reach for the beers. Directly behind him, Zach yelled, "What the hell do you think you're doing?"

"Derek, I mean the boss, said I should serve them. I told them I was underage and would get you, but he told me to do it anyway." Ben felt close to tears and that made him even angrier.

"Asshole," the chef muttered. "I'm out of here for sure. We could lose our liquor license if he lets minors serve drinks!"

Ben backed away, and the chef grabbed a tray, putting the drinks on it. He pushed the half shutters into the dining room open and said over his shoulder, "Watch the fryer."

He was back in a few seconds, even angrier, if that was possible. " 'Oh, Chef, we were so looking forward to your fabulous lobster ravioli, couldn't you make a few for us to taste?' " he said, imitating a high, squeaky female voice. Ben and Jim, the only other member of the kitchen crew still there, stood still. This was getting scary. Zach Hale looked at them and smiled. "Don't worry, children. I'm not pulling a nutty on you. Take the food out and let's close this place down before Cary gets here and pulls it down." Seeing their eyes widen, he added, "Again, calm down. I've been in way worse weather, and this place will be fine. If anyone wants dessert we have pie and that's all."

The group lingered. Derek was seeing to the drinks now, and Ben was kept busy removing empty bottles. The Englishman had ordered blueberry pie and pronounced it "inedible." He'd announced that no one, not even the French, could beat his country for "pudding" and told Ben he'd give the chef a recipe for "Spotted Dick." The table erupted in raucous glee. Ben had no idea what he was talking about and decided to hate him, too. Hate them all. He stood well away where he could see what he might need to do but not be seen. Derek was offering them a place to stay for the night, but they were refusing. Ben heard Sophie's name—Felicity was saying something about her—and tuned back into their conversation. He had liked his old babysitter, and it had been great to see her again.

"Ah yes. Sophie. Not that I need a reminder." Ian was smiling broadly. "Got a job to do, Derek old man. And nice work if you can get it. Forbes and Barks lured me to this godforsaken island, sorry that's what it is. Nothing going on and nothing much to eat. Big contract at stake and all I have to do to increase my cut is train my charms on little Sophie once again. Tonight is the night. Has to be. Have to get back, but she's easy, if you know what I mean."

So this Ian had been a boyfriend of Sophie's, Ben gathered, and now because of some deal with those two he was going to "charm" her again. How could her cousin Rory sit there and let them talk about her that way? Forbes and Felicity were her cousins, too. Some family. He had to figure out a way to warn Sophie, even with everything else on his mind now.

The chef strode into the room. "Mr. Otis, the kitchen is closed. I've sent most of the staff home. We need to clear this table."

"Theeze are my frens," Derek said. He was clearly drunk. "Good frens."

Forbes stood up. "We were just leaving, Chef. Thank you for an unmemorable meal."

Ben stepped from the shadows and started to pile the plates, ignoring the rules for proper table service. He looked at Zach Hale, expecting an explosion. Instead Zach said with exaggerated politeness, "Exactly the same for me." And left the room.

Ben and Jim quickly filled the dishwasher and ran it. "Jimmy, you get going," Chef Zach said. Jim lived a short way down the road from the Lodge and biked to work. "Ben, your mother is picking you up, right? Better call her—then I need to talk to you, but first we have to put that miserable excuse for an innkeeper to bed."

Derek had a room on the second floor of the Lodge and the maids were always complaining what a chore it was to clean. Derek could walk—barely—and they guided him up the stairs. Ben opened the door, and they managed to get him into bed, rolling him on his stomach so, Zach said, "He doesn't choke on his own puke, tempted as I might be to let him."

The maids hadn't been to the Lodge today and the room was a pigsty. Ben was tempted to take a picture with his phone to show his mother the next time she complained about *his* mess. The outside shutters had been nailed shut by the maintenance crew, and Ben could hear them hammering the large plywood covers over the picture windows on the main floor now that the dining room was empty.

"Come on, Ben," Zach said. When they reached the kitchen, the chef pulled Ben's knapsack from behind the door. "I should fire you for this, but if—and that's a big if—we stay open, it would be hard to find someone to replace you. As usual every restaurant from here to Camden is looking for workers."

Ben dropped his head.

"How long has this been going on?" Zach asked.

"I—I . . ." Ben stammered.

"Hi, honey. Hi, Chef. Ready to go? I'm sure you don't have any guests left. The whole island is closing down."

Great. It was his mother.

The chef looked as if he was considering a few options. He chose one.

"What would you do in your business, Mrs. Fairchild, if you discovered an employee was stealing food?"

"Get rid of the person immediately, of course," she said. "If you can't trust the people who work for you, your business will fail before you can say bon appétit!"

Zach nodded. "Ben needs to learn this. I'm giving him one more chance, but only one. If it happens again, he's out the door and no *bon* at all."

"Wait a minute! Ben has been stealing from you, from the Lodge?"

The chef opened Ben's knapsack wide and revealed an entire roasted chicken that Ben had carefully wrapped, a Baggie with rolls, another with the chef's double chocolate brownies, several small containers of other food, and a cold pack.

"I imagine you have your own utensils."

Ben looked from the chef to his mother and back again.

"I thought with the electricity probably going out this would go to waste and . . ."

His mother gave him the look. The look he had known well since early childhood. The "can you look me straight in the eye and say that" look. He couldn't, and his voice faltered.

The chef handed him the knapsack, still full. "I'm going to assume this is the first and last time. Get going now and stay safe."

When they were in the car, Ben pleaded, "Don't say anything, Mom. Just don't."

She didn't.

Sophie was relieved that her cousins, Barks—such a stupid name—and Ian were not at The Birches when she got back from Granville with her slim pickings— no batteries; a large bag of brown rice, not an island staple; and several cans of condensed milk that must have been overlooked, as it *was* an island staple. She continued with storm preparations and the more difficult job of avoiding Will, who was in and out of the house, using the back door. Each time his eyes seemed to bore into her head, accusing her of she knew not what. No, she had to admit to herself; she knew exactly what he was thinking. What she didn't know was what *she* was thinking—or doing.

Ian Kendall was the one man, one person, she had hoped never to run into again for the rest of her life, and by putting an entire ocean between them, this had seemed a reasonable belief. But the old Kevin Bacon thing had smacked her right in the face, truly knocking her senseless. And senseless was how she was behaving. Ian was a total shit. She *knew* this. She could still hear Gillian's parting words about the family "heirloom" ring: "He's got a drawer full of them."

Where was her self-respect? How could she ever trust him? Yet, remembering the way he looked at her last night—and his words—produced the same effect they had when she'd first met him. Other memories flooded back. His touch, his smile, the way they had seemed to be one person in thought, word, and deed. Except, she reminded herself, she would never do what he had done to her.

Sophie looked down. She had peeled a potato almost to the size of a pea and was about to start on her hand. She shook her head to try to clear it.

It didn't work. Will. What about Will Tarkington? Their mutual attraction had become clear to both of them. Hadn't it? He was wonderful to Uncle Paul, a decent, loyal man. Right? Ian was a snake. Will was a pussycat. No, that wasn't right. Too tame. Her thoughts froze for the moment at "Will is . . ." and then moved on. It was a sentence she couldn't complete, because she had absolutely no idea who Will was. What he did, where, even who . . . ?

Her luck didn't hold, and an hour later, Ian found Sophie on the shore after he returned with the others. She thought she'd be safe from everyone, especially him, and could try to gather her wits in the calm before the storm. It had seemed like perfect timing.

She'd been sitting by the lighthouse, thinking back to her other life, B.I.—Before Ian. Just a year ago she was steadily climbing the ladder of success by all sorts of measures—job, apartment, clothes—especially shoes. Great shoes. She'd tossed it all away for love. And it *was* love. At least on her part. She looked up at the lighthouse, long since decommissioned and replaced by an automatic light and horn on the rocky shoal farther out that ships were meant to avoid. She hadn't avoided the rocky shoal that was Ian and the sad part was that all the lights, bells, and whistles in the world wouldn't have saved her.

When she was little, the lighthouse was open and they used to play in it. Several years ago there had been some sort of accident. A death. She kept meaning to ask Faith Fairchild about it. Apparently she had been involved. Now the lighthouse was kept locked up tight. Sophie got up and pressed the brass door handle, worn smooth over time. She was surprised when the latch clicked and she could push the door open. She pulled it shut, wondering whom she should tell. It needed to be locked again, but she wasn't sure whether her family or the Rowes owned it.

She was starting to walk back to the house when she remembered there used to be a spare key on a hook, hidden by the beach roses that had grown up on the sides of the lighthouse. It was rusty, but it was still there. For a moment she thought about weathering the storm inside, watching from the top where the light with a Fresnel lens—now in a museum—had been. It would be safe in more ways than one. Instead, she locked up and was thinking she should be getting back to The Birches when Ian's voice intruded.

"Tuppence for your thoughts?"

Sophie quickly pocketed the key. It could give Ian ideas—ideas that she just might be too weak to resist. Remember the drawer filled with rings, she told herself. Remember the redhead in his arms.

"Sorry, they're not for sale," she said and started walking.

He grabbed her wrist. "Sophie! A day hasn't gone by that I haven't thought of you and the way I treated you. How I totally blew my only chance for happiness. The girl you saw was a temp at the firm and meant nothing. What you saw was a one-off. Honestly."

Sophie pulled free. "A 'one-off'? In this country we call that kind of book a 'stand-alone,' and I believe it's my cue to leave."

Suddenly she felt extremely happy. Euphoric. She began laughing. The first real laughter she could recall for months.

"You're hysterical. It's the weather. The storm." Ian clearly thought she was unhinged. "We'll talk later. This isn't over. I won't give up. I love you!"

"Oh no you don't. But I hope you think you do, because then you'll have a taste of your own medicine, as you 'stand alone.' Oh, I sound like a teenager. I feel like a teenager. Thank you, Ian!"

She pulled off her sandals and ran down the beach, her bare feet leaving footprints on the wet sand. She felt free as a bird. The gulls were screeching like mad overhead, and she thought they had never sounded so sweet.

The storm began that night at around eight. The muggy, still air suddenly released a torrent of rain, just like a tent that has filled up and sent its contents streaming over the sides into the ground. No wind, just a downpour like other summer downpours. A tease.

Paul McAllister had been right and almost everyone had gathered in the living room. The radio was tuned to the local channel, which was broadcasting storm updates. Sophie was washing up with Sylvia and Autumn's help, much to her surprise.

"We can put some plates of cookies out and lemonade," Sophie said. "People always get hungry waiting for something to happen. A storm, a party, a baby . . ." She was babbling.

"Why don't you do that, Sophie? I want a word with Autumn," Sylvia said.

Autumn clearly did not want a word with her mother, but Sylvia barred the way after Sophie went through with the food and drink.

When Sophie returned whatever "word" Sylvia had said had produced an Autumn Sophie had never seen. Her face was a mask of fury. Sylvia's back was to her, and Sophie stood still, not wanting to interrupt what was clearly a private mother/daughter conversation. Make that argument.

"The answer is no, Sylvia. Plain no," Autumn said, spitting each word out. Sylvia's older two children had used her first name for as long as Sophie could remember. Autumn's inflection made it sound like an expletive.

"Is it asking too much for you to simply be nice to him? You always liked him and Aunt Priscilla. I'm sure he thinks you're avoiding him. That you don't want to be with an oldie. You haven't said two words to Paul so far as I know. Simon and his family are bending over backward to include him in their vacation and you can't be bothered. Because you're so busy doing God knows what. Where you go I don't know and I don't want—"

"Shut up! Just shut up," Autumn hissed. She could see Sophie but didn't stop talking. "I didn't want to come to Sanpere this summer. You know that. I wanted to stay close to my sponsor and meetings. And for your information, I've been clean for eight months—in rehab and out. But you had to produce the perfect family in order to get The Birches. Heaven forbid Uncle Paul should leave it to someone else. I don't want it! And if you don't leave me alone, I'll tell him I don't. Rory will, too. I don't know how much you paid him to come, but I know what you gave me and you can have it back. As soon as the storm is over, I'm flying home to California. I never should have caved."

Sylvia turned slightly and saw Sophie. "Just a little tiff, Sophie dear." She left the kitchen abruptly.

Sophie immediately went over to her cousin and put her arms around her. Autumn was so thin, Sophie was afraid if she hugged her as hard as she wanted to, she'd break the fragile bird bones.

"I'm so sorry. I wish I had known. Wish I could have helped."

Autumn's head fit under Sophie's chin, and her soft, shining hair smelled like lilies.

"I was the only person who could help me and that's what I finally did—and am doing. One day at a time. There was nothing you or anyone else could do. Later I'll tell you the whole story, but the short version is I started a lot of stuff when my dad left—no excuse, just a fact—and by the time I was out of high school I was using. Sylvia never noticed except when she had to call the EMTs or whatever, and then I'd get locked up in my room with lectures and a ton of brown rice to cleanse my toxins."

Sophie decided to ditch any brown rice concoctions unless they got desperate.

"Rory talked me into going into rehab—he'd been trying for years, but at last I was scared for real. And tired. So tired. He made Sylvia pay for it. He's been amazing."

"I'm here for you now, too. On this coast or out on yours."

"You are a sweetheart, Sophie. Always were." Autumn straightened up. "I've been walking miles since I came—that's where I've been—and I lied to Sylvia. I *do* love Sanpere, and The Birches, but I don't want it. None of us do, although Daisy is too young to know what she wants. Believe it or not, Rory is kind of like the dad in our family, and he's worried about Daisy being with Sylvia. Sylvia's got a new guy and we don't think he wants a kid around. Unfortunately, Daisy's dad didn't, either. I guess none of ours did. I couldn't get custody or legal guardianship, whatever, but Rory is going to try."

This had been the longest train of thought, and most heartfelt, Sophie had ever heard from her cousin. She realized they were both crying a little. She hugged Autumn again and whispered, "Whenever you need me, call. I'll come."

"Thanks. That means the world. Oh, and Sophie— Will knows. I don't know how, but he confronted me when I first got here and told me the same thing. That he was here for me if I needed him. He's been great. 'No judging.' That's what he said."

After she finished, Autumn said she wanted to go to bed and headed for the bunkhouse, promising to come back if the storm got worse. Sophie couldn't bring herself to go into the living room. Too many people she wanted to avoid.

And one she didn't.

Over at The Pines, the kids had draped blankets over some chairs to make a kind of cave. They were inside playing Uno, darting out occasionally to check on the weather.

"Call this a hurricane," Amy said standing near

the window and peering out through the crack between the shutters. "Humph!" She'd picked up the expression, and hands on hips pose, from Gert Prescott.

"I'm afraid my children thrive on storms, the more dramatic the better. Amy won't be satisfied until the thunder and lightning start," Faith said to Ursula.

"A few times *my* very foolish children used to dash out to get a closer look. It's a wonder they never got struck," Ursula said.

"We used to get annoyed when the power *didn't* go out," Pix added. "One of the signs of aging. Praying we don't lose power and hoping storms pass us by."

Down in Massachusetts Faith knew the Fairchilds were probably functioning as Storm Central for the neighborhood. Tom had told her that his mother was demanding to be discharged so she could see the storm with her family. As if it were one of her beloved special exhibits at the Museum of Fine Arts or the Gardner. Her doctor wasn't swayed and apparently Marian was having to content herself with surfing between the Weather Channel and New England Cable News. Faith had assured Tom that all was well, and so far it was. Upstairs Ben was probably reading manga on this laptop. She wasn't pressing him to join the rest of them. This was definitely a time he needed to be by himself. Aside from a walk, a brief phone call to Tyler, and a hastily eaten dinner, he'd stayed put since they returned from the Lodge.

"Wind is picking up," Sam Miller said. "Starting to come down the chimneys."

Amy, Dana, and Daisy scuttled out of their hideaway and rushed to the windows, trying to peer out through the storm shutters. The lights flickered.

"Wow," Daisy said. "This is great!"

The wind picked up even more, and what had been a pleasant sort of "whooo" coming down the chimneys became more of a howl. The electricity flickered once more and went out completely. After Faith helped light the lanterns and candles, she grabbed a flashlight. She knew it didn't make sense, but she wanted Ben down with the rest of them.

"Be back in a minute. I'll get Ben. He'll want some of the hot chocolate Samantha is making."

Upstairs she knocked on the bedroom door and went in. The room was empty. Ben's laptop was closed; the battery power was glowing, and the sleek silver case seemed almost alive in the dark.

"Ben?" Faith could see he wasn't in bed, but something made her call out anyway.

He must be in the bathroom, she told herself. But he wasn't. He wasn't in any of the other rooms, either. Silently she went back to the room where he was staying, her fears mounting. She opened the closet door and trained the beam on the clothes. There weren't many and Faith immediately saw his rain gear was missing. She pointed the light onto the floor. So were his boots.

The next clap of thunder was so close Faith felt the house shake.

Her son was out in the hurricane.

Chapter 11

The storm had caused an unexpected change in Mandy's plans. The plan she had shared with Ben Thursday as he had made his way back to The Pines from work was that she'd be off the island well before Cary arrived.

He'd been tired and his steps had slowed after he'd passed the Hitchcock house. He was startled—and relieved—when Mandy darted out, pulling him into the birch grove, well away from the road.

And then she'd told him everything. Starting with why she'd left work so suddenly. Going into the kitchen for more silverware, she'd overheard one of the maintenance crew who was also a volunteer with the ambulance corps tell his buddy he had to answer a call—"Looks like Dwayne Hitchcock has finally bought the farm."

Mandy had immediately taken off for Little Sanpere, leaving her car behind her neighbor's house, knowing they weren't home, before going around through the woods to the back of hers. She'd raced inside and gone upstairs to her room, which was in the front. Through the open window she could see and hear everything happening in the yard.

"It looked like he'd been shooting up and that's what they were saying. Heroin overdose," she'd told Ben. "I knew right away that wasn't possible. Dwayne would pass out if you waved a safety pin at him. No way would he stick a needle anywhere in his body. Somebody else did it and they must have knocked him out with something first. Mom is at work, so they're going to think it was me."

Ben had started to contradict her—how could anyone possibly think Mandy was a killer?—but she'd cut him off and haltingly told him why she would be the main suspect. What her father—if he really was—had been doing for years. Ben thought he would explode. If Dwayne Hitchcock hadn't already been dead, Ben swore to himself he would have done the deed. Right away he had asked Mandy why her mother hadn't stopped Dwayne from hurting her. All Mandy had done was shake her head and say, "She's pretty good at not seeing, if you know what I mean."

Mandy had proceeded to explain her plan. She'd already moved her car to a clearing behind a summer person's house she knew was unoccupied. She wasn't about to break into the empty house but instead would hide in the lighthouse while she tried to get in touch with an older girl she had waitressed with last summer. Sally lived near Waterville and had told Mandy if she ever needed help to call. She had guessed about the source of Mandy's bruises and urged her to leave home. They'd been in touch all year, and Mandy had pretty much made up her mind to take Sally up on her offer even before today. She'd wanted to make some more money at the Lodge first, though.

Sally wasn't answering her phone, even texts, all day Friday. Mandy had finally reached her this morning, but Cary's arrival meant she had to stay put until after the hurricane. When she'd told Ben, she'd added, "Maybe the Staties will find the real killer by then."

Ben had immediately thought about telling his mother and had even told Mandy about some of the murders Faith had solved, but Mandy wasn't convinced.

All night, first when it started to rain heavily and later as the winds picked up, buffeting the house, shrieking in the trees, Ben had been worried about Mandy alone in the lighthouse. Once the thunder and lightning arrived and the electricity went out, Ben couldn't stay inside any longer. When he had brought Mandy the food, she had been sure she'd be safe and sound in the lighthouse.

"It would take more than a hurricane to bring it down, Ben. Don't worry. Think of all the storms it's been through."

But Ben wasn't so sure. The lighthouse was the tallest thing around. What if it got struck by lightning? What if Mandy was looking out one of the windows at the top or the smaller slits along the stairs and a bolt came shooting through, striking her? He had to make sure she was all right. Convince her to leave. The Pines had back stairs—no one would see them—and she could stay in his room until the storm died down.

Outside the wind was fierce and the lightning was like a giant strobe. Ben ran down the long path to the beach and across to the lighthouse. He pushed the handle down and shoved the door. It didn't budge; he tried again.

It was locked! Had Mandy locked it from the inside? He pounded his fists against it and screamed her name. And then he saw her face at one of the small windows, the one lowest to the ground, but still far above his head. She looked terrified. He waved to reassure her. She'd shown him where the key was hidden and Ben ducked around, slipping on the wet rocks. The huge beach rose bushes were bent sideways from the wind. He trained the flashlight on the lighthouse wall and reached for the key with his hand.

It wasn't there.

He got down on his knees and felt along the ground, knowing that he wouldn't find it, but he had to try. The key had been attached to a ring embedded in the stone itself. The strongest wind couldn't dislodge the carabiner-type clasp. Someone had taken it.

Mandy was locked in.

After the power went out, Sophie tried reading by flashlight. She hadn't been able to get back to *The Goldfinch*, and it was calling to her. But it was awkward holding the light and the thick book, plus she felt her eyelids start to droop. She gave in, put the book down, and turned off the flashlight. Outside her window, which wasn't shuttered—none of the back ones were—the hurricane was starting to fulfill all the most dire predictions. But soon Sophie was asleep, sound asleep, blissfully unaware and deep in a pleasant dream. She felt lips brush her cheek and then seek her lips. A hand was pulling back the bedding. "Will?" she murmured.

Her eyes flew open as the kiss became harder and the hand cupped her breast. She reached to turn on the light before remembering the power must still be off. Sitting up and struggling out of bed, she took a breath and smelled a familiar smell. An expensive one. She didn't need the flash of lightning that lit up the room to know who it was.

"Ian! What do you think you're doing? Stop it!"

He didn't—murmuring endearments instead—and just when she thought she might have to start screaming or try to do some serious damage to his person with her flashlight, her door opened. More lightning flashed briefly, and another male voice said, "No means no, mister. Maybe not where you come from, but it does here. Sophie, I need you to help me. Get your rain gear. I'll explain on the way."

Ian jerked away sputtering, "What the hell!"

"Ben Fairchild, is that you?" Sophie said.

"Yes, it's me. Sorry, I forgot to turn my flashlight on. I'm trying to save the batteries. But please just come! And don't listen to this guy. He has some deal going with your cousin and his friend. He's supposed to 'charm' you. That's why he's here. They hired him or something. I heard them at lunch. Now hurry! Please!"

There was no escaping the desperation in Ben's voice, and Sophie started reaching for more clothes.

When he couldn't find the key, Ben had tried frantically to think who might have one or know where one was. When Sophie Maxwell took care of them, they often came to this beach and went inside the lighthouse, which was open in those days. Sophie was his best bet. Once decided, he took off with a final wave to Mandy. Besides, Sophie was the adult he thought would help without a lot of fuss, and The Birches was the closest house. He just hoped he could get Sophie alone. He hadn't really thought how he could explain what he was doing there otherwise. He headed straight for the back door. When he'd walked Daisy back one time, Sophie had come out of her room, which was right off the kitchen. He prayed she was there now—and by herself.

Well, part of his prayer had been answered. He wanted to explain more and say something about the lighthouse key, but he didn't want that Ian guy to hear. "Chap" he guessed was a better word. That Ian chap. He was the type who'd call the police and tell them where Mandy was. Ben knew Sophie wouldn't.

"I think you should leave now. Go back to your own room," Ben said.

"Sophie! Who is this kid?" Ian was furious. "What's going on?"

"You tell *me* what's going on, Ian! Or rather, don't. I can guess. Now, you heard Ben. Get out."

Ben held the door open and waited until Ian was beyond earshot.

"Mandy's locked in the lighthouse. She's been there since her father got killed. But she didn't do it." Ben's words were racing together. He slowed down and got to the point. "Do you know where there might be a key?"

Sophie had been pulling her jeans on in the dark. She grabbed her flashlight, flicked it on, and directed it toward her pocket.

"It just so happens I have one right here. Let's go!"

A figure stood looking out the window as Sophie left the house. The lightning was coming in waves; the entire yard was bathed in brilliant Technicolor, then, as if a switch was pulled, the scene plunged into darkness. Ben, following behind, didn't make it on-screen. Now where could she be going? She's headed for the woods, not the bunkhouse. Everyone is in bed. It can't be a tryst. Not in this weather. If I hurry, I can do it now! I'm getting so good at this. It was smart to practice on Bev. And Dwayne was plain fun. Slow down, little Sophie, I'm coming.

Fortunately The Pines was well stocked with foul-weather gear. Thinking she must look like the old salt on the Gorton's fish sticks package, Faith made her way to the beach. Ben may have overheard Ursula say how her children used to go out in the storm. Doing so would certainly fit her son's current mood, and she pictured him sitting on a rock, letting the elements act out what he was feeling inside.

She'd grabbed the largest flashlight she could find, and it threw a long beam up and down the shore. Nothing.

It was hard to keep her balance. The gale almost knocked her down twice, and she went back up the path to the point where it branched off toward The Birches—the path that led through the grove of the trees.

The place she had found Sophie leaning over Bev's dead body.

Maybe Ben went to The Birches. But for what? Certainly not to see Rory. Or maybe to see Rory. To have it out with him again. Did Ben suspect the man had something to do with Mandy's disappearance? Faith tried to run, but the force of the wind slowed her steps.

"Oh, Ben," she cried aloud. "Where are you!"

Sophie tripped on a root and landed flat on her face, her arms splayed out, having tried in vain to cushion her fall.

"Are you okay?" Ben yelled in her ear. She could scarcely hear him over the storm.

She shook her head no and gingerly got to her knees. She didn't know whether her face was bleeding or wet from the rain, but her right cheek hurt like crazy and she was pretty sure she'd sprained her right wrist as well.

She dug in her pocket with her good hand. "Take the key!" she yelled back. "Bring her to the bunkhouse. I'll make sure Rory and Autumn understand what's going on. And, Ben, be careful!"

"Rory?" A lull made Ben's doubtful voice audible.

"He's a good guy. Don't worry. You two just got off on the wrong foot. Now go! It's only going to get worse out!"

Faith saw the two figures and quickened her pace, pushing herself as hard as she could. She realized one was Sophie when the sky filled with a bright flash of light. She couldn't make out the other, and then the two separated. Lightning flashed again and she could see it was Ben coming straight toward her! Faith stood still. A few seconds later, he almost knocked her down.

"Mom!" he cried. She didn't know whether to hug him or maybe smack him. She went for the hug and heard his voice in her ear saying, "Oh shit . . ."

Sophie started back toward the house. Branches were falling like pickup sticks. She cradled her wrist while trying to hold the flashlight beam steady. She didn't want to fall again. With her gaze on the ground, she missed seeing a person step from behind a tree in front of her.

But she didn't miss the person's tough grip as two hands came from behind and two arms wrapped around her body, pinning her own arms to her sides. Her first thought was that Ian had followed her. She tried to jerk free, screaming over the wind, "Stop it, Ian. Let me go!"

"It's not Ian," a familiar voice said close to her ear. Sophie relaxed. Of course they had noticed she wasn't in the house and sent out a search party.

"I'm okay. It's a long story, but I'm coming back in now. I think I hurt my wrist, though." The wind had died down, producing a deceptive moment of calm, and her words were clear. So was the answer.

"Oh, I don't think you need to worry about your wrist." Sophie twisted around, saw the syringe, and looked into a face she had known all her life, the face, she now realized, of someone who was totally insane.

She was going to die.

Cousin Sylvia was about to kill her.

Again the wind howled. Finding energy in the sound, Sophie kicked hard at Sylvia, but the woman was surprisingly strong. Possibly all those years of yoga? With a sure hand, she pulled up the loose sleeve of Sophie's rain jacket and aimed for a vein.

"Noooo!" Sophie let herself go limp and pulled her cousin to the ground, trying to roll away from her. The next flash of lightning revealed she had rolled closer instead. The hand with the needle was coming down, down, inexorably down.

And then it stopped. Two sounds, not from nature, filled the air. A gunshot—and a more familiar voice.

"Stop it this instant, Sylvia. And Will, what in God's name are you doing with my gun?"

It was Mother. Babs had made it to The Birches.

Hurricane Cary was not in and of itself one for the books, but no one in the two houses—or the lighthouse—on the Point would ever forget it. Sunday dawned clear and crisp. The sound of chain saws filled the air as island residents cleaned up the storm damage and all the supposed blowdowns by the shore that had been blocking their views. "Blowdowns" that no one could challenge and levy a fine for clear-cutting.

While Babs had guided her daughter back to The Pines, Will had followed, keeping a firm hold on Sylvia, who was almost foaming at the mouth. Deirdre, a traveling pharmacy, had produced a strong sedative to knock the murderess out until the storm abated and the police could take over.

Sophie took a lighter dose and woke many hours later, to find both Will and her mother by her side.

"Faith Fairchild, her little boy—not so little—and Mandy Hitchcock are here waiting for you to wake up. The riffraff is gone, specifically that Brit. And darling, he is very dishy, but really you didn't put two and two or more together? That he just happened to turn up with Barclay—no, I will not call him 'Barks'? He's gone, and Felicity, too. The wedding is back in New York. Apparently Barclay wasn't as keen as she was. Something about the smell of the beach at low tide."

Sophie let her mother's words wash over her, feeling incredibly happy—and safe. Maybe it was also because Will was holding her hand.

"Are you hungry? Faith brought chicken soup," he said. "If you are up to talking, we can move into the living room. But there's no rush." He squeezed her hand. "Sylvia has been arrested for the two murders and one attempted—you." His voice cracked.

Sophie sat up straight. "Two! Whose?"

"Come on, sweetheart," her mother said. "Throw some clothes on and let's all sit down. We'll fill you in—and you can explain how Will came to have *my* gun. I would have thought he had his own."

Curiouser and curiouser, Sophie thought. Someone—she hoped it had been Babs, or maybe she hoped not—had stripped off her wet clothes last night, and she was wearing sweats and a long-sleeved tee. She slipped her sandals on and a cardigan that had been Aunt Priscilla's.

Uncle Paul immediately got up when she entered the living room and led her to a spot next to him on the couch after hugging her fiercely.

The room was full, but it was also interesting to note that many of the cast of characters from these last weeks were gone. Obviously Sylvia, but also Rory, Autumn, and Daisy. Forbes must have hitched a ride on Barclay's plane as well. Her aunt and uncle were still here.

As if reading her mind, Will said, "Rory and Autumn are making arrangements for the three of them to fly back to California tomorrow. Daisy is over at The Pines with her new friend Amy, a friend she will keep forever, a 'BFF' according to the two of them."

"This is Mandy, Sophie," Ben said shyly. "We feel bad. If I hadn't come over here last night, you wouldn't, I mean—"

Babs interrupted him. "She's safe and sound. So is Mandy—and we're going to keep her that way. Besides, Sylvia was bound and determined to bump my little girl off. She would have succeeded if she had picked a less dramatic time. Now, I'll start. After a hellish cab ride—which cost me a fortune—I arrived to discover Sophie wasn't here, and that rat Ian told me she was out in the storm, so I went after her—just like your mother did after you, Ben—someday you'll have children of your own to put you through this sort of thing I can only hope. It was lucky Will came along, though I didn't know he had my piece. Sylvia dropped the syringe when she heard the shot, and Will had better have been intending the next one for her heart if she hadn't."

"It must be the sleeping pills or whatever you gave me, but I'm still very confused," Sophie said. "Two murders? Who did Sylvia kill?"

Will answered. "It's hard for us to comprehend, but she killed Bev to see whether a method she found on the Internet would work."

Sylvia a geek, who knew? Sophie thought in astonishment.

"She isn't saying how she got Bev to the birch grove—probably told her someone needed help and they had to go quickly—and she'd been stockpiling syringes from . . . someone." He paused. "She had loaded one with potassium chloride. A very soluble salt substitute widely available. She pumped Bev full of the stuff, and it mimicked a fatal heart attack. Potassium chloride is undetectable in an autopsy, since we have so much salt in our blood naturally. She had prepared an even higher concentration for you, and there was a thick branch near where she had been standing that suggests she also planned to bludgeon you. The storm was taking trees and limbs down, so there would have been no cause to think that your death wasn't accidental."

The blood had drained from Sophie's face, and she was feeling a little faint. She thought of the used syringe she had stowed in the Lexus's glove compartment and then promptly, maybe purposely, forgotten about. And of course it must have also been Sylvia herself who planted the Beanie puffin in her own bed.

Faith Fairchild appeared as if by magic with a steaming mug of soup. "Sip this, and there's plenty more."

"The second murder was Dwayne, right? Sorry, Mandy," Sophie said.

"Don't be. I'm not. I think the reason I freaked in the lighthouse—which was the safest place to be on the island last night, I'm beginning to realize—was because I've been on edge and worse for so long. When the thunder and lightning started, I kinda went to pieces."

"But what did Sylvia have to do with him? And maybe I'm missing something, but why kill me? It can't be because of the house."

Paul McAllister looked grim. "I should have listened to my friend Ursula and ignored Priscilla's wishes. The Pandora's box, the letter, let a great deal of evil into our lives. Sylvia thought by eliminating the competition she'd be the last man standing, so to speak."

Sophie was horrified. "She was going to keep on going?"

"I'm quite sure she was putting something in my food. Ipecac to start. I found the empty bottle," Deirdre said. "There's no other explanation for the way I've been feeling."

Will looked over at Sophie and made a slight drinking gesture with his hand. She started to giggle, then focused back on the serious matters to hand.

"But Dwayne Hitchcock. He isn't related to us."

"Dwayne saw Sylvia inject Bev and was blackmailing her. He regularly went into the birch grove to pick up loose pieces for stove wood—as well as stealing some from our woodpiles—and he caught her in the act. Sylvia doctored one of his cans of beer and watched until he passed out. She obviously didn't know about his needle phobia."

"Which leaves?" Babs looked pointedly at her brother. "The Ian debacle."

"Uncle Paul. Sophie," Simon said pompously, perhaps an adherent of "the best defense is offense" school, "I had *no* idea whatsoever that Forbes and the others had cooked up the plan to bring Sophie's ex here to keep her from getting involved with someone else, someone close to you, Paul."

"And if you believe that, I have a bridge you might like to buy," Babs said.

"Mother!" Sophie started to object. It was over. Well and truly over. Enough was enough. She was more tired than she had ever been. Even when she was shooting for twenty-four billable hours.

Faith stood up. "We just wanted to make sure you were all right, Sophie. Mandy and Ben have to get to work. Mandy is staying at The Pines until school starts, and then she has a number of options to consider, including a move to Massachusetts. Ursula would like to have someone in the house and would love it to be Mandy." Sophie noticed that Ben was beaming while his mother spoke.

After The Pines contingent had left, the room grew quiet. Sophie, with Will on her other side now, had started to drowse off.

"I guess it's as good a time as any to put an end to the mess I started eleven days ago in this same room," Paul McAllister said.

Sophie opened her eyes; Simon and Deirdre had stiffened. Her mother was adopting an unconvincing nonchalant pose.

"I'm sorry, Simon, but I'm giving the house to Babs. I know you have the funds to maintain it, but so does she. And I know you love it, but I'm afraid it comes down to the next generation. Sophie reminds me of Priscilla in so many ways, especially her kindness. The whole time she has been here she has been chief cook and bottle washer with very little help from any of us, I'm afraid—except for Will. My lawyer will be drawing up the necessary papers and Babs's acceptance is contingent on agreeing to leave The Birches to Sophie."

Simon took it well. "I understand, sir," he said. "We'll be out by morning."

"Oh, don't be such a doofus—and cut the martyr crap," Babs said. "Next thing we know you'll be doing Sydney Carton's *Tale of Two Cities* speech."

Sophie started to giggle again—she really had to get some sleep—thinking of Uncle Simon's Declaration of Independence performance.

"Of course you can stay—for as long as you like," Babs continued. "Whenever you like, and that goes for your impossible children, too. And their children, although what Felicity will produce with Barclay is beyond imagining. Puppies?"

Babs was on a roll.

Will slipped his arm around Sophie, and she found herself fitting neatly against his chest. As she started to lean back, her mother's words from the night before returned. She tilted her head to look at him squarely in the face. "What did my mother mean about you having your own gun, and why did you take hers from the car?"

She shot her mother a look that clearly said "More about that later."

Will looked a bit sheepish. "I need it for my work at times. Don't worry. It's all legal." He grinned down at her. "I'm not some kind of hit man. And taking the gun from the car was part of doing my job here."

"But *what* are you? And *who* are you? I couldn't turn up a 'Will Tarkington' anywhere in the state of Georgia."

Paul answered. "I got an odd anonymous letter before coming up here—Sylvia sowing early seeds—it warned me to watch out for family members. I showed Will, who is a private investigator, and that's all it took for him to clear his caseload and come with me. I think he's no doubt very happy he did."

"So do you have some horrible name that you want to keep secret?" Sophie asked.

"I thought it best to come incognito in case anyone did exactly what you did and Googled me, discovering my profession. 'Will' *is* my first name but 'Tarkington' is my middle name—and we are distantly related to the author. My last name is . . ." He was smiling broadly, as were Babs and Paul. " 'Maxwell!' "

Sophie was stunned, and all the events since she'd left Connecticut—no, make that since she'd left London—came crashing down on her. All that had happened, and kept happening. All of it incredibly hard to believe.

"I've met Will often visiting Paul and Priscilla in Savannah. You'll like it there, Sophie," Babs said. "And this certainly makes life simple. You won't even need new writing paper, and the monogramming on your towels—easy peasy. Now, what does a lady have to do to get a drink around here? Deirdre, have you left any Stoli?"

Sophie moved from her comfy spot on the couch. "I'll be right back."

She went into her room and sat on the bed, gazing out the window for a while at the tall pines casting deep shadows on the yard. All at once she knew what she had to do. Wanted to do.

Ten minutes later she was diving from the dock. The instant she hit the cold salt water she felt herself again. That Sophie Maxwell. When she surfaced, she began a leisurely breaststroke out toward the Reach. She had the feeling she could keep swimming for miles. She turned over and the sky above was like the bright blue cereal bowl Aunt Priscilla always put out for her. She felt her body grow weightless, closed her eyes, and decided to let the tide move her back and forth, washing away the last year and especially this summer.

Then she heard a splash that she was sure wasn't a harbor seal.

"Sophie!" Not far off a slightly anxious voice called. "Shug, I'm here."

She smiled at the puffy white clouds above—like the spots of milk left at the bottom of the bowl—turned over, and swam toward Will. Will Maxwell. Her beloved.

The Blue Hill Fair, one of the last old-time agricultural fairs in Maine with "Some Pig" celebrated in E. B. White's *Charlotte's Web,* marked the end of the summer. Faith noted the fact to herself, as she did every year when she walked around the fairgrounds with a bittersweet mixture of pleasure and regret.

Some of the swamp maples by the sides of the roads had already started to turn, scarlet swatches against the green. Tom had been back and forth several times, bringing his parents to Sanpere with him for four days at the start of August. Marian had made almost a full recovery, and the new addition to the cottage meant plenty of room for guests.

Despite Derek's ineptitude, the Lodge had remained open—although without its young boss, whose stash of pills was discovered by his parents. He'd voluntarily entered McLean's residential substance abuse program in Massachusetts. The Otises hired a manager recommended by the chef. Word spread; The Laughing Gull became a prime destination for dinner and lodging both. Zach Hale had agreed to return the following summer, as did the new manager. Zach asked Ben and Mandy to consider returning as well.

Mandy was staying on the island for her senior year. She and her mother were in therapy, which Ed Ricks had arranged. The hope was for the two of them to eventually live together again, but for now Mandy was with Freeman and Nan Hamilton, some sort of cousins. The gifted girl's future was looking much brighter than it ever had before.

Only Sam and Pix were still at the Miller cottage. Faith had seen them a few minutes ago. They said they were on their way to the grandstand to watch the iron skillet toss and told the Fairchilds they would save them seats.

In the aftermath of July's momentous events, Pix had finally taken her brother to breakfast, and he had told her, much surprised, that of course things would stay the same—so long as Dana would be able to come as he got older if he grew to love the island as much as the rest of them. It hadn't occurred to Arnie that the new addition to the family would cause any changes in Ursula's plans, which he told his mother as soon as he had wolfed down three of the gargantuan strawberry pancakes and returned to The Pines.

"I love this fair," Faith said, one hand holding her husband's, the other picking at the fries from the King and Queen's stand—formerly Thelma the Fry Queen's alone—that Tom had balanced in his free hand.

"Even though it means summer is over?" Tom teased her. "You said last week you didn't want this one to end."

"True, but the fall is wonderful, too." She thought of the sudden rush of all the vegetables that New England's late growing season pushed into September. She wasn't looking forward to the part of school that meant homework, but she *was* looking forward to the way it kept her children occupied, leaving her free to pursue her catering jobs.

They walked past Ben, who was with Tyler and a group of island friends, including Mandy. He had surprised his parents by saying Amy could join them. Faith waved but knew enough not to actually approach her children, who were headed for the Rescue Dog Frisbee show.

Faith thought back to the Fourth of July and the realization she'd had that her kids weren't kids anymore, with its accompanying sense of loss. Watching them go off with their friends, she felt a similar twinge, but also something new. Pride, yes, but anticipation. What were these rapidly changing—each had seemed to add inches to their heights this summer—human beings going to be like this time next year, and the next, and—

"I think I need another strawberry shortcake before we watch the toss." Tom's voice interrupted her wistful thoughts.

Him, she knew—and no changes there.

Dusk was falling and she could see Blue Hill, the small mountain that gave the town and the fair its name, silhouetted behind the giant Ferris wheel with its flashing lights. Flashing lights. Lightning flashes.

It had been an illuminating summer.

Author's Note

I started this book with one of Oscar Wilde's gems: "After a good dinner one can forgive anybody, even one's own relations," and families are what this book is all about, aside from murder and food, of course.

Families. So many possible configurations. So many complications. A dance that can be a waltz, a tango— or the twist. I find families endlessly fascinating, in fact and in fiction. Especially fact, as what goes on in a family is almost always harder to believe than any fiction. You cannot make this stuff up. Particularly when it comes to inheritance.

Since Esau, famished after a hard day's work, sold his birthright to his twin, Jacob, who was second in line from the womb, for a mess o' pottage in Genesis, and probably earlier, people have been at odds with their near and dear over who gets what. And the range in the sizes of legacy wrangling is enormous. Brooke Astor's Mount Desert Island, Maine, estate was as large a bone of contention for her family and heirs—the end result prison for her eighty-nine-year-old son—as was the quarrel between the two brothers over a small cottage on "Sanpere," with several acres mentioned in these pages (names and much more changed). When it comes to personal effects, an heirloom smaller than a bread box can cause not just estrangement, but also litigation. I know one family where a teapot truly caused a tempest. Years later, the two sides are still not speaking, despite regularly running into one another in the bank, at the market, and elsewhere.

With real estate, it may come down to money, but more often it isn't about the money at all. Family summer places, the ones that have been handed down over several generations most of all, become family totems. These dwellings *are* the family for the siblings or cousins who grew up there, faithfully following the traditions established by the first rusticators. In Maine this means swimming in frigid water, reveling in the slightly musty odor of places closed up most of the year, and a cuisine that celebrates the fruits of the sea, but also items like Habitant canned pea soup and now sadly unavailable Crown Pilot biscuits. Even the youngest

family members wear Mr. Bean's Duck Boots, only a few pairs purchased in the twenty-first century. After all, if they need repair, just take them to Freeport 365 days a year, open twenty-four hours a day.

However grand, or minuscule, sharing the summer cottage can be murder. Drawing from a hat for dates. Figuring out who pays for what repairs. And hovering not far in the backs of the younger generation's minds is the question "What will Mom and Dad do?" With its heartbreaking corollary "Who's the favorite kid?"

There has been a spate of *New York Times* articles recently about this very thing—how an estate can divide a family. The Boomers are aging, even the ones who plan on not going. They have decisions to make, painful ones at times. Having to pick the child who can afford the upkeep over the child who loves the cabin, camp, cottage, yurt, warts and all, is wrenching. Parents in the process of these decisions were interviewed and their responses ran the gamut from "I'm not going to be here to witness the mayhem, so they can duke it out"—leaving the place to all the sibs—to a kind of King Solomon decision: "We're selling it and leaving the money instead."

In general, death is not a popular topic—many polls put the fear of death second after fear of public speaking. Speaking to one's parents about their mortality with a "By the way, what do your wills say?" may rank third in the list. Somewhere there must be families like the one in the book who get it together and form an association or create a similar solution without rancor. I put that up there with the tooth fairy and leprechauns (maybe not leprechauns). For better or worse, richer or poorer, sickness and health, large or small, our families are with us for life. And at those moments when we feel they might be too much with us, there's always that other quotation I considered using at the beginning of this book: "Friends are God's apology for families." Needlepoint or stencil it on a pillow. Once you're done, punch it hard, and then go call your mother, father, sister, brother, son, daughter, aunt, uncle, cousin.

Have Faith in Your Kitchen

by Faith Sibley Fairchild
with Katherine Hall Page

Dilled New Potato Salad

2 1/2 pounds small red
   (new) potatoes
3 tablespoons olive oil
1 tablespoon balsamic
   vinegar
1/2 teaspoon Dijon
   mustard

1/2 teaspoon salt
1/4 teaspoon freshly
   ground pepper
1/2 cup sliced scallions
1/2 cup chopped fresh dill
Dill frond for garnish, if
   desired

Scrub the potatoes. Quarter them and steam until soft, but not mushy. (You may also boil them starting with cold water.)

While the potatoes are cooking, whisk the oil, vinegar, mustard, salt, and pepper together in a large bowl.

Add the potatoes when done and stir to coat well. Let sit, stirring occasionally, for 8 to 10 minutes.

Add the scallions and stir. Add the fresh dill and stir. Let sit, again stirring every once in a while, for 10 minutes and serve at room temperature or refrigerate, bringing the salad to room temperature before serving.

Serves 6 amply.

Faith likes to use garlic scapes, or curls, instead of scallions when they are in season early in the summer. Any of the many varieties of Kozlik's mustard made in Canada make this dish extra special: www. mustardmaker.com. Canada produces 90 percent of the world's mustard (who knew?)!

Summer Corn Chowder with Bacon

3 slices of bacon, cut in half

1 tablespoon olive oil or unsalted butter

1 small yellow onion, diced

1 small garlic clove, minced

2 tablespoons flour

2 cups chicken broth, preferably low sodium

1 large potato (Yukon Golds are good), diced (approx. 1 cup)

4 ears of corn, kernels
   cut from the cob
   (approx. 4 cups)
2 cups half-and-half
1/2 cup heavy cream

Salt and freshly ground
   pepper to taste
Fresh parsley, chopped, for
   garnish

Cook the bacon until crisp in a soup pot (this is why you have cut the slices in half). Drain bacon on a plate covered with a paper towel. Crumble and set aside.

In the same pot, add the olive oil or butter, draining any excess bacon fat, and sauté the onion and garlic until soft.

Add the flour and coat the onion and garlic.

Add the chicken stock and diced potato. Bring the mixture to a boil, then reduce the heat and simmer until the potatoes are soft.

Add the corn kernels, bacon (reserving some to sprinkle on the top of each bowl), the half-and-half, and the heavy cream. Simmer for 10 to 12 minutes.

This soup improves if it sits for 5 minutes before serving. You can also add shrimp or crab to it.

In the winter, frozen corn kernels may be substituted.

Whatever the season, it is a nice thick chowder with corn as the star.

Serves 4.

Smoked Turkey Puff Pastry

Parchment paper

2 sheets frozen puff pastry
(Pepperidge Farm is
fine)

Roasted garlic onion jam,
red pepper jelly, or a
mustard

1/2 pound thinly sliced
smoked turkey

1/2 pound loosely grated or
sliced sharp cheddar

1 large egg, beaten

Preheat the oven to 375 degrees. Place a sheet of parchment paper on a baking sheet.

Roll one sheet of the pastry to about 1/8 inch and put it on the parchment-covered baking sheet.

Using a pastry brush, spread a thin coat of the jam, jelly, or mustard on the pastry, leaving about a 1/2-inch border at the edges.

Layer the turkey on top and then the cheese. Brush the edges with half of the beaten egg.

Roll the second pastry sheet to the same thickness and place on top, sealing the edges well, pressing with your fingers. Brush the top with the remaining beaten egg.

Place another sheet of parchment paper on top and a second baking sheet on top of that. This keeps the dish from puffing up too much as it first bakes. Bake for 20 minutes.

Remove both the second baking sheet and parchment

paper. Continue baking for 10 to 15 minutes until the top is golden brown. (Keep an eye on it.)

Cool for 10 minutes and cut into bite-size squares, if using as an appetizer, or large portions as a first course or main dish (great for a luncheon with a salad).

Serves 8 to 10 as an appetizer, fewer as a first or main course.

This is a versatile recipe. You can use other meats or just cheeses as the filling. It can be made ahead, even the day before. Follow the recipe and stop before brushing the top with the beaten egg. Cover with plastic wrap and refrigerate.

Nan Hamilton's Chocolate Drop Cookies

8 ounces bittersweet chocolate, finely chopped

1 1/4 cups flour

1/2 cup unsweetened Dutch process cocoa powder

2 teaspoons baking powder

1/4 teaspoon salt

1/2 cup unsalted butter, room temperature

1 1/2 cups packed light brown sugar

2 large eggs

1 teaspoon vanilla

1/3 cup whole milk

1 cup granulated sugar

1 cup confectioners' sugar

Parchment paper

Melt the chocolate in a double boiler. Set aside to cool. Sift together the flour, cocoa powder, baking powder, and salt in a bowl.

Beat the butter and brown sugar with an electric mixer on medium speed until pale and fluffy. Mix in the eggs and vanilla and then the melted chocolate. Reduce speed to low. Mix in the flour mixture in two batches, alternating with the milk. Divide the dough into four equal pieces. Wrap each in plastic and refrigerate until firm, about two hours.

Preheat the oven to 350 degrees. Divide each piece into sixteen 1-inch balls. Roll in granulated sugar to coat. Then roll in confectioners' sugar to coat. Space the balls 2 inches apart on baking sheets lined with parchment paper.

Bake until the surfaces crack, about 14 minutes, rotating the sheets halfway through the time. Remove the cookies from the baking sheets and cool on wire racks. When cool, they can be stored for four days in airtight tins or a cookie jar.

Old-Fashioned Lemonade
(With or Without a Twist!)

1 cup sugar
7 cups water
Zest of 1 lemon
6 lemons

Mint and/or lemon slices,
   for garnish (optional)
Vodka or gin (optional)

Stir the sugar and 1 cup of the water together in a small saucepan and bring it to a boil. Add the zest and simmer for 5 minutes. Cool in the fridge until room temperature. Strain the zest out and reserve.

While the sugar/water/zest mixture is cooling, squeeze the lemons (one of the six will be the one you used for the zest). Strain the seeds out if you use an old-fashioned glass squeezer, as Faith does.

Put the remaining 6 cups of water in a large pitcher and add the lemon juice and 1 cup of the reserved syrup. Stir well and taste. Add more water or all the leftover syrup, if needed, but this 6-to-1 ratio seems to taste perfect to the Fairchilds. You may use mint or lemon slices as a garnish.

For the grown-up version, add a jigger of vodka or gin to a tall glass with some ice, fill with lemonade, and stir with a swizzle stick.

Squeezing lemons is easier if you roll the whole lemon on a hard counter to release the juice before cutting it in half and squeezing.

Makes about 2 quarts or 6 to 8 servings.

About the Author

Katherine Hall Page is the author of twenty-one previous Faith Fairchild mysteries and a collection of short fiction, *Small Plates*. She has won multiple Agatha Awards and has been nominated for the Edgar, the Mary Higgins Clark, the Maine Literary, and the Macavity Awards. She lives in Massachusetts and Maine with her husband.